By Your Side

Phil Giunta

RAGING SEAS PRESS

My sincerest thanks to Sue Frey, Amanda Headlee, Deb Lesko, Lynn Murphy, Susanna Reilly, Sylvia Steigler, and Sandy Zier-Teitler for your considerable proofreading and critiquing skills. You gals have eyes like hawks!

To Steven H. Wilson for your tireless support, encouragement, mentoring, and friendship.

To Howard Weinstein for taking the time over the years to answer my pesky writing questions and provide helpful—dare I say perspicacious—feedback on my work.

Under the topic of music to write by, I'd like to thank Jerry Goldsmith, James Horner, John Williams, the Moody Blues, Phil Collins, Genesis, Journey, David Glasper, Julia Fordham, SEAL, Grey Eye Glances, and especially DIDO, whose beautiful, invigorating music and exquisite voice filled my heart and healed my soul during one of the darkest times in my life. That makes you a hero in my book. I hope I can thank you in person someday.

CHAPTER 1

NIGHT AT THE ZOO

Miranda Lorensen was about to watch her brother die—again. Golden sunlight through sheer curtains gave soothing warmth to the dining room, warmth that belied the anguish of its occupant. She stood over Colin as he folded his suicide note and slipped it into an envelope addressed to his wife, Rebecca. With a trembling hand, he reached across the table and leaned the letter against a clear blue vase. Colin had gone to the florist earlier in the day for a bouquet of carnations and roses, Rebecca's favorites.

The sunlight was brighter now through the windshield of Colin's car. He pulled out of the garage, braking for a wild rabbit that darted across the driveway. He leaned over the steering wheel and watched as it ducked beneath a lavender plant in the neighbor's front yard. As Colin turned onto the street, Miranda called his name, pleaded with him to listen. As usual, he didn't acknowledge her. Still, she had to try—again. She'd been assaulted with visions of her brother's final hour at least once a week for the past six months, though she wasn't with him when it happened.

I should have prevented this. Miranda reached for his hand, but her fingers passed through the gearshift as if she were a ghost. *Why should this time be any different?*

He took the final left turn and slowed to a stop at the top of the hill. Miranda followed his gaze to the bottom where four concrete abutments supported the highway bridge that ran above the road. Colin removed his seatbelt. The dashboard chimed in rhythm with the blinking warning light.

Miranda twirled a lock of her long blonde hair, a nervous habit she had developed as a child. *Did the drivers on the bridge feel anything when it happened—a jolt, a vibration? Maybe it hadn't registered at all.*

Behind them, a driver leaned on his horn. Miranda glanced at the pickup truck in the passenger side mirror. Same one as always. This stranger had been the last person to see her brother alive. Tires screeched. The pickup shrank in the mirror.

Colin turned the wheel to the right, putting his car in line with the abutment. "This is it."

"RANDY?"

Miranda awoke with a start. Her face was cold, drenched by beads of sweat chilled by the car's air conditioner. She let out the breath she'd been holding. Beside her, Colin was gone. In the driver's seat was friend and fellow paranormal investigator, Marc Malkasian.

"This is it. We're here." Marc pointed at the sign affixed to a stone wall. "Emery Zoo."

"Yeah. Sorry. Must have dozed off."

"You're the only person I know who can sleep with her eyes open." Marc paused. Then, in a softer voice, "The vision again?"

"What else?"

"Well, hopefully, getting back into the swing of things will make it stop."

"I don't know. I think Colin's trying to send a message but I'm just not getting it."

"If so, you're not going to figure it out sitting in the car." Marc adjusted his glasses and peered through the windshield at a group of four milling around near an SUV. "Team's waiting."

"Remind me. Who are we meeting here?"

Marc reached behind her to the back seat and retrieved his Baltimore Orioles cap. He'd begun wearing it months ago to conceal his thinning hair. "Stanley Peyton. He's the night security guard. He got permission from the board of directors to have us investigate. Though I suspect this whole thing might just be a publicity stunt. Oh, word of warning, Stanley seems like an eccentric character."

"How so?"

_____

"It's when the chimps go crazy, that's when I know the ghosts are here. It's not like when they get agitated at the visitors. That's different. I know because we're close, the chimps and me."

Marc and Miranda followed Stanley along the main trail to the Primate Playhouse, an enormous habitat divided into two sections. The enclosed structure was a simple, three-walled rectangular room with climbing bars along the ceiling, drooping ropes, and ladders made of faux tree branches.

That section was completely unoccupied as all three chimpanzees were enjoying themselves in the outdoor area known as the Playground. *My kids would love this place.* Miranda stepped up to the chain link fence as one of the chimps twisted

3

up and over the monkey bars then swung down and grabbed one of the rungs with acrobatic aplomb. A smaller chimp sat on a rope net devouring a lettuce leaf. High above, several loose ropes crisscrossed one another as they spanned the length of the Playground.

In the center of it all, a mound of heavy rocks formed a rough pyramid atop which sat the largest of the chimps, a king of his hill taking in all he surveyed. He scanned the newcomers with a stern gaze that drifted from Marc and settled on Miranda.

"That's a little creepy," she muttered.

"He seems to like you," Marc said. "Must have good taste."

Miranda shook her head. "I don't think the look in his eyes is a friendly one. Animals can sense the presence of spirits or those who've been touched by them and they don't always react well."

"Right around this area is where most of the activity's been happenin' the past three nights." Stanley tilted his head toward the trail which wound its way up a slight incline to a quaint garden filled with various flowers and a cluster of weeping willow trees that provided generous shade to a pair of park benches. Beyond the trees, the chain link fence marked the zoo's perimeter.

"When I make my evening rounds," Stanley continued. "I hear voices comin' from the garden up there. They sound like kids and sometimes I see shadows movin' around." Using both hands for emphasis, he pointed to the ground. "This is as far as I go after dark. Up there is about where those two boys died back in fifty-seven. I think it's them I'm hearin'."

"What can you tell us about that?" Miranda asked.

"Well, before the zoo bought up all this land in the late sixties, it used to be Paradiz Farms. Right up there, where the Weeping Willow Garden is now, stood a huge red barn.

According to the story I heard, two young boys were workin' in there one day. The oldest was up in the hayloft while the younger one was leadin' a horse in. They say somethin' spooked the horse and he bucked. The boy lost control of him and got kicked in the head. While he was knocked out, the horse trampled him to death. The older boy saw what happened and ran for the ladder to climb down, but slipped and fell from the loft. Broke his neck when he hit the floor and died instantly."

"God, that's terrible." There was a shuffling noise from the Playground behind Miranda. She ignored it as Stanley went on.

"To this day, I think those two boys are still up there in the garden. That's why I don't go anywhere near it. Don't want any part of that."

"Is there any other activi-hey!" Something struck the back of Miranda's head. As she brought her hand up to her ponytail, a sharp stone pelted her between the shoulder blades.

"Reno!" Stanley kicked the fence. "Cut that out, you little bastard."

The king chimp shrieked back at him from atop his mountain. He picked up another handful of stones and hurled them at Miranda. Marc pulled her away as Stanley threw his arm over his head and stumbled back. Most of the stones clanged and pinged off the chain link fence. The ruckus excited a second chimp who bounded from the back of the habitat and joined the other one atop the rock pile.

"Damn!" Miranda scurried up to the garden, well out of the primate's firing range. She tore off her hair tie and dislodged a small jagged stone that had grazed her scalp. She pressed her fingers to her head but there was no blood.

"You okay, Randy?" Marc asked.

"I'm sorry about that, miss," Stanley said. "I've never seen them go *that* crazy before."

"It's okay. I'm fine." Miranda gathered her hair together and replaced the tie. "First time for everything."

"Guess you were right about how they react," Marc said.

"Either that or my ponytail looked like a big yellow banana."

"And I thought only gentlemen preferred blondes."

Stanley threw his hands up. "No idea what the hell got into him, but I'm definitely reportin' this. They'll be inside the sanctuary overnight, so they won't bother you."

By this time, Reno had turned his back and ambled away to the far side of the habitat as if nothing had ever happened. The second chimp was nowhere in sight.

"What I was asking before being rudely interrupted." Miranda shot a sidelong glance at the hirsute attacker. "Was whether there was activity elsewhere in the zoo?"

"Well, the story goes that the mother of the two boys, Nellie Paradiz, was so devastated that she hanged herself from a tree on the other side of the property, where the reptile house stands now. You know them little boxes where you push the button and it plays a recorded message about the animals? Well, more than once they turned on all by themselves in the reptile house. I thought someone was in there. I went in, looked around, nobody."

"Good, that's where I'll start tonight. Marc, this side of the zoo is all yours."

"NOBODY GOES ANYWHERE ALONE."

Three hours later, an unseasonable chill in the night air replaced the blazing heat of the August sun as all five members of the team gathered inside the zoo's entrance.

"I know most of you don't need to be reminded of that." Miranda glanced at her team's youngest member, Eddie

Reynolds. What the nineteen-year-old lacked in stature, he overcompensated for with attitude and boundless energy, which sometimes worked against him.

The rest of the team followed Miranda's gaze until Eddie unfolded his lanky arms. "Hey, quit staring at me. I didn't do anything."

"Not yet," another voice chimed in. At just over six feet, Amy Healy was second to Marc as one of the tallest members of the team. She was also the newest recruit. Miranda had been impressed with her unswerving confidence, even when it meant confronting her fears head on. On the flip side, Amy's self-assurance brought with it an unrestrained candor that always managed to target Eddie. "What happened at Purcell Antiques last week?"

"Oh no," Marc groaned.

Eddie held up a hand. "You broke the rule on that one. You left the room and went upstairs without telling me."

"Don't blame me because you got scared of the dark. What was it again, two thousand dollars in Depression glass you knocked over when you ran out of there?"

"That rack was across the room from me when it fell over," Eddie said. "You know, sometimes things move by themselves when a place is haunted. You were the one who left as soon as the activity started. You tell me who got scared."

"I went upstairs to investigate the footsteps—"

"Enough!" Miranda barked. "First of all, I was only kidding, Eddie. Secondly, let's act like the professionals I know you to be. Put the past where it belongs and focus on this case, please.

"This is a large zoo, but we only have two hot spots reported by the security guard. One is up along the fence at the Weeping Willow Garden." Miranda pointed past the ticket booths to the trail that led off to the right. "Stanley claims to hear disembodied voices of what he thinks are two teenage boys who died on the property decades ago when this was a farm. Marc and T-Ron will go there first.

"The second hot spot is about halfway up the opposite trail in and around the reptile house. Amy and I will tackle that. As always, we'll take shifts so everyone gets a chance to investigate the hot spots while one of us gets a break and keeps an eye on our screen in the security office."

"T-Ron and I already set up the new wireless IR camera in the garden," Marc said. "This'll be its test run. Eddie volunteered to take first shift on the monitor and while he's at it, do a little research online to confirm Stanley's stories. Any questions?"

The group was silent, responding only with shaking heads and shuffling feet.

"OK. Let's get on it."

"I'D SAY we have spirits of a different kind here."

Twenty minutes later, in the Weeping Willow Garden, Marc held up an empty beer can. "Milwaukee's Best?" He laughed. "Definitely kids. Stanley was partly right."

He ran the beam of his flashlight along the ground until he found more cans strewn about near a hole in the fence. It was large enough to crawl through.

T-Ron shook his head. "The place is a damn mess." At forty-three, Tyrell Ronald Riverside—a.k.a. T-Ron—was the oldest member of the team and one of its co-founders. He and Marc were responsible for much of the electronic equipment. Together, they had invested some of their own money in the monitors, video cameras, digital voice recorders and, most recently, the infrared camera.

"I want to test something," Marc said. "Do me a favor, go back to the chimp habitat. Stanley said he's too scared to go past that point on his patrol. I'd like to know what you see in this garden from there. I'll move around and make some noise."

T-Ron sauntered down the trail until all Marc could see was the glow of his flashlight as it bobbed farther away then turned in his direction. It did little to illuminate the area through the sagging branches of the weeping willows.

Marc moved back and forth in front of the hole in the chain link fence. "Can you see me from out there?"

"You say something?"

"Yeah, can you see me?" Marc shouted.

"The trees are dense. I'm only catching glimpses of movement. The branches are casting shadows everywhere."

"Okay, I'm coming down."

A few minutes later, T-Ron and Marc made their way toward the security office carrying the IR camera and cables.

"Well, that should calm Stanley's fears," Marc said.

"Probably embarrass him, too. We should recommend they add a lamppost up there."

"Are you really out after this?"

Marc's best friend of fifteen years sighed. "Yeah, man. I may come back once in a while, but all the travelin's taking a toll on my marriage. I'm on my third one and I'd like it to last this time, you know? I ain't gettin' any younger."

"I hear ya, brother. Been through it once myself. You are coming to Randy's for dinner this weekend, right?"

"Damn straight. There's a woman who knows how to cook." T-Ron cocked his head at Marc. "I suspect both in and out of the kitchen if you know what I'm sayin'."

Marc smiled. "Yeah, I do."

"Then what the hell you waitin' for, bro? You need to make a move. Y'all ain't gettin' any younger either."

"I'm working on it," Marc said. "I wonder how Randy and Amy are doing on the other side."

"Maybe they found better beer."

"DUDE, we're totally scraping bottom here. Investigating a freakin' zoo." Back at the security office, Eddie pounded away on the keyboard of his laptop as he searched the web for anything on the history of the land. "We better find some serious activity here or I'm not even posting this case on our website. Every paranormal group in the world will bust our balls unless we get some irrefutable shit out of this."

"Why're you so concerned about what other people think of us?" Marc's voice betrayed annoyance, something that surfaced all too easily when dealing with Eddie.

"'Cuz I don't want to end up the laughingstock of paranormal investigators."

T-Ron snickered. "Too late."

Though tonight's case was an exception, T-Ron had often been paired with Eddie, the team's resident computer geek and webmaster. It hadn't taken him long to learn why no one else wanted to spend much time around the boy. Yet, despite the kid's callow attitude, T-Ron did his best to tolerate him.

On most occasions, his best wasn't enough.

"Wow, look at this," Eddie pointed at his screen. "It says that when the zoo was being built, construction crews unearthed the bones of a dinosaur known as the T-Ronasaurus."

T-Ron snapped his fingers. "You know, I thought I heard someone say the lion's den was haunted. Why don't you go put your head in its mouth and see what happens?"

"Why don't you jump in the gorilla cage and see if anyone can tell the difference?"

T-Ron leapt to his feet. "I think I see someone who's about to *become* a ghost."

Marc slipped between them and raised his radio. "Randy and Amy, come in, ladies." After a moment of silence, he tried again but there was no reply.

"I think Eddie's gonna go look for them," T-Ron said.

The boy raised an eyebrow. "Oh, am I now?"

T-Ron's expression was deadpan as he took a step forward. "Yes, I am."

ON THE OPPOSITE side of the zoo, Miranda and Amy made their way to the Reptile House by the light of the lampposts. It was a long one-story brick building with four windows along each side. During their guided tour earlier in the evening, Stanley had promised to keep the place unlocked until their investigation was over. No sooner had Miranda touched the handle of the glass door than her flashlight dimmed for a moment before going dark.

"Mine, too," Amy said. "And these are new batteries."

Miranda unclipped the walkie-talkie from her belt. The LCD display was off. She twisted the power knob to no avail. "Check your radio and mini DV."

After a moment, Amy shook her head. "Same. What the hell? There's no way everything could shut off at once." As if on cue, the closest lamppost winked out. "I stand corrected. I don't scare easy, but this is creepin' me out."

It was a popular theory among paranormal investigators that as spirits attempt to manifest, they draw energy from their surroundings. In doing so, they can drain batteries, as well as any heat in the immediate vicinity. Amy shivered as a chill wrapped itself around her. "Oh, my God, Randy, did you feel that? I think we have a cold spot."

Something flashed in the pale moonlight that crossed the entrance to the reptile house. Amy realized she was alone.

"Randy?" She stepped up to the door and pulled the handle. It was cool to the touch, but refused to budge. She cupped her hands around her eyes and pressed her nose to the glass. It was impossible to discern any details inside, save for the reflection of moonlight on various surfaces. A shadow passed in front of a window on the opposite side of the building.

"Randy!" Amy pounded on the door to no avail. She backed away until the air was warmer, and pulled her radio from her belt. It was still dead. She considered making her way back to the security office but couldn't bear to leave Miranda alone. The question was, how long could Amy bear to be alone?

IN THE BLINK OF AN EYE, moonlight through the windows brightened into the amber rays of the afternoon sun. Straw crunched beneath her feet. Somewhere behind her, a woman called her name.

Amy? The barn door slid aside, stopped midway, then continued as if requiring great effort to open. The silhouette of a young boy appeared. He held an oil lamp in one hand and in the other, a leather strap that led to the halter of a brown horse, young and sturdy. Except for a white patch between its eyes, it had no other markings.

"Come on, Bluff," the boy said. As he drew near, Miranda estimated his age at ten, perhaps eleven. "It's too hot out today. We'll ride tomorrow."

Miranda went unnoticed as the boy led the horse past her. He placed the oil lamp atop a wooden barrel and used his free hand to unlock the stall door and swing it open. At that moment, there was a loud thud from the hayloft, startling both boy and horse. Bluff jerked his massive head to one side as if preparing to retreat through the barn doors. The boy stroked the horse along its taut neck, but this only served to aggravate it all the more.

"It's okay, Bluff. It was nothing. Probably a squirrel or a bird." He pulled on the strap as hard as he could to turn the horse back toward the stall, but Bluff wouldn't have it. The horse reared up, yanking the strap from the boy's grasp and whipping him against the door of the neighboring stall.

The boy shrank away and for a moment, Miranda hoped his fear would keep him frozen in place, allowing the horse to bolt freely from the barn. Instead, the boy charged forward.

"No!" Miranda cringed as Bluff's left hoof slammed down on the boy's head, knocking him to the floor in a crumpled heap. The horse then bucked, kicking the barrel with its hind legs. The oil lamp tumbled to the floor, igniting a patch of dry hay. At that, Bluff bolted from the barn, leaving the boy unconscious and helpless against the spreading flames.

Within minutes, the fire had consumed the stall and the boy with it. The entire right side of the barn was soon ablaze. There was nothing Miranda could do. She was merely a spectator in this vision of the past, a dark and immutable event in the land's history.

On the hayloft, an older boy gazed over the edge on his hands and knees. He appeared to be drowsy and disoriented, as if he'd just awakened from a nap. At the sight of the flames, he pushed himself to his feet and swatted bits of hay from his hair and clothes. The fire had spread beneath the loft, scorching the underside of the wood. He had barely taken two steps toward the ladder when his left leg punched through the floor. His face contorted in agony from the pain of the jagged wood that sliced into his calf and the flames that singed his bare foot and ankle.

Miranda knew he had no chance. He sat back on the floor and pulled his leg up through the hole. He crawled toward the ladder, but the floor could no longer support him and gave way, sending the boy plummeting to his death in the inferno below.

Miranda dropped to her knees and wept, ignoring the fire that raged out of control around her. Above, wood beams cracked and groaned. She threw her arms over her head as the roof collapsed.

When she opened her eyes a moment later, Miranda found herself in the Reptile House once again—along with the two boys. The room was oppressive, as if it still retained the inferno's heat.

"We didn't know anyone could see us," the younger boy said.

His older brother stepped forward. "We've been trying to get through to people for a long time, but no one would listen."

"I'm listening now." Miranda wiped the sweat from her nose and chin.

"We're lost. We don't know how to get home or where our parents are."

She took their hands. They were cold, but she gripped them and spoke in a soft tone. "You never left. The farm is gone. There's a zoo here now. You—"

The younger boy's eyes widened. "What happened to our mom and dad?"

"They moved on."

"To where?" he demanded.

His brother placed a calming hand on his shoulder. "Please, can you tell us where to find them?"

Failing to hold back her tears, Miranda nodded. Discussions like this were never easy, especially with children. "Yes, I can."

ALL THE LAMPPOSTS turned on at once.

Amy shot forward on a park bench beside the Reptile House, nearly sending the video camera tumbling from her lap. She caught it and noticed the red glow of the power light. Flipping open the screen, she aimed the camera at the light of the lamppost. It worked, but not for long. The batteries were nearly dead.

"Amy."

She whirled to find Miranda leaning against the side of the building. "Randy, what happened? You're drenched in sweat. Are you okay?"

Miranda swallowed hard before finding her voice. "The barn was here. Whole thing burned down. Those boys died right where I'm standing, not back there." She waved in the direction of the Weeping Willow Garden.

"You had a vision."

"I need to sit down."

With some help from Amy, Miranda lowered herself onto the bench. She rocked her head back and closed her eyes. "Hot in there."

"You were only in there for a few minutes."

"A few minutes in Hell."

"There you are." Eddie emerged from the shadows along the trail. "What happened? We've been trying to get you on the rad—whoa, Randy, you okay?"

"Just peachy."

"She had a vision," Amy said. "All of our equipment lost power. Even the lampposts went out."

"No freakin' way."

"She's not lying," Miranda confirmed. "It's been a few years since I've had a vision that powerful."

Eddie took a seat at the edge of the bench. "So what did you see?"

Amy sneered at him and shook her head.

"If you feel up to talking about it, that is."

"Stanley was partly correct," Miranda said. "Although his location was off. The brothers did die in a barn—"

"—but the barn was here." Eddie finished. "Right where that Reptile House was built."

"How did you know?" Amy asked.

"Google."

Miranda chuckled.

"Seriously, you wanted me to research the history of the area, right?" Eddie said. "I found a website of some local historian and he had all the details of what happened here, so your vision was accurate. Though it sucks that you had to watch some kids die. Oh, and as for the mother, Nellie, she didn't hang herself from a tree, she died in a nursing home seven years ago at the age of eighty-nine. The father, Leonard, died from a heart attack eleven years before that."

"Nice work," Miranda said.

"Maybe we should send two other people back here," Amy suggested. "Set up video and audio inside the Reptile House. We might catch those speakers turning on by themselves like Stanley said."

"I'll stick around," Eddie patted his jacket pocket. "I got my digital voice recorder in case those dead kids have something to say. Just send someone back with fresh batteries in the video camera."

"'Those dead kids?' You're so rude." Amy turned to Miranda. "You feel up to walking back?"

"Absolutely."

The women started off along the trail toward the security office. Before they were too far away, Miranda turned to ask Eddie if he was sure he'd be all right by himself for a few minutes. It was, after all, against the rules to go anywhere alone. But Eddie was speaking into his voice recorder. This was not unusual. It was common practice to provide a brief introduction, so you know what you're listening to later when you review the evidence.

What was unusual were the ghosts of the two boys seated on opposite sides of him. They waved at her before vanishing.

"You worried about leaving Eddie alone?" Amy asked.

"Nah. He'll be fine. There's nothing to fear in the Reptile House, aside from that albino crocodile that was eyeing me up for its next meal."

CONCERNED that T-Ron would feed Eddie to that same crocodile, Miranda asked him to accompany Amy to the Weeping Willow Garden for further investigation while Marc joined Eddie at the Reptile House. However, the remainder of the night passed without incident and by two thirty in the morning, the team decided to pack it in and wish Stanley a good night.

It wasn't until she was halfway to the hotel that Miranda realized they'd forgotten to alert him to the hole in the fence and the sprawl of beer cans. It was just as well. She and Marc would be returning the following afternoon once Amy, Eddie, and T-Ron spent the day reviewing all of the audio and video footage, a task that Miranda didn't miss.

"The zoo was definitely haunted." In the passenger seat of Marc's SUV, she wiped tears from her eyes. The memory of those boys burning to death started her crying all over again. "At least the Reptile House was."

Marc nodded. "I believe you."

"Really?" Miranda said. "Because what I saw is no good without evidence and all of our equipment shut down."

"Eddie and I have footage from the Reptile House to review," Marc reminded her. "I used the IR camera and he set his voice recorder in there for a few hours. We walked around inside and out with the mini-DV, too, so there's going to be a lot to go over. If we come up empty, well, you know the drill better than anyone. Personal experiences are great but they're not evidence unless we capture them."

"What happened to me was a hell of a lot more than your run-of-the-mill personal experience," Miranda insisted. "I watched two kids die before helping them move on. At the very least, I want to mention it tomorrow when we present our findings."

"I agree, but I'd like to back you up with some evidence," Marc said. "Otherwise, you risk the typical skepticism that anyone gets when they claim to be a psychic or a medium... or both."

"But even without proof, do you believe the zoo was haunted?"

Marc turned into the parking lot of the hotel. "I said I believed *you*."

It was no secret that Marc had developed a crush on her almost from the time they met over four years ago at a paranormal investigators conference. To this day, she could see it in the way his aura changed whenever they were alone together. As a result, Marc always treaded lightly when it came to Miranda's visions.

"I'm sure the zoo was haunted," he continued. "Flashlights, cameras, and lampposts don't all turn off at once. That goes beyond coincidence. I know how frustrating it's been for you on past cases when we had no evidence to back up your visions, but when we did you came out a star. People were blown away."

"I don't need to be a star."

"All I'm saying is that everyone on the team believes in you as much as I do. In fact, I think Amy's got a little hero worship going on. But in the end, it's like anything else in life. You can't win 'em all."

"I never expected the evidence to back up my visions every single time. The paranormal's not an exact science. We've had plenty of cases where I didn't see or feel a damn thing, but we captured some evidence. I can't just turn it on and off like a switch. It depends on what the spirits want to reveal."

"I get it, and I know you think that if you could control your gift, your brother might still be alive."

Miranda let that comment go, although Marc was right. "Point is, I think I'm comfortable mentioning my experiences, whether or not we captured anything to show. This one was too vivid, too real, for me to ignore. I owe it to those boys to say something. Besides, our job is to disclose everything we find. We've taken the time to mention physical encounters— being touched by something unseen or feeling sudden cold spots—why not psychic encounters? Every time we decided not to talk about those, I felt like we were suppressing evidence."

Marc parked the car and turned off the engine. "You don't need my permission. You're a co-founder of the team."

"I'm not asking for your permission. I just want your support."

"Go for it."

RETURNING to the zoo that afternoon, Marc and Miranda took seats at a picnic table beneath a cloudless sky. The weather brightened Miranda's mood and she felt confident about revealing her vision from the night before.

Seated opposite them were Stanley and Emery Zoo's president, Andy Nearhouse. The latter's rumpled suit, salt and pepper beard, and imposing height gave him the air of an academic. According to the zoo's website, he held master's degrees in Zoology and Animal Biology.

For Miranda, those were the only redeeming qualities about the man. When Nearhouse had called them to schedule the investigation over a month ago, he made his disbelief in the paranormal all too clear. He'd admitted that while Stanley had reported numerous strange occurrences, his main goal in permitting this "charade" was to earn publicity for the zoo.

In short, Nearhouse hoped that a report from so-called experts would raise interest and in turn, boost lower than average attendance. Nevertheless, Marc and Miranda had agreed that Stanley's reports warranted investigation regardless of the president's motives. When the team had arrived last night, Nearhouse welcomed them with obvious disdain before departing in haste.

"So, is the place haunted?" He raised his hands to form air quotes.

"We'll get to that," Marc began. "I just want to take a few moments to review what happened."

Nearhouse glanced at his watch.

"You're both going to want to hear this," Marc continued. "The first place we investigated was the Weeping Willow Garden. You should get someone over there to repair the fence. Stanley, I'm afraid the voices you've been hearing are not ghosts, just some underage drinkers. We walked all the way to the back of the garden to find that the fence had been cut and bent inward. The area's littered with beer cans."

Stanley's pasty complexion reddened under Nearhouse's burning gaze. "As soon as we're finished here, you and I are taking a walk. I want to see this for myself."

"Yes, sir," Stanley replied.

Miranda spoke up in his defense. "It's no one's fault. That area is dark and creepy at night. Stanley's right not to go up there. What if those kids had a gun or a knife? If I may suggest, adding more lighting to that area would discourage this from happening again."

Nearhouse nodded. "I'll see to it. What else?"

"Amy and I investigated the Reptile House. There were reports of the audio players turning on by themselves, cold spots, and shadows. When we approached the building, all of our equipment turned off at once, including flashlights, video camera, and radios."

"Wow," Stanley whispered.

"And the lampposts," Miranda added.

"What?" Nearhouse drew back. "That's ridiculous."

"The two lampposts closest to the Reptile House went dark about a second after our equipment shut down."

"So what did you do?"

"Amy and I were separated. I went into the Reptile House and the door locked behind me. Amy was forced to wait outside. She said she felt a cold spot right beside the building but when she backed away, the air became warmer."

"I've never experienced that," Nearhouse said. "Stanley?"

"Uh, no. Can't say I have."

"Tell me, Ms. Lorensen, you think ghosts are responsible for the loss of power to your equipment?" Nearhouse asked in a way that reminded Miranda of a prosecutor baiting a suspect on the witness stand. "And could ghosts have generated these cold spots?"

"I can't say with absolute certainty that—"

"Is the zoo haunted, yes or no?"

"We don't... we don't have concrete evidence one way or the other."

"Thank you for your time." Nearhouse rose from his seat and checked his watch again.

As he turned to leave, Miranda called out. "One more thing. The story of the two boys who died in the barn was true, but Stanley's details weren't entirely accurate. First of all, the barn was not built near the Weeping Willow Garden. It was on the exact spot where the Reptile House stands now.

"Secondly, while it's true that a young boy was kicked in the head by a horse and his older brother fell from the loft, the missing detail is that the barn burned to the ground with the boys still inside. The horse kicked over an oil lamp, which ignited hay on the floor. The fire spread quickly. The older brother wasn't able to escape the loft in time before part of it collapsed. Those boys burned to death."

"And I suppose their ghosts told you all that?" Nearhouse asked.

Miranda steeled herself. "Google," she blurted. "Our researcher found a local historian's website. It provided details about the history of the property."

Nearhouse smirked. "Real-world answers win every time. Have a nice day."

"MY FOOT UP his ass could be a real-world answer," Miranda said as they made their way back to the parking lot.

"I thought you were going to tell him about your vision," Amy said.

"Given his attitude, that would've opened me up to more ridicule. Everyone I ever met who worked with animals was pretty cool, but this guy's a belligerent prick."

"You want me to go back and kick his ass?" Eddie asked. "Seriously, T-Ron, go kick his ass."

T-Ron nudged Marc. "Can he ride home on the roof?"

"Hey, who was it that validated Randy's vision?" Eddie said. "Screw that guy. It's just a friggin' zoo. Who gives a shit?"

"For once, the kid's right," Marc agreed. "Let's put some miles between us and this place."

CHAPTER 2

THE BOY AND THE HOUSE

It had been two hours since the boy awoke. No one was certain how the seven-year-old with an advanced brain tumor had managed to survive two comas in the past six weeks. The nurses, who had come to adore the sweet, hazel-eyed tot, attributed it to his strength of will or perhaps, a miracle.

Dr. Tammy Schell, the newest and youngest pediatric oncologist at Irvine Cancer Center, was hard-pressed to come up with a better explanation.

Matthew Meade had been admitted nearly eight months ago after being diagnosed with diffuse pontine glioma, an inoperable brain stem tumor. Initial radiation therapy had proved only temporarily successful, but that was expected.

Just before lapsing into his second coma, Matt had suffered from the worst of the symptoms including frequent headaches, vomiting, and loss of motor functions. He'd been unable to chew or swallow food. In short, Matt had been close to death. Bearing all of that in mind made his current condition all the more surprising.

"Matt, your parents are on their way back." Tammy cupped her hand over his. "How are you feeling?"

"Okay," he whispered. "But Lori's in trouble."

Tammy leaned closer to the bed and pushed a lock of auburn hair behind her ear. "Sorry, who?" This was probably another of his dreams or delusions caused by the tumor.

"I know that Tom Urban died here yesterday."

"Uh, yes he did. How do you know that? Did you overhear the nurses talking?"

"No." Matt shook his head, or tried to with what little energy he could muster. "Those two girls told me. They said we need to protect his wife, Lori."

"Protect her from what? Which girls?"

"The twins. They were standing right where you are." The boy turned his gaze to the ceiling. "It's too late. Lori's coming, but she won't make it." The wail of sirens in the distance grew louder as he spoke.

Tammy ignored them at first. Before she moved to this semi-rural town, she had lived and worked in Baltimore and before that, Philadelphia. Such sounds had been daily background noise, no more or less distracting than car horns or street music. Tammy knew the approaching ambulance was headed for the emergency room of Lancaster Hospital across the street. Though she would never admit it, the noise brought a sense of comfort, like being home again.

"She's here," Matt said. "But she's slipping away."

It was beginning to seem less likely that this was a delusion, which piqued Tammy's curiosity. She hurried from Matt's bedside to the window and opened the blinds. Two floors below, a cluster of nurses crossed the glass-enclosed bridge that connected Irvine Cancer Center to Lancaster Hospital. On the street, the ambulance was just coming into view, turning into the driveway toward the emergency room.

"How do you know that's Lori Urban?"

"The girls told me she was in trouble," Matt replied. "But the ambulance got there too late."

"When did they tell you all this?"

"I don't know... just before you got here."

"Matt, I checked with the nurses when I arrived. No one's been in this room since your parents left a few hours ago."

"It doesn't matter." Matt closed his eyes. "She's gone. Lori's gone now."

Tammy paused for a moment before returning to Matt's bedside. She waited for more information, but he was already drifting off. "Get some rest, I'll be back soon."

———

"I'M SORRY." Matt awoke with a shiver. It took a few moments for his eyes to focus on the woman standing near the window. "Tammy?"

Her short blonde hair was disheveled and tears streaked her face. It was definitely not Dr. Schell. The woman was taller with a slightly heavier build. Somehow, Matt knew it was Lori Urban.

"Why am I here?" The air grew frigid as she approached Matt's bed. "Can you help me?"

He tugged at his blanket. "It... it wasn't your fault."

"I couldn't stop. I couldn't control it." Lori sobbed. "It was like someone else took over and made me want to die." She wrapped her arms around herself and massaged them. "I'm so cold."

Matt wasn't surprised, considering she was wearing nothing more than a t-shirt and panties. The last time he'd seen a girl so barely dressed, it was a Halloween night. He had snuck into his cousin's room and hid in her closet wearing a werewolf mask. What he hadn't expected was that she'd get undressed to change into her costume before opening the closet door. Needless to say, both of them got a good scare that night.

"Tom is waiting for you," he told her.

"Where?"

"Go to the light. It's warm there."

Behind her, a glowing portal appeared, dim at first but it soon washed out the entire wall. Lori made her way toward it. Before stepping through, she glanced over her shoulder and waved. "Thank you." With that, she was gone. The portal faded.

Matt stared at the wall. "Wow."

THERE WAS little activity in the emergency room. A few scattered people sat in tan and green chairs in the waiting area. A pair of toddlers played with toy cars on the floor near their mother while the television, mounted high in the far corner, blared canned laughter from some indistinguishable sitcom.

At the reception desk sat an elderly man with blood-stained gauze wrapped around his left hand. Tammy moved to the next counter and tapped on the window, catching the attention of a burly, middle-aged nurse flipping through a thin stack of paperwork. With mild annoyance, she slid the window aside.

"Yes?"

"I'm sorry to bother you," Tammy began. "My name is Doctor Schell. I'm an oncologist from across the street. Can you tell me if a young woman was just brought in by ambulance maybe five minutes ago?"

"Yes."

"Was her name Lori Urban, by chance?"

"Sorry, Doctor, I'm not sure. I just came on shift when they rolled her in."

"Any way you could find out for me?"

"Are you a family member?"

Tammy shook her head. "No. Her husband recently died from cancer. He was one of our patients. His wife wasn't coping well and someone on my floor told me she was being brought here."

"I'll see what I can do. What was the name again?"

"Lori Urban. Thank you."

The nurse closed the window. Outside, the ambulance was still parked in the driveway. One of the crew was leaning against the back of the vehicle taking a drag from a cigarette, phone pressed against the side of his head. Tammy knew him only as Mickey, which was all she wanted to know. He had been introduced to her in the local coffee shop by one of the nurses from her floor. Since then, Mickey had taken a bit too much interest in Tammy. He'd always come across as desperate and the stench of cigarettes repulsed her.

Nevertheless, an idea occurred to her that was far more expedient to getting the answer she needed. Although Tammy didn't want to encourage Mickey, the circumstances called for a direct approach. With a fleeting glance at the reception desk, she charged outside, the doors barely parting in time as she barreled through.

Mickey paced beside the vehicle deep in conversation. His strawberry blonde hair was platinum under the stark street-light. He couldn't have been more than thirty-five, but the dark bags under his eyes and gray stubble added more than a few years. To his credit, he maintained a slim build, but that probably had more to do with chain smoking than proper diet and exercise.

After several seconds, Mickey noticed her and realized she was waiting for him. He dropped the cigarette butt and crushed it under the heel of his boot. "I have to go. Talk to you later." He slipped the phone into his shirt pocket. "Well, well, Doctor Schell, or can I call you Tammy?"

"Sure."

"How's life in the cancer center?"

Tammy nodded at the smoldering cigarette butt. "Keep puffing on those and you'll find out soon enough."

"Right," Mickey grinned. "Walked into that one. So, what brings you down here at this hour?"

She forced herself to step closer and lowered her voice. "Well, I shouldn't even ask you this and I'll completely understand if you refuse to answer, but what can you tell me about the woman you just brought in?"

Mickey hesitated. "How do you know it was a woman?"

"Just a hunch."

He pointed toward the ER. "Why don't you ask in there?"

"They seem to have a full house tonight. I don't want to get in the way. I saw you out here and thought you might be willing to help."

"Well, how can I resist those gorgeous green eyes? You didn't hear this from me."

"You have my word."

"Tall blonde, not much older than me. She coded about five minutes ago. It'll be a miracle if they can revive her."

"Is her name Lori Urban?"

Mickey nodded.

"What happened?"

"When we got to her house, she was lying on her bed in her underwear. We found half empty bottles of Keppra, Xanax, and OxyContin. She had powder on her lips. I think she crushed the OxyContin and swallowed the powder—a lot of it."

"Who called 911?"

"Her sister found her and made the call. She followed us here. I think she said the OxyContin was hers."

Lori had epilepsy, which explained the Keppra. She had also begun taking Xanax to cope with the stress of watching her husband die of cancer. How could Matt have known? "I don't believe this..."

"I'm sorry. Was she a close friend?"

"Thanks for your time, Mickey. Don't worry. This conversation never happened." As she sauntered off, Tammy tried to wrap her mind around the events of the last fifteen minutes. It all seemed impossible, like something from a movie or a dream. *Or the* Twilight Zone. *How the hell could Matt have known about Tom, let alone his wife?*

It wasn't outside the bounds of reason that, while in his coma, he could have overheard someone discussing Tom's death and Lori's emotional state. Perhaps all of that had made its way into Matt's subconscious and re-emerged as a dream in which he met a man that his mind identified as Tom Urban.

Glancing up and around, Tammy realized that she had walked halfway around the building. To return to work, she would need to either double back to the ER and take an elevator up to the bridge or cross the street to Irvine's main entrance. She stifled a yawn and rubbed her eyes. Tammy didn't need a mirror to know that they were red and bloodshot. *Christmas eyes.* She smiled at the term her father had used when she was a child.

Tammy's most striking feature had always been her bright green eyes. When she'd rub them red, her father would call them Christmas eyes. "Tammy must be tired," he'd say. "She's got Christmas eyes again!" *Damn right I'm tired.* She thought about Matt and hoped he was resting peacefully. *At this hour, at least one of us should be.* She'd always found it easier to raise the shield of clinical detachment with her adult patients than with children. Truth be told, she'd grown fond of Matt.

Tammy yawned again and realized her exhausted mind was wandering all over the place. By now, Matt's parents, Robert and April, were well on their way. Although Maureen, one of the nurses that had been managing Matt's daily care, would be there to meet with them, Tammy knew she should be as accessible—and alert—as possible.

She leaned against the cool brick wall of the hospital. Before talking to anyone, she needed a boost. Fortunately, she'd been walking in the right direction. The coffee shop at the corner was open twenty-four hours. As she pushed herself off the wall, Tammy resolved to mention nothing of tonight's events to anyone. Even if she were so inclined, who would believe her?

SOMETIMES, when she walked the streets of downtown Lancaster, Tammy was reminded of the surrounding Amish countryside and its rural towns with funny names like Bird-In-Hand, Fertility, and the ever-popular Intercourse. Even after six months here, she still did a double take when a horse and buggy trundled by, usually trailed by a line of irritated motorists. But Lancaster was losing its grip on quaint. Modern housing developments, with their cookie-cutter designs, had already outnumbered the distinct vintage country homes.

In the center of town, Irvine Cancer Center had become the most intrusive sign of the times. The eight-story concrete and glass facility stood out almost in defiance of the old-world charm of Lancaster's gothic churches, antique shops, family hardware store, and the corner grocery.

The new hotel and convenience store were still under construction two blocks away, largely due to the presence of Irvine. Almost all of the patients at the cancer center were from out of town and their families required a place to stay while they underwent treatment.

Tammy often wondered what the Amish thought of all of this, with their simple lives of horses and buggies and hand-made quilts. She wondered how they managed the changes that their society had endured as the world around them moved forward.

Forward! In line at Apollo's coffee shop, Tammy shook herself out of another bout of mental meandering and stepped up to the counter to place her order. Less than a minute later, sipping from a twenty-ounce cup, she turned to leave when someone called her name. A hand waved her over. It belonged to Jackie, one of the oncology nurses at Irvine. She sat across a table from her sister, Lena, a radiologist at Lancaster Hospital.

"Fancy meeting you here, Doc," Jackie said.

"Good evening, ladies." Tammy set the cup on the table and tore open two sugar packets. "Tell you what, if I didn't get this, they'd hear snoring from one of the empty beds tonight."

"The twelve-hour graveyard shift will do that to you," Lena said. "Especially if you're not used to working nights."

Tammy took another sip and closed her eyes for a moment. "Thankfully, this is the last week for it. I'm off tomorrow then back to day shift next week. So, what's new with you two?"

Lena held up half of a chicken salad wrap. "Lunch break. We usually meet up here at least once a week. Check this out." She slid a page from the local newspaper across the table. "They finally finished construction on that house at the old Vernon property. I can't believe anyone would want to live there. Way too creepy."

Jackie nodded as she swallowed her food. "Of all the available land in the township, why would this guy... what's his name?" She leaned over to scan the article. "Elias Gray. Why the hell would this guy build a new house there?"

"Maybe he's a horror freak," Lena said.

"What's the old Vernon property?" Tammy asked.

"Remember, I only moved here six months ago. I don't know who's who yet."

Lena and Jackie started to reply in unison.

"You barely touched your sandwich, woman," Lena said to her sister. "You eat, I'll talk for a change."

Jackie gave her a playful sneer as Lena launched into the story. "When we were kids, Jackie and I and our friends used to go into the original house that was there before they tore it down. I'm talking twenty-five years ago. On one particular occasion, we had the guts to go there at night. We lasted about ten minutes."

"What happened?" Tammy asked.

"When we went in, we heard a woman crying and footsteps above us, pacing back and forth. Then everything went quiet for about thirty seconds until we heard a gunshot. A woman screamed like someone was torturing her. We bolted out of there and never went back."

"So what's the deal with the house?"

"The township demolished the place years ago. This Elias Gray just showed up and bought the property from the county late last year. He's asking for trouble. That scream we heard was Nancy Vernon's ghost, no doubt about it."

"You didn't tell her the whole story," Jackie said. "In the late seventies, Jeff Vernon got caught embezzling from his company. He was acquitted, but I guess he cracked. One day, he grabbed a rifle and shot his two daughters then himself. Nancy came home from work and found them. About a week after their funerals, she killed herself in the basement. The kicker is, our dad used to work with Jeff Vernon. They were good friends."

"Well, I guess every town has its haunted house."

"Not much of a believer in the paranormal, I take it," Jackie said.

Tammy shrugged. "Never really gave it much thought. I have a friend back in Baltimore who's into it, though."

"So, how's Matt?" Lena asked. "I heard he's out of the coma."

Tammy stopped in mid sip and glanced at her watch. "Damn, his parents are probably there now. I better get moving."

"Is Maureen there to greet them?"

"Yeah, and she'll take them to Matt's room, which gives me time to get myself as alert and energetic as possible. As for Matt, he's awake and surprisingly cognizant."

"Has he spoken at all?" Lena asked.

"Yeah, you could say that."

———

THE HEADLIGHTS that shone through the kitchen window and glided across the wall startled Elias Gray. As he folded his newspaper and tossed it onto the table, he made a mental note to get curtains. There were still a few such minor furnishings left to complete. Elias had just moved into the house two weeks prior. Since then, he'd been busy arranging far more important matters—such as the visitors arriving at this late hour. It was nearly 3:00 in the morning. Right on time, as usual.

Elias took one last sip of tea and rose from his chair. He glanced out the window into the darkness as headlights approached the house. The pop and rumble of tires over gravel reminded him to call the contractor about having the driveway paved. He started across the kitchen toward the door to the basement stairs. It had been closed and locked a moment ago but was now wide open.

"This again." The bizarre event had started two days after he moved in. As of yet, Elias had no explanation for it. He dismissed it as he continued down to the basement and unlocked the metal doors that opened to the backyard. He pushed them outward until they stood vertical and locked them in place just as two armed men climbed out of a large, nondescript white van.

The driver, Leland, was the older and shorter of the two. Though only in his late forties, his thinning black hair and sagging, stubbled jowls added years to his appearance. The second man was his nephew, Hagen. Even at twenty-eight, he was referred to as "the kid." Though he was the tallest of the three men, Hagen's round, boyish face and unruly blonde hair complemented his often puerile behavior.

Without a word, Elias joined them at the van. Together, they unloaded several framed paintings of various sizes, all wrapped in canvas cloth or bubble wrap. They carried each piece down into the basement and leaned them against a wall.

"Well, that was easy enough," Hagen said, once all of the cargo was inside.

"There were no heavy wooden crates this time," Leland added, his voice betraying a slight German accent.

"And there won't be ever again," Elias said. "It's all paintings from here on out. No more marble busts or statues."

Hagen spun and crept to other side of the basement.

"What's wrong, kid?" Elias asked. "Looking for something?"

Hagen held up a hand. "I heard what sounded like a woman crying. It was faint, but it got a bit louder while we were talking."

"I didn't hear anything," Leland grumbled.

"Actually, I heard that sound down here a few days ago," Elias said. "Among some other strange things I couldn't explain."

Leland waved a dismissive hand. "You're both crazy. Whatever it was, it came from outside, a stray cat or something. We should close those doors."

As if on cue, they slammed shut with a thunderous boom. All three men exchanged startled glances.

"Probably... just the wind," Leland suggested, although by his tone and expression it was clear he didn't believe it himself.

"What wind?" His nephew said. "There was barely a breeze out there and those steel doors were propped—"

"Whatever! This is going to be one of our biggest payoffs. We're near the end now so it's understandable if we're a little tense. Just relax." Leland turned to Elias. "What possessed you to talk to the newspaper about the house, Janos? You're not supposed to draw attention to yourself."

"His name is Elias now," Hagen corrected.

Leland snickered. "Elias, Marcus, Karl, whatever you're calling yourself this month, whatever you look like today, you were born Janos Skorzeny. We go back thirty years and to me, you will always be Janos."

Elias placed a reassuring hand on Leland's shoulder. "And you haven't changed a bit in all that time, my stoic friend. The newspaper reporter came to my door. I had little choice but to talk to him. I thought if I did, he'd be satisfied and leave me alone. However, I refused to have my picture taken."

"Wouldn't have mattered," Hagen remarked. "How many plastic surgeries have you had in the last ten years? Your barely look like yourself with raised cheekbones and curved-in nose and you're wearing blue contact lenses to hide your violet eyes. Very clever."

"That and shaving my head were the easiest parts of the disguise," Elias smiled. "As for the paper, the article was printed at the bottom of some obscure section of local news. No harm done."

"What do you have to drink around here?" Leland asked.

"I wouldn't mind seeing the rest of your cool new house," Hagen said.

"*Alone among the dead.*"

All three men turned their gazes to the top of the steps. The door was open and light from the kitchen illuminated the upper half of the staircase.

"Is there someone else here, Janos?"

"No." Elias shook his head. "But then, you read the article."

Ever the pragmatist, Leland had never believed anything beyond the perception of his five senses. Which was why, when they heard footsteps in the kitchen above, he pulled his gun.

Hagen did the same and motioned for Elias to remain as he followed Leland up the stairs. When they were three steps from the landing, a shadow passed the doorway. Leland bolted into the kitchen. Seeing no one, he continued into the dining room. As Hagen emerged from the basement, Leland signaled for him to check the back door. It was locked. They made their way through the rest of the house but found no intruders.

"There was someone here," Hagen insisted later when the three regrouped in the dining room. "We heard the voice. We saw the shadow."

"Welcome to my world," Elias said. "That door in the kitchen that leads to the basement opens and closes on its own. I've locked it before going to bed only to find it wide open in the morning. I've heard the crying in the basement, but this voice up here... that was new. As for the shadow, it could have been caused by passing headlights through a window."

"This is a nice house you've built, Elias," Hagen said. "But what if it really is haunted?"

"Oh, for Chrissake!" Leland holstered his gun.

"If so, I won't bother them so long as they don't bother me, and if it becomes a problem, I'll deal with it. Keep in mind, Leland and I are from Germany where every place is haunted."

"So why all the cloak and dagger with these paintings?" Hagen asked. "Why do we need to bring them here in the middle of the night? Why can't we take them straight to your gallery?"

"You weren't hired to ask questions, kid," Leland snapped.

"No, it's quite all right," Elias said. "I suppose we can let our young partner in on our secret—over drinks, of course."

A few minutes later, the trio was seated in the living room. The dull hum of the central air unit could be heard beyond the side wall of the house. "How much do you know about the second World War?"

Hagen downed a shot of whiskey. "Mostly the highlights. I'm no history buff. Never really cared that much."

"Then let me tell you a story. I'll keep it short to accommodate the limited attention span of your apathetic generation. In 1931, my great-uncle, Otto Skorzeny, joined the Nazi army in Austria. He fought all over Europe, including the Russian front and gained a reputation as a daredevil. Otto was fearless, so much so that he quickly became noticed and was assigned to several commando teams. He participated in a few famous missions toward the end of the war, including the rescue of Mussolini from Northern Italy in 1943."

"Mussolini was an Italian dictator who threw in with the Axis powers," Leland added. "In case you didn't know."

"But he was arrested and incarcerated by his own people in July of that year," Elias continued. "The Italian military shuffled Mussolini all over Italy for two months. It was my great-uncle who tracked their movements to a ski lodge in the Apennine Mountains and staged a successful rescue without firing a single shot."

"Sounds like a fun guy," Hagen quipped.

No one laughed and Hagen fell silent under Leland's burning gaze.

Elias leaned forward in his seat. "Now, here's where it gets interesting. Otto was tried by the Allies after the war. They attempted to convict him on charges of violating some vague laws. I won't bore you with the details, but even though he was acquitted, the Allies kept him in prison until he escaped in 1948 and made his way to Spain, where he lived the rest of his life, becoming an engineering consultant for many world governments. He died in Madrid in seventy-five, after amassing quite a fortune.

"Now, all of this information can be found online. It's public knowledge, but what I'm about to tell you is known only to a privileged few. Throughout the war, Otto accumulated over three hundred pieces of artwork confiscated by the Nazis throughout Europe. Paintings, busts, statues, you name it. He kept them stored in an underground facility somewhere in Austria. To this day, no one knows where, but that doesn't matter because in 1952, Germany granted him amnesty."

"Actually, they called it de-Nazified," Leland interjected.

"This allowed Otto to return to Austria, along with two other former Nazi officers, and with their help he moved all of the artwork to Spain, completely unnoticed."

Leland raised his shot glass. "A risk-taker to the end."

"I have no idea how they managed it," Elias continued. "But in payment for their help, Otto gave a few pieces of art to each of those officers. It's said that the pieces were valuable, but we don't know what they were. After the collection was entirely in Spain, Otto began selling it off to private collectors in secret, fetching millions. The prevailing theory in the family was that his buyers consisted of the rich and powerful among the nations for which he consulted.

"By the time he died, a third of the collection had been

sold. Through the years, my family sold off another third or so to maintain their lifestyle and the rest has fallen to me."

Hagen was astonished. "You're telling me that everything we've been smuggling is already yours?"

"Give the kid a cigar," Leland said.

"Then why all the sneaking around?"

"While not strictly illegal," Elias said. "Selling art with such a controversial history tends to upset certain parties and they make their protests very public. Should the descendants of victimized families discover us, there could be complications. I can't afford that kind of attention and believe me, you can't either."

"It's a hell of a lot less dangerous than what we used to do, kid," Leland said.

"Which was?'

"You don't want to know."

Hagen gave an understanding nod before changing the subject. "I just thought of something. What if it's not your house that's haunted, but the artwork we've been bringing in? Maybe it's the ghosts of the original owners all pissed off that we're selling their stuff."

"Would you shut up," Leland growled.

"Well, if that's the case, Hagen." Elias poured another shot of whiskey. "We won't have to worry about it much longer. In two days, the art will be on its merry way and the only concern we'll have is what to do with our new fortunes."

CHAPTER 3

STRANGE HAPPENINGS

Disappearing acts were nothing new to Miranda. Apparitions vanishing into walls, shadows fading into dark corners, hovering mists that evaporate into thin air were all exciting events to any paranormal investigator.

However, when Miranda put something down and walked away, she expected it to be there when she returned, especially in her own home. Thus, when an entire tray of homemade Mexican lasagna disappeared into the mouths of her voracious teammates, her shoulders slumped. "Thank God I made two of them. You think you can save some for the chef this time?"

The team had gathered to celebrate T-Ron's retirement from ghost hunting and officially welcome Amy aboard.

"Sorry," Eddie muttered, a string of melted pepper jack dangling from his lips.

Amy leaned toward Miranda. "He already had seconds."

"I did not. Shut up!"

"Can't take you kids anywhere." T-Ron's wife, Linda, circled her fork over her plate. "Thank you, Randy. This is incredible. You always make the best stuff, although it pains me to admit it."

"She'll ask you for the recipe later," T-Ron said.

Marc raised his hands after clearing his plate. "One serving's enough for me. I dropped over thirty pounds since March and I want to keep it that way."

"You look fine," Miranda said. "Now if you'd just shave off that damn goatee. I hate facial hair."

"I'm reinventing myself."

"Translation—midlife crisis," T-Ron said. "Next it'll be a Ferrari."

"Lamborghini."

Linda shook her head. "Boys and their toys. So, Randy, what part of Europe are the kids in today?"

"Rome. They just got there from Paris. Next, it's two days in England, then Ireland, and they'll finish up in Madrid at World Youth Day."

T-Ron took a second helping of lasagna. "Your ex-husband has them on a whirlwind tour. Are they sending pictures?"

Miranda nodded. "By the ton. We can look at them after we eat."

"Oh, to have summers off again," Linda said.

"Come back to the classroom. We're losing our other social studies teacher next year. He's taking the vice-principal spot."

"Uncle Sam pays better."

"Maybe, but you couldn't pay me enough to put up with D.C. traffic." Just then, her phone chimed from the kitchen. "I better get that. Could be the kids." Miranda excused herself and snatched her phone from the table. "Tammy, how are you? Long time, no hear from." The two had been neighbors for a few years until Tammy moved to Lancaster.

"I'm doing all right. Is this a bad time?"

From the urgency in Tammy's voice, Miranda sensed that this was more than a social call. "I have dinner guests here right now. Can I call you back later tonight?"

"Sure. I think I may have a case for you."

"Really?" Miranda was intrigued. "Never thought I'd hear those words coming from you."

"Same here, believe me, but I think we've exhausted all other options."

"We?"

"Call me later and I'll give you all the details."

"Well, hold on. My entire team's here stuffing their faces. They can entertain themselves for a little while if you want to give me the low down."

"Are you sure? What I have to tell you is going to sound dramatic and probably a little crazy."

Welcome to my life. "Try me."

Tammy launched into the events at the hospital on the night that Matthew Meade had awoken from his coma and predicted the death of Lori Urban.

"I didn't know what to think at the time, so I let it go. Then two days later, a known alcoholic, Arnold Weiss, was driving drunk when he ran a red light and hit a guy named Mike Leigh. Mike died on impact. Arnold lost control of his car, drove up onto a sidewalk and straight into a brick wall. Needless to say, he wasn't wearing a seatbelt."

"I'm sorry to hear that," Miranda said.

"It gets worse. In fact, it gets unbelievable. Mike Leigh had two daughters. One of them is an oncology nurse on my floor. Her sister works at the hospital next to us. The day after the incident, Matt became agitated and warned his nurses that both Arnold's son and one of Mike's daughters were in danger. He insisted that someone check on them right away. I wasn't there at the time, but the nurses took it as a sign that he was declining, getting confused, losing his grip on reality. Matt *is* declining but patients with brain tumors don't develop psychic abilities."

"How long does he have?" Miranda asked. Another child with no chance, like those boys in the barn.

"He probably won't make it to the end of the week. He's going to hospice care in the next day or two."

"That's terrible. I don't know how you do it, Tammy." *Watching children die.*

"It's worth it for the ones we save. Anyway, a week after Arnold's funeral, his son hanged himself."

"Charlie," Miranda blurted. "No, one syllable like Chet... Chad? Is it Chad? Sorry, I had this name forming in my head."

"Yeah. That's right."

"Hold on." Miranda started pacing in her kitchen. She massaged her forehead as fleeting images assaulted her mind. This wasn't unusual. In past phone conversations, Miranda had gleaned information through sensations and images, some more intense than others.

"What about Mike Leigh's daughters?" she asked.

"The one who took his death hardest was Lena. She's a radiologist at the hospital. I got to know her through her sister, Jackie. In fact, Jackie's staying with her for a while to help her through this. Lena seemed like she was coping at first until she had a breakdown after their dad's funeral."

An audience had gathered in the kitchen doorway in the form of Eddie and Amy. "Short hair, bleached." Miranda turned away from them without breaking stride. "I see a woman in her early forties, average height, full figure. Does she drive a tan or gold SUV?"

"Yeah. Lena drives a tan Chevy Tahoe. Christ, between you and Matt, I'm getting even more freaked out. I don't believe in clairvoyance, but this is remarkable."

"Ever have a bad feeling about something or trust your

instincts?" Miranda asked. "That's a form of clairvoyance. Everyone has some measure of it."

"I guess. I don't know about the others, but Lena's always been strong. Still, with everything that's happened lately..."

"In other words, she's on a suicide watch."

"We didn't want to say that, but yes. Matt warned Jackie that something was going to happen to Lena. Jackie said she didn't believe him, but I think she was more rattled than she let on."

"Has Matt been able to predict every death?"

"Only the suicides," Tammy replied. "And only within a few hours before they happened, which makes me wonder if we would've had time to prevent anything even if we had believed him. Try getting the police to buy a suicide that's about to happen somewhere in town. It isn't like Matt provides addresses, just names, and by the time I look them up, it's too late. I keep hoping to wake up one morning and laugh all of this off as a bad dream."

"What do Matt's parents think of all this?"

"They don't know yet. I think he's too scared to tell them, and we don't know *what* to tell them. As you can imagine, his parents are dealing with enough right now. There's no precedent for this. It's devastating enough to know that your child has maybe a week to live."

Miranda knew Tammy was no stranger to death, but the bizarre circumstances unfolding in Lancaster were enough to put even the most clinical minds on edge. She sensed that someone—or something—was at work in the town, and it wasn't finished. Its motives were unclear, but its presence and energy were formidable. In her pacing, Miranda turned away from the kitchen doorway without looking up. She knew Eddie and Amy were still there. So why did her mind register two young girls in bell bottom pants?

She glanced back. Eddie and Amy were now bickering under their breath.

"Does Matt have siblings?" Miranda asked.

"No, he's an only child."

So who were those two girls I just saw? "Do you think his parents would let me meet him?"

"I can talk to them. I guess it's about time I told them what's happening."

Miranda stopped pacing and summarized the situation in thoughtful, deliberate words for the benefit of her eavesdroppers. "So, each natural or accidental death is accompanied shortly after by the suicide of someone close to the deceased."

At that, Eddie and Amy scurried off. Miranda allowed a fleeting smirk as she imagined the conversation that was about to ensue in her dining room. She turned her attention back to Tammy. "What are other people saying? Police, mayor, religious leaders. Anything from them?"

"Well, the cops are just reacting," Tammy said. "Not much else they can do, but the story has already hit national news. You probably would've heard about this soon enough on TV or online. The only cleric that said anything so far is a Catholic priest at Heart of Christ church. Small article in the local paper with the standard quote, 'thoughts and prayers for the victims and ask God to bring an end to this string of tragedies', etcetera, etcetera.

"Look, no one knows I'm calling you and I don't think anyone else is putting a paranormal spin on this, so if there's any way you could come here and work your mojo quietly. Last thing I want to do is draw media attention by bringing in a psychic. No offense."

Miranda chuckled. "None taken. I understand, but our first rule is to never go anywhere alone. At the very least, I'd like to bring two other people. We'll be discreet. I'll have them do some research into the town's past and see what they come up with while I talk with Matt—if his parents allow it, of course."

"I'll see what I can do. No guarantees, but at this point, we're open to anything."

Miranda ended the call with the assurance that she would contact Tammy in the next few days with her plans. After hanging up, she rejoined her team in the dining room. All conversation ceased as she entered.

"Sorry about that, but I have something that might pique your interests. You remember Tammy Schell who used to live three houses up?"

"The hot doctor?" Eddie asked.

Amy rolled her eyes. Everyone else laughed.

"The hot oncologist to be precise," Miranda replied. "She just called with an incredible story, some of which you might have already heard from my little eavesdroppers."

"Sorry," Amy said. "We just went in to get drinks. Next thing you know, it's deaths, suicides, psychic predictions. No sense trying to be coy about it. You knew we were there."

"Yeah, yeah." T-Ron waved. "You two were hoping to sneak a smooch where we couldn't see you."

"Ew!" Amy grabbed a pillow from the couch and hurled it at him.

Miranda dropped into her favorite recliner. "Good thing I wasn't talking to my gynecologist."

Eddie's face contorted into a pained expression. "Now that warrants an ew."

"So, what's this 'incredible story'?" Marc asked.

Miranda told them, interrupted by the occasional "wow," "what?" and "no way!"

"I told her I'd call her back soon. We need to keep this low key. I only want one or two volunteers."

Amy and Eddie raised their hands.

"What a surprise."

"We do have the McCarren house on Tuesday night in Towson," Marc reminded them.

"Is that the old lady with the footsteps in the attic?" T-Ron asked. "And doors that open and close on their own?"

Marc nodded. "Martha's ninety-one and lives alone. I figured I could take a quick run after work and check it out for her."

"I'll bet we can debunk most of that," T-Ron said.

Linda raised an eyebrow. "We?"

"Oh, right. I guess you're on your own, man."

Marc smiled. "Well, I'd much rather be going to Amish country, but I'm not fortunate enough to have my summers off."

Eddie raised his hand again. "How do we investigate something like this? It's one thing if a specific location is haunted, but that's an entire town."

"I know it." Miranda leaned forward in her chair. "But I got strong images and impressions during that phone call and I suspect they may be even stronger when we get there. If we're lucky, the answers might just present themselves."

THREE HOURS LATER, after her guests had departed, Miranda rinsed off the last plate and slipped it into the dishwasher. After pouring detergent into the dispenser, she closed the door and noticed a blurred reflection in the stainless-steel door. It moved from left to right before coming to a halt in her peripheral vision. It made no sound as it glided along the tiled floor, which became cold under Miranda's bare feet.

She ignored the presence at first, continuing with her chores. She had learned years ago not to be frightened by the appearance of spectral visitors, nor would she drop everything to attend to them. Death should not give license to be discourteous. Miranda wanted to help them, of course, but she would not allow them to disrupt her life. She was a single parent with three children, a career, and a home to maintain. These were her priorities.

Still, the kids were away for now and if this gentle presence was the return of the little girls she'd seen earlier this evening, then Miranda was all too happy to give them her attention. She dried her hands with paper towel as she turned to address her guest. "Yes, what can I—"

It had been twelve years since she last saw the tall, gaunt man who stood before her. He'd appeared to her just after the birth of her twin boys. Before that, it had been the birth of her daughter. He hadn't come to her wedding. Miranda's mother had joked that he probably didn't approve of Brian.

"Dad."

"How's my Miranda Panda?"

"You haven't called me that since I was eight."

Her father shrugged. "I miss my little girl."

"I miss you, too."

"I checked in on the grandkids. They're safe with Brian. Despite his other shortcomings, he turned out to be a good dad."

"Yes, he is."

Her father looked just as he had in the months before his emphysema—healthy and robust. As always, he was clean-shaven and his light brown hair spiked as it had been since his days in the Marines.

"I've been having visions of Colin," Miranda said.

"I know."

"Is he okay?"

"He'd be better if you'd move on."

"How can I? He took his own life, and I could have saved him if—"

"Depression took him. It wasn't his fault."

"Then why am I having—"

"Guilt is what you're having. Needless guilt. Let go, Miranda. Give him peace."

Tears welled up in her eyes as her father continued. "Now, as to why I'm here. You're going to help those people that your friend called about, but you don't realize how dangerous it is."

"Dad, my ability is dangerous in and of itself. I never know who's going to show up or when. The things I've seen... If I can't help people, what's the point of it all?"

"You can't save the world, Miranda."

"No, but I can damn well try."

"At what cost?"

"We've both seen the cost of not trying."

"You didn't know the depth of your brother's depression," her father said. "No one in the family understood it."

"You did. If you could come here tonight to warn me about going to Lancaster, you could have warned me about Colin." Miranda turned away and reached for paper towel to dry her eyes. "I could have helped him."

She glared at her father, but he was gone. "I could have saved him."

"THERE's something shady about that Elias Gray and his art gallery."

"Who?" Detective Denny Teelko asked before inhaling a forkful of mashed potatoes.

Seated across from him in a booth at The Pressroom Restaurant, retired newspaper reporter Frank Knedlhans leaned forward over his pasta. "The art dealer that bought the old Vernon property."

"Frank, you think everyone's shady."

"I don't think you're shady."

"That's comforting."

"I drove out there last week to check out the place. I was just curious to see how it looked with a new house. It was after two in the morning and I see this white van parked there and these guys unloading boxes and crates and stuff wrapped in sheets."

Denny shrugged his broad shoulders. "So?"

"I didn't think much of it, but I drove by a few nights later and the van was back with more guys unloading the same type of stuff. All of this after midnight. Don't you think that's a little weird?"

"The guy runs an art gallery, Frank. I doubt they ship their more expensive pieces via FedEx or UPS. A lot of it's probably picked up by the proprietor or delivered by the seller. Nothing weird about it. Honestly, Frank, I think you're bored. I understand, believe me. You were an investigative reporter for twenty-five years and now you manage newspaper archives at the Historical Society. Big difference."

With a dismissive wave, Frank slumped back in his seat.

"No, hear me out. This isn't the first time. Della's Deli last year. You thought Al Purdella was dealing drugs out the back door, so you called the cops only to find out Al was giving food to the homeless."

"Honest mistake," Frank said. "He was handing out packages wrapped in white paper. It looked suspicious. How was I supposed to know? Besides, you would've thought he'd mention something like that."

"Al's a humble guy. He doesn't like to brag." Denny took a sip of iced tea. "But you jumped to conclusions without getting the facts. All those days you were spying on Al, did you ever see money changing hands?"

Frank had no reply. He shifted his gaze to the window. The sun had set beyond Steinman Park and his moon-faced reflection, with its sagging jowls and sunken eyes, stared back from the darkened glass. *Denny's right. You're getting too old for this, Frankie.*

"Look, you saw something suspicious and called the police. In your own way, you did the right thing, but if you'd actually followed any of those homeless people, you probably would have seen them rip open those packages and start chowing down. Take my advice, Frank, leave the art dealer alone, okay?"

Frank sighed. "Fine."

The waiter returned with new drinks. Denny took that moment to change the subject.

"So, how's Ginny?"

"The Barefoot Contessa's doing all right. She finished her junior year at college and now she's back working at the library for the summer. Made the dean's list again this past semester. Still, she's the only girl I know that hates wearing shoes. Goes to class barefoot half the time like some damn hippie."

Denny shrugged. "My oldest girl has a friend that never wears shoes when she comes over. As for Ginny, she's always been a free spirit."

"Gets that from her mother."

"That and the fact they're both redheads. Have you talked to Gwen recently?"

"Christ knows where she is these days. Last I heard, she was somewhere in the Netherlands with her new sucker, uh, I mean husband. Good luck to him."

A few minutes passed as the men ate in silence.

Frank snapped his fingers and pointed at Denny. "Hey, what's going on with all these people dying left and right the past few weeks? Seems to be a run on suicides lately."

"Yeah, but none of them seem to be related, at least not yet. First guy dies of cancer then his young wife ODs. Then, two guys get killed in the same DUI. The car hits a pedestrian first then a brick wall. A week later, the drunk driver's son hangs himself in his house. Find a pattern in that."

"There's got to be a common denominator."

"We're working on it."

The waiter delivered the check to their table and wished them a nice day. Denny snatched it up as Frank reached for it.

"My treat, brother. Just promise me you're not going to stake out that art dealer every night."

"You have my word."

JACKIE LEIGH AWOKE with a start and leapt from the reclining chair. She damn near hyperventilated as she paced the family room. It was three o'clock in the morning and she chided herself for falling asleep. She'd been drinking black coffee all night to stay awake after a twelve-hour shift.

Jackie had dreamt of being trapped in a sealed glass tank. As she began to suffocate, two young girls appeared outside. She had pounded on the glass for help, but the girls merely stared at her. Even now, Jackie had no idea who they were, only that they'd been identical twins of about nine or ten years of age. Even their clothes matched, much the same way Jackie and Lena used to dress at that age.

Lena...

Jackie trudged up the steps to the second floor. After their father's funeral, and Lena's subsequent breakdown, Jackie had offered to stay with her sister for a week or two. Lena had refused at first, but Jackie's persistence won out. Of course, she would never admit that Matthew Meade's frantic warnings were the main reason she was here.

Lord knows that Lena had always been the stronger one and would eventually recover, but with recent events in town,

Jackie was taking no chances. As she dashed down the dark hallway toward Lena's bedroom, a low, mechanical humming caught her attention. At first, she dismissed the sound as the central air intake in the ceiling, but as Jackie crept into the bedroom, the sound grew louder. Two things struck her at once —Lena was nowhere in sight and the humming was that of a car engine. The master bedroom was directly above the garage.

Dammit!

Jackie charged down the steps and through the house to the laundry room. She unlocked the door to the garage and pulled, but it wouldn't budge. She tugged on the knob repeatedly to no avail. It was as if someone was on the other side, holding the door closed. Jackie pounded on it and screamed her sister's name. When there was no response, she bolted through the family room, threw aside the sliding door, and crossed the patio along the back of the house. Both garage doors were closed.

Jackie tried the window. It was locked, of course. The garage was dark save for the interior lights of Lena's SUV, but her sister was not in the vehicle. Jackie turned right and left, searching for something to smash the window. She recalled the new landscaping that her father had done for Lena in the spring. He had dug up a few massive rocks and some were left in the garden as accent pieces.

Jackie ran around to the front of the house and returned a moment later, carrying a rock the size of a steering wheel. She hurled it at the window. It shattered the first pane but only cracked the second. Another try successfully broke through. Reaching in, Jackie unlocked the window and threw up the sash. She climbed in, ignoring the shards of glass that cut and scraped the soles of her bare feet.

Gritting her teeth against the pain, Jackie limped past the SUV and slapped the button to open the garage door. Overhead lights flashed on as she reached into the vehicle and turned off the ignition.

"Lena!"

Her sister lay motionless behind the vehicle, dressed only in a powder blue nightshirt. She had no pulse. Jackie dragged her out to the driveway and began CPR, though she knew it was too late. No doubt Lena had been inhaling carbon monoxide long before Jackie woke up. When her sister was non-responsive, Jackie ran back into the house for her phone. Her hands trembled such that tapping three simple digits was a challenge. After calling 9-1-1, she knelt over Lena's prone form and spoke with the dispatcher. She ignored the barking dogs and the neighbors who were just now hurrying across yards and driveways in her direction.

All Jackie could think of were the two girls from her dream who stared at her as she suffocated.

CHAPTER 4

JUST IN TIME

"Heather..."

Matt was alone when he awoke panicked and disoriented. It had been a few days since Lena's death. He had hoped it was all over, but the ghosts weren't finished with him yet. Matt heard a name in his head but wasn't sure if he'd spoken it aloud. He just knew that he had to help Heather, whoever she was. He had to tell someone about her *now*. He pressed the call button strapped to the bed rail. Even such a simple motion had become an effort as of late and he let his arm drop to his side. A moment later, Matt was relieved when Jackie hurried in. She was his favorite and she treated him likewise. Her wavy red hair smelled of strawberries and was soft against his face whenever she tucked him in.

"Hey, Matt. What do you need, sweetie?"

"Heather's next. You have to get to Heather."

"Relax, honey." Jackie reached for his hand. "Who's Heather?"

Matt closed his eyes and whispered. "They told me, the twin girls. They told me her last name... Marceta. Her last name is Marceta. She's going to kill herself."

"You had a bad dream. That's all."

"No, this wasn't a dream. None of them are dreams. Heather's in trouble. Someone's coming for her. The same one who took your sister."

Jackie backed away from his bed. "I asked you not to talk about..." She trailed off, her voice raspy. "Lena... killed herself, Matt. Nobody else took her life. Now, I just buried two people I loved dearly. End of discussion."

"The ghosts are killing people," Matt went on. "They took your sister and now it's Heather's turn. You have to believe me this time."

"Stop it!"

On the day before Lena's death, the twins had warned him that she would be the next to die. Jackie had refused to believe him, but she spent the night at Lena's house anyway. Now, Matt was afraid that Dr. Schell and the nurses would start blaming him for these suicides. No one had made an accusation, of course, but it was in their eyes. He could sense it and he was afraid of what they thought—or what they might do.

Matt was moving to hospice care soon, which meant he was going home, but he wondered if someone might hate him enough to make sure he didn't make it. He knew that one day, the portal of light would open for him—but he wasn't ready yet. The girls had told him that there were a few more deaths to come. Then, all would be settled. Whatever that meant.

Another nurse, Lilly, leaned into the room. "Everything all right in here?"

"Yep." Jackie forced a smile. "Everything's fine now. Matt was just upset about a nightmare he had."

"Please, Jackie," he pleaded. "Call Doctor Schell. She believes me now. She told me to let her know if I had any more..." He shot a glance at Lilly. "...nightmares."

Jackie sighed. "OK. Lilly, can you get Doctor Schell on the phone, please? I'll be right there."

"I'm sorry about Lena," Matt said. "I liked her a lot."

"She liked you, too. We all do. So, who's Heather Marceta?"

"I don't know, but at least this time, I know where."

"And where is that, exactly?"

Miranda glanced at the screen on her dashboard. "According to the GPS, it's the next turn."

"What, are you deaf back there?" Amy jabbed.

Eddie ignored her. "That was ten minutes ago."

"This is the country," Miranda reminded him. "The next turn could be five miles and two farms up the road."

"Quit complaining," Amy said. "It's beautiful out here."

"It's boring out here."

"You're just mad 'cause I called shotgun."

As if on cue, the baritone male voice of the GPS chimed in. "In point two miles, turn right onto Wagon Wheel Road."

In the backseat, Eddie leaned forward. "About time."

"Can we strap him to the roof rack on the way home?"

Miranda shook her head as she made the turn. "Don't make me regret bringing you two. Tammy said she's about halfway down the street on the right just before the woods."

"Drive point one mile to your destination," the voice announced.

A moment later, a seemingly endless cornfield opened up to a low-cut lawn surrounding a modest two-story stone home. It sat slightly off center on the property, with a larger section of lawn on the left side that bordered dense woods.

"Dark red door and shutters," Miranda observed. "This should be it."

"You have arrived at your destination."

"Thank you." As Miranda pulled into the driveway, the

front door of the house opened, and Tammy stepped out onto the slate walk to greet them. She was barefoot, wearing jeans and a flattering yellow tank top. Her brown hair was pulled up in a ponytail.

"Oh, yeah, this is definitely the place," Eddie said.

"Down, boy," Amy warned. "She's way out of your league."

"What do you know about my league?"

"It's the pee-wee league and you're the shortstop."

Miranda laughed as she opened the door and waved to Tammy.

"Just try not to embarrass yourself... or us," Amy said as she and Eddie climbed out of the car.

"Hey, lady." Miranda smiled as she and Tammy embraced. "You look great. How's country life treating you?"

"Well, it took a while to adjust. The solitude out here was eerie at first, especially at night when you really notice how quiet it is. Between the woods and the cornfields, it felt like a horror movie. Plus, this is an eighty-year-old house complete with all the usual creaks and groans. Took me nearly a week to get a decent night's sleep."

Miranda gestured toward her teammates. "You remember Eddie. And this is our newest member, Amy."

"It's a beautiful place," Amy said as she shook Tammy's hand.

"Oh, it's amazing for a rental. Come on in, I'll show you around. Want anything to drink? I have iced tea, lemonade—"

No sooner had they started toward the door than Tammy's phone buzzed.

"Sorry." She glanced at the screen. "It's work. Go on in, I'll be right there. Feel free to raid the fridge. Glasses are in the cupboard to the right."

Miranda led the others inside as Tammy paced in front of the house, phone pressed against her ear.

"So rustic," Amy said. "I like it."

The walls of the living room and dining room were covered in mahogany-stained wood paneling. Family pictures and a few vintage movie posters contrasted the dark red. The floors were hardwood with well-placed area rugs. Modern double hung windows were wide open while ceiling fans spun, pushing down a welcome breeze.

Tammy bounded into the house behind them. "That was Jackie who called, one of our nurses. Matt had another vision. There's a woman that lives about fifteen minutes away named Heather Marceta. She lost her fiancé in Iraq. His name was Nick. His body was shipped back here, and the funeral took place a few days ago."

"That's terrible," Miranda said.

Tammy nodded. "I don't know Heather personally, but I do know her brother, Kyle. He owns the gym in town and we've been on a few dates. Long story short, Matt just claimed that the 'ghosts,' to use his term, are going to kill Heather today."

"Did you call her brother?" Miranda asked.

"I was going to do that on the way, though I'm not sure what to tell him. My car's in the garage, if you want to pull out—"

"That'll take too long. I'll drive if you navigate."

"Deal." Tammy slipped on a pair of flip flops just inside the door. "No offense, but Heather's going through hell right now and I don't want to show up with a gang of total strangers."

"We understand," Amy agreed. "Maybe Eddie and I could get started researching the town's history to see if anything like this has ever happened before."

"That works," Tammy said. "Wi-Fi's wide open at the moment, I haven't gotten around to securing it yet. Didn't think the Amish would be rolling by with laptops looking for a signal. Spare bedrooms are upstairs at the end of the hall to the right. Bathroom's on the left before that. One bedroom has a futon, the other has an air mattress folded up in the closet. Sheets are on the top shelves. Got all that?"

"Sounds good," Amy nodded. "Please call if something happens."

"We will." On her way out, Miranda turned back. "Oh, and try not to kill each other."

"WELL, THIS SUCKS," Amy said as she and Eddie made their way upstairs. "As soon as we arrive, all hell breaks loose and we have to stay behind."

"It ain't so bad." He flipped the hallway light switch. "Paranormal events happening all over town and it's gonna be dark in about two hours. It's kinda… romantic."

Amy held up a hand. "Oh, no. We are *not* going there. I don't mind the innocent flirting we do from time to time but that's where it ends."

"What? No. I didn't mean it that way… well, then again…"

Amy raised an eyebrow, her expression sheer ice.

"All I meant by 'romantic' was that this is every ghost hunter's dream."

"Yeah, well, I don't want to know what you dream about." Amy stalked into the bedroom to their right and opened the closet doors. "Ah, smells like cedar. I love it. Futon or air mattress? I'll let you pick since I called shotgun for the ride here."

"I'll take the futon," Eddie replied. "Since you and Randy will be sharing a room, you should take the air mattress."

Amy left the closet doors open and brushed past him. "Then this is your room. The futon's folded up in there."

"Hey, why don't we investigate this house while we're here?"

"Because we didn't ask Tammy for permission and we're already on a case. Focus, Eddie." Amy dragged the air mattress out of the closet in the neighboring bedroom and connected the air pump. "Let's finish up here so we can get back downstairs and start researching."

"All work and no play."

"You'll need to move up to the big leagues before you can play with me, shortstop."

"Is that an invitation?"

Amy said no more as she switched on the air pump.

WHILE EN ROUTE to Heather's apartment, Tammy called Kyle only to learn that he had been with his sister for a few hours. Heather was devastated over the death of her fiancé, but according to Kyle, she was a "tough girl" accustomed to holding her own.

"He said Heather hasn't shown any indications of being suicidal."

"Neither did the others," Miranda said. "At least from what you told me."

"True."

Heather lived in a second-story garden apartment with a private entrance and a balcony that overlooked the street. As Miranda pulled up to the curb, a slim, dark-haired man with a goatee peered down at them from the sliding glass doors. After a moment, he stepped away.

"Was that Kyle?"

"Yeah." Tammy hesitated before unbuckling her seatbelt. "You know, I'm way out of my element here. This is going to be awkward."

"Don't worry. I'm used to that. We better get in there."

"Getting any vibes?" Tammy asked.

"Vibes?" Miranda chuckled. "No. No vibes yet."

Kyle appeared in the doorway as the women stepped out of the car. He was a head taller than Miranda, wearing black running shorts and a sky-blue polo embroidered with the logo of his gym. "Hey, Tammy. Thanks for comin', although I'm not sure I understand what's goin' on."

"I'll explain once we're upstairs."

Miranda extended a hand as Tammy introduced her. "I'm sorry for your sister's loss, but we shouldn't leave her alone for too long."

"Yeah, sure. Come on in." Kyle motioned them inside.

As Miranda climbed the steps, she sensed an hostile presence waiting at the top. Something didn't want her there. Pressure behind her eyes intensified until her vision blurred. She clutched the railing against a wave of vertigo but pressed on until she reached the apartment. By the time she turned the corner into the living room, her vision cleared and the pressure in her head diminished to a tolerable level. Whatever this entity was, it had backed down—for now. In the doorway below, Tammy and Kyle conversed in whispers.

"Trust me." She gave him a quick kiss before starting up the steps.

"Well, since you put it that way." He closed the door and followed. "But I'm tellin' ya, Heather's coping just fine. The Marcetas are a strong family. We can handle whatever life throws at us... or takes away."

In the living room, several flower baskets were lined up on the floor in front of a cherry wood entertainment center. A haphazard array of sympathy cards flanked the TV where an old black and white movie was playing. To the right, a throw blanket lay in a heap in the middle of a tan leather sofa as if someone had been sitting there a short while ago.

"Huh, she was just here," Kyle muttered.

From somewhere down the hall, a door slammed. When Kyle started toward the sound, Miranda turned to Tammy. "Getting a vibe."

"Heather?" Kyle called. He nearly collided with her as she emerged from the laundry room. "Sorry. We didn't know where you were."

"Just putting clothes in the dryer, jeez!" She peered over her brother's shoulder at the visitors. "Are these the two who think I'm gonna off myself?"

"No one's sayin' that exactly."

Heather ran a hand through her sandy blonde hair, pushing it away from her face. With a sidelong glance at Kyle, she stepped around him and introduced herself to Tammy and Miranda.

Heather was a few inches shorter than her brother, with what could have been considered a full figure. She wore no makeup and her hair was damp and uncombed as if she had just showered. Drooping eyelids betrayed fatigue and sorrow as much as her slouched posture. A well-worn T-shirt and frayed denim shorts completed the look of someone far too preoccupied with grief to be concerned with appearances.

"So you're the doctor that my brother can't stop talking about. Now I see why."

Tammy blushed.

"Sorry," Kyle said. "She has a habit of embarrassing me every chance she gets."

"What are sisters for? Why don't you fetch these ladies something to drink?" Heather gestured toward the living room. "Make yourselves comfortable. So, my brother told me you were coming here because you think I'm gonna commit suicide."

"Well, we're concerned," Tammy replied. "We wanted to see if there was anything we could do."

"We?" Heather shifted her gaze to Miranda. "Not that I'm ungrateful, but we don't even know each other. Are you a grief counselor or something?"

"Not at all." Miranda had been trying to think of a reason for their visit, something that wouldn't sound as outlandish as the truth. The last thing she wanted to do was upset someone already in a fragile state. "Actually, I'm a high school history teacher."

"Oh. Around here?"

"No, in Baltimore.

"Randy and I used to be neighbors," Tammy added. "Before I moved here."

"I see."

"Maybe I should start from the beginning." Tammy imparted the events of the past week, including Matt's predictions, and revealed the true purpose of Miranda's visit. By the time she reached the end of the story, the color had drained from Heather's face.

"I know you're going through hell," Miranda said. "But you can imagine that with everything Tammy just told you, we had to come."

"No. This is absurd." Heather rubbed her bloodshot eyes. "Let's say I believed you. If Nick was really able to communicate from the other side, why wouldn't he talk to me instead of some kid we never met? It doesn't make sense."

"I honestly don't know. There must be something special about Matt—"

"You don't know? I thought you were the psychic or medium or whatever. I thought you were the so-called expert."

"When it comes to the spirit world, I don't think there's any such thing as an expert."

"Well, then maybe there's no such thing as my dead fiancé sending messages from beyond."

"Heather, calm down, please," Kyle said. "They came here because they care—"

"It's none of their damn business." She leapt from the sofa and pointed at Kyle. "You know what I'm going through. I haven't slept in a fuckin' week, I barely made it through Nick's funeral, and now these two show up with some bullshit story as if I don't have enough to deal with. What the hell do you people want?"

"I'm sure they just want to help."

"Heather." Tammy leaned forward in her chair. "Please believe me when I tell you that we didn't come here to add to your grief and we certainly don't want anything from you. We're here because a little boy has been making some frightening predictions and so far, they've all come true. I know this a horrible time for you, and this is a lot to unpack, but we just want to be sure you're safe."

Heather closed her eyes and took a deep breath to regain her composure. "OK, fine. I'm sorry for freakin' out."

"You don't need to apologize," Miranda said.

"I appreciate your concern, but I'm not suicidal. I don't have thoughts of killing myself. Lord knows, losing Nick was the worst thing that's ever happened to me, but I know I'll get through this. I have faith, not to mention a supportive but sometimes blockheaded brother. What I am is exhausted, mentally and physically. If you don't mind, I'm going to crash for a while." Before leaving the room, she thanked Tammy and Miranda and welcomed them to stay as long as they liked.

When the bedroom door closed at the end of the hall, Kyle sighed. "That went well."

"We didn't mean to upset her," Tammy said. "But I had to tell her the truth. Look, Miranda can testify that I'm the biggest skeptic in the world when it comes to the paranormal but right now, no one has an answer to what the hell's going on in this town and a lot of folks are scared."

"How many people know about the kid's predictions?"

"Not many. The nursing staff is sworn to secrecy."

Kyle turned to Miranda. "And you're here to see if this is some kind of supernatural event?"

"I came here with two members of my team, who—" The pressure that Miranda had felt earlier returned with a vengeance. She winced and doubled over against a wave of nausea. Hands gripped her shoulders.

"Randy, what's wrong?" Tammy asked.

When Miranda opened her eyes, tunnel vision and vertigo overcame her. "Kyle, get in there. Get to your sister now."

"Why? She's just taking a nap."

"She's in trouble. Go!"

He bolted down the hall and knocked on Heather's bedroom door.

"Can you stand?" Tammy asked.

Miranda pushed herself off the sofa and dropped to her knees.

"Take it slow."

"I have to get in there. There's an entity here. Matt was right. It's after Heather and it's trying to keep me out of the way."

With Tammy's help, Miranda forced herself to stand. The nausea had passed, and the tunnel vision was beginning to dissipate. "I'm good. Let's go."

As they started down the hall, sobbing from Heather's bedroom grew louder. Her brother opened the door and peeked into the room.

"Leave me alone!"

In the doorway, Kyle raised his hands. Tammy and Miranda stopped a few steps behind him. The meager glow of a streetlamp through mini blinds provided the only illumination in the room. Miranda could see Heather kneeling on her bed. She held something outstretched in one hand, but it was indistinguishable in the darkness.

"Stay away from me." Her voice quivered. "All of you, just stay the hell away from me."

Kyle moved his hand toward the light switch. The movement was enough to allow Miranda to see the silver gun in Heather's hand.

She backed away from Kyle and pressed herself against the wall in the hallway, out of Heather's line of sight. She brought a hand up close to her chest, thumb and forefinger outstretched in the symbol of a gun. Tammy's eyes went wide.

"Heather," Kyle said. "I'm turning on the light. Maybe we can—"

"I want it dark. Just get out."

"Why? Please, tell me what you're doing."

Heather doubled over, sobbing. Kyle glanced over his shoulder at Tammy and Miranda. He waved them back with his raised hand. "Heather, please let me help you."

His sister caught her breath before she spoke again. When she did, her voice was hoarse and tired. "You can't stop what's happening. None of you can, not even the medium. Believe me, I never wanted this, but I have no choice."

"I don't understand."

"This doesn't involve you. Please, just leave. Take your girlfriend and the medium with you. I don't want to hurt any of you."

"Of course this involves me," Kyle insisted. "I'm your brother. You and I are all the family we have. I don't want to lose you. I'm putting my hands down now, but I'll stay right here if you want."

Tammy pulled Miranda into the laundry room. "We need to call the cops."

"That isn't Heather in there."

"What?"

"She's not in control of her actions."

"Are you saying she's possessed?"

"Possibly since before we got here. I'm not sure. I need to get to her."

"What we need to do is call the cops."

"If they show up, this could end badly. If I can contact the entity that's controlling her, I might be able to talk her down."

"And if not?"

"Get out of here as quietly as you can. Wait by the car. If you hear gunshots, call the cops."

Tammy shook her head. "I'm not leaving either of you."

"We need someone far enough away to be able to call the cops if she starts shooting."

"I'm sorry I got you involved in this."

"This isn't my first dangerous case and it won't be my last. Now go." Miranda nudged Tammy toward the door before making her way back to Kyle.

"Heather, where did you get the gun?" he asked.

"From Nick. He gave it to me before he deployed. We went to the range. He taught me how to use it. I want to be with him again. I don't want to live without him." Heather turned the gun and pressed the muzzle to her chest.

"No!" Kyle lunged forward.

Miranda chased after him, slapping the light switch on her way in. Heather yelped as Kyle seized her wrist and twisted her arm downward. The gun dropped to the carpet. Miranda grabbed Heather's flailing legs, but not without taking a random kick to the side of her head. She was grateful that the woman was wearing only socks as she wrapped her arms around Heather's calves, binding them together.

"Get the fuck off me!" With her free arm, Heather pummeled Kyle between the shoulder blades. "I want to die. Dammit, just let me die!"

"Leave me alone." Matthew Meade struggled against his mother's embrace. "Just let me die!"

His father, Robert, hurried into the room with Jackie in tow. "I'm not sure why he's doing this."

"Matt, honey, please calm down. It's going to be OK." April glared up at Jackie. "What are you people doing to my son in here?"

"He's been having occasional nightmares and hallucinations," Jackie said. "But they've never been like this."

"Why didn't you tell us?"

Heather had stopped screaming but continued to struggle. She squirmed her way toward the edge of the bed, bringing herself within arm's reach of the gun. Miranda tightened her grasp on Heather's ankles and dragged her back. This served to infuriate the woman all the more.

Kyle winced under her ruthless pounding. A dark stain formed on his shirt. "Now what?"

"For one, that's going to stop right now." Clutching Heather's wrist, Tammy forced her arm down to the bed. With one last futile effort to yank her limbs free, Heather realized defeat. As her body went limp, she turned her face away and sobbed.

"Oh, thank God." Kyle lowered his head, sweat rolling down the side of his face.

"Don't let up," Miranda warned. "She could be playing us."

A dull throb started in her head, either from the stress of the night's events or the kick to her temple. She straightened herself and felt the sides and back of her shirt peel away from her damp skin. She shifted Heather's ankles until she held them together under one arm. "Tammy, I thought you went outside."

"And miss all the fun? Are you sure we don't need the cops?"

"I just want to talk to her," Miranda said. "Heather, look at me. Look at me right now."

Heather regarded her with a vacant expression. Without much effort, she liberated her arm from Tammy's grip and slipped out from beneath her brother. Neither of them moved. They were frozen in place. Time seemed to stop as the air around the bed turned frigid. The woman pushed her hair back to reveal a face that was not Heather's. Whoever this was, her features were older, softer, and her brown eyes were filled with trepidation.

"Who are you?" Miranda asked.

"I don't have long." The woman's low voice conveyed urgency. "He's close. He forces me to do these things. There will be no peace until they're all dead."

"Who is he?"

"I can spare this one. She's not that important, and she's so young. She really didn't have anything to do with it."

"With what? Please help me to understand."

"He's close. I can't stay." Heather collapsed onto her brother.

"Wait," Miranda said. "Just give me a name."

"What the hell?" Tammy gaped at her empty hands.

All eyes turned to Heather as Kyle eased her head onto a pillow. "What's happening?" she whispered.

"I'm not sure," he said. "How do you feel?"

"Nauseated... and a little dizzy."

"It'll pass soon. You were having a nightmare," Miranda said. "You were shouting so we came in to check on you."

"I remember saying things I didn't mean."

"You were... talking in your sleep," Kyle said. "It's OK now. Everything's fine."

Heather frowned at Miranda. "Then why is she holding my legs?"

SEATED in the dining nook ten minutes later, Miranda pressed a cold compress to the side of her head. It was little more than three ice cubes wrapped in a damp washcloth. "She should be fine after a good night's sleep. I doubt you'll have a repeat incident."

"How do you know that? Ow!" Across the table, Kyle straddled his chair. He had removed his shirt and was leaning forward as Tammy treated the wound between his shoulder blades.

"Your sister was possessed."

Kyle sat up. "What?"

"Stay still." Tammy ordered as she applied a bandage.

"Look, I don't know what your beliefs are," Miranda said. "But I'll tell you what I learned tonight. First, there's the spirit of a woman who claims she's being forced by a man to go around killing people. Now I'd venture a guess that this man is also a spirit, but I'm not a hundred percent certain yet."

"Wait." Kyle held up a hand. "Heather told you this? Or should I say the ghost that possessed her? When did she say all of that?"

"After she managed to free herself from the two of you. It was a brief conversation. I didn't glean much, but she promised to spare Heather because your sister was, and I quote, 'not that important,' whatever that means."

Kyle laughed. "I can't believe this."

"Whether you do or not, it's happening. You probably

think I'm crazy. Maybe you think I'm lying. I'm not unaccustomed to either."

"All I care about is my sister. We're all the family we have. There's no one else left." Kyle tapped on the semi-automatic lying in the middle of the table. "And this thing's going where Heather can't find it until I know she's all right."

Tammy massaged his shoulders. "You're a good brother. We know you'll take care of Heather." Her phone buzzed. She unclipped it from her belt and gazed at the screen. "Sorry. I need to take this." She rushed through the living room and out onto the balcony.

Kyle slipped on his shirt. "You said my sister was possessed by the ghost of some woman who's being forced to kill people."

"Correct," Miranda replied. "And if my theory's right, these ghosts are responsible for the recent spate of suicides around here. I need to talk to Matt, the boy in the hospital. He may know more."

"I like a good ghost story as much as the next guy, but I never believed in much of anything. I'm not religious at all. That's Heather's gig, but if what you're telling me is true then there's a Catholic church on the other side of town called Heart of Christ. Heather and Nick were going to be married there. If you end up going to a priest for help, ask for Father Rourke, and if you need some backup, let me know. I'll be your witness."

"Thank you, that's good to know."

"How would you like to talk to Matt tonight?" Tammy returned to the dining nook. "That was Jackie who called, one of my nurses. You're not going to believe this. At about the same time we had to restrain Heather, Matt's parents were visiting him. For no apparent reason, he started freaking out and screaming at them. His mother had to hold him down to keep him from hurting himself. He said he wanted to die."

"Let me guess," Miranda said. "He calmed him down about fifteen minutes ago."

Tammy nodded. "I'm going there now to talk to his parents. They're waiting for me. It's about time I tell them the truth, and I think this may be the perfect opportunity for you to meet him."

CHAPTER 5

BROKEN FAMILIES

With assurances from Kyle that he would keep watch over Heather until morning, Tammy and Miranda said their goodbyes. On the way out, Miranda tossed her car keys to Tammy so she could call her team and exchange updates on the way to Irvine Cancer Center.

"How do we handle this?" Amy asked after Miranda had imparted the events of her evening.

"First thing we do is gather all the information we can. Did you and Eddie find anything yet?"

"As a matter of fact, we did. There was an article in the local paper two weeks ago about a guy who just built a house on what had been an abandoned lot out in Amish country. There's a dark history to the property and it's reportedly haunted. Back in the seventies, a couple lived there for nearly twelve years until one night when the father shot his daughters, then himself. His wife committed suicide about a week later. The house remained empty for another ten years before it was demolished by the township."

A hint of pressure returned in Miranda's temples. There was a connection here. "Can you give me some names?"

"The family's name was Vernon," Amy replied. "Give me a moment to scan through the article again. Yeah, here it is. Nancy and Jeff Vernon. It doesn't mention the daughters' names in the article, but I found a local historian and I thought I'd call him tomorrow to arrange a visit."

"Good idea," Miranda agreed. "Bookmark that article. I want to read it when we get back."

"Are you on your way now?"

"No, we're en route to the hospital to see Matt, the boy with the premonitions. He apparently had some sort of episode at the same time we were struggling with Heather. His parents witnessed whatever it is that's happening to him and they want answers. If they let me meet him, maybe I can help."

"Eventful night for you," Amy said. "How's Tammy handling all of this?"

"Well, I wouldn't say she's a believer yet." Miranda shot a sidelong glance at her friend. "But I think she's getting a whole new perspective on things."

Tammy snickered "You ain't kiddin'."

"We'll regroup later to compare notes and figure out our strategy moving forward. I think you're onto something with that article. You and Eddie getting along?"

"I haven't killed him yet," Amy said.

IT WAS dark by the time Tammy pulled into the parking lot at Irvine. She handed the keys back to Miranda as they made their way to the building's entrance. A few minutes later, they marched into the pediatric oncology ward on the fifth floor.

Jackie glanced up as they approached the nurses' station. "Hey, Matt's parents are in with him now."

"How is he?" Tammy asked.

"Perfectly calm, like nothing ever happened. Robert and April, on the other hand..."

"Yeah, I'll bet." Tammy introduced Miranda and explained that she was there to talk to Matt about his visions.

"Are you a psychiatrist?"

"Funny," Miranda said. "You're the second person today to ask me that."

"Jackie, I'll fill you in later," Tammy promised. "For now, I think it's best that I go in alone. Miranda will wait here until I call her in. I want to explain everything to the Meades as gently as I can."

"That works," Miranda said. "I could use a few minutes of quiet."

"You and me both."

DURING THE RIDE TO IRVINE, Tammy and Miranda had discussed—and dismissed—a number of methods for approaching the Meades about their son's newfound ability. There was no easy way, so Tammy resolved to take Robert and April aside, well out of earshot of the nursing staff, Matt, and Miranda.

"A psychic-medium?" Robert was incredulous. "What the hell is that? You can't be serious. Of all people. You're a doctor. Don't tell me you believe in this crap."

"Until recently not at all, but honestly, Bob, I can't explain how Matt knows what he does about the people who—"

"My son doesn't know a damn thing about those people," Robert said. "You want an explanation? One that makes sense? Maybe Matt overheard your nurses or a visitor talking about them. Maybe he saw news reports on the TV in his room and all of that caused him to dream about those people."

Robert's voice cracked as he spoke, and his eyes brimmed with tears. "Or maybe he's having nightmares because he knows he's going to die in a few days."

Tammy had no response. The last thing she wanted to do was press the issue with parents whose emotional states were scoured raw by a coarse and hopeless reality. They were already in mourning and had been for weeks.

Nevertheless, she knew that something must be done or more lives would be lost. Taking a deep breath, she tried a different approach. "When Jackie called me to come here, Miranda and I had just prevented a young woman from committing suicide. She was a complete stranger, and we only knew it was going to happen because your son predicted it in enough time for us to save her.

"Now, I know you're both going through hell, and I completely understand if you don't care about the people that have died over the past few weeks, but somehow your son has made a connection to them. Matt saved a life tonight. If we could understand what's happening to him, maybe we can find the pattern in these deaths and put a stop to them.

"I've known Randy for years. She has three kids of her own. She's a sweetheart and has a soft touch. I guarantee she won't do anything to upset Matt. You can be here the entire time, and we'll back off if he starts getting stressed out."

There was a moment of tense silence before April squeezed Robert's hand. "I'm OK with this, provided it won't take too long."

"It won't. I promise," Tammy said.

Robert's shoulders slumped, but he lodged no further protest.

A FEW MINUTES LATER, Tammy led Miranda into Matt's room. She nodded politely at his parents standing by the window. April whispered a "hello" while Robert cast a stern gaze.

"Tammy." Matt's eyes opened wide. "Is Heather all right?"

"Yep. She's fine thanks to you, Matt. Maybe when she's feeling better, she can thank you in person. Would you like that?"

"Sure. I'm just glad she's OK."

He appeared so fragile. Had his brief surge of excitement earlier tonight drained him? Miranda couldn't imagine watching without hope as one of her children deteriorated.

"Matt, I brought along a friend who would like to—"

"Talk to me about my visions. I know." Matt craned his neck to peek around Tammy at Miranda. "You helped save Heather."

Miranda stepped forward. "Yes, I did. Did your parents tell you that?"

"No, the girls did. You're very pretty."

Miranda could have melted where she stood. She wished she could trade in her abilities for the power to heal. Instead, all she could offer was a warm smile. "Thank you. About these girls, what are their names?"

"They didn't tell me, but they said that you see things like I do."

"Sometimes, yes. Did they tell you I was coming?"

"Yeah."

"Can you tell us what they look like?"

"They're older than me, a little bit. They're twins. Long brown hair and they always wear the same clothes. Big jeans with white shirts."

"Big jeans?" Tammy asked.

"Bell bottoms," Miranda said. These girls were the same ones that had appeared in her kitchen during her phone conversation with Tammy two nights ago. Another piece to the puzzle.

"Bell bottoms, right," Tammy repeated. "So, Matt, when these girls show up, do they come in through the door?"

"I don't know. Sometimes they wake me up. Sometimes I look around and they're standing there. I think they're ghosts."

Miranda glanced at his parents. They were riveted. "Why do you say that?"

"Because they told me their dad shot them both with a big gun."

"Oh my God!" April blurted. She cupped a hand over her gaping mouth.

"All right, that's enough." Robert glared at Tammy. "Get this freak away from my son right now or so help me, I will go straight to the president of this place."

"I'm sorry," Tammy said as she and Miranda turned to leave.

"Dad, wait," Matt said. "There's more. The girls—"

"That's enough. Matt!"

His son ignored him. "More people are going to die."

"Who?" Tammy asked, despite Robert's burning gaze.

"I don't know yet. I'm sorry," Matt said. "The girls only tell me so much at a time and I only see the other people after they're dead."

"Stop it!" April shrieked. She collapsed onto a chair and sobbed.

"You satisfied now, Doctor?" Robert snarled. "You managed to upset my wife and my son." He pointed to Miranda. "You don't come near my family again or I will sue you and this hospital. Am I clear?"

Miranda lowered her gaze. "Of course. I'm sorry. You have a wonderful boy. I'm... I'm so sorry." With that, she dashed out of the room—and didn't stop until she reached her car.

TEN MINUTES HAD PASSED before Tammy realized that Miranda was no longer in the building. She found her lying back in the driver's seat of her car, staring through the windshield at the light of a nearby lamppost.

Tammy opened the passenger door and leaned in. "You OK?"

"Yeah."

She climbed into the seat and closed the door. "I'm sorry you had to deal with that."

"I'm used to it," Miranda said. "In fact, I'm used to a lot worse, but I don't blame Robert at all. These are the last few precious days they have with their son. The last thing I want to do is cause them even more pain."

"You didn't. None of this is your fault." Tammy lowered the back of her seat, bringing herself level with Miranda. "If anyone should feel terrible it's me. I brought you into this. Christ, you could've been shot today."

"But I wasn't, and we saved a life, so the night wasn't a total loss. Still, I don't know how you do it, watching kids wither away and die."

"They don't all die. Many pediatric cancers are treatable, but certain specific tumors, like Matt's, well... treatment can only do so much for so long. He has what's known as a diffusely infiltrative brain stem glioma."

"Now you sound like a doctor, Doctor."

There was a moment of silence before Tammy asked, "How are your kids?"

"They're traveling through Europe with their father," Miranda replied. "I talked to them yesterday before we left to come here. They're having a fantastic time, but I'll be glad when they're home. I worry about them. Brian's a great dad and I trust him, but sometimes they can be a handful, especially the twins—wait a minute."

"What?"

"Just thinking about twins. Matt said that the girls who visit him are twins. Remember, he said that they look and dress alike. He also said their father shot them both."

"I remember," Tammy said. "I don't think I'll forget, and neither will his parents. What are you getting at?"

"When I talked to Amy on the phone earlier, she read a few lines from a newspaper article about a father who shot his two daughters, then himself. The mother committed suicide a week later. Amy didn't say the girls were twins, but it can't be a coincidence. We need to get back to your place so I can read that article."

"Only if we stop and pick up some pizza first. I haven't eaten since breakfast."

"THIS ARTICLE DOESN'T HAVE a lot of detail. It references past events having to do with the Vernon family, but I can't seem to find anything more about them online. Still, it's a wild story."

In Tammy's dining room, Eddie finished off a slice of mushroom pizza before turning his attention back to his laptop. "This article in the Intelligencer was written by a guy named Frank Knedlhans who happens to work at the Historical Society now. Back in the seventies, he was the main reporter covering the story, but this article I found was written in 1985 as a retrospective." He turned the computer around to allow Miranda to read the screen.

"Oh, my God." With her mouth full of pizza, it sounded more like "oh rye cod." She swallowed and pointed to the article. "That's her!"

"Who?" Eddie asked as everyone gathered around.

The caption underneath the photo read, *Nancy Vernon, one year prior to her death.* "That's the woman I saw at Heather's apartment tonight, the spirit that possessed her."

"No freakin' way." Eddie turned to Tammy as if seeking confirmation.

She held up a hand. "Don't look at me. I didn't see anything like that. All I know is that one second, I had Heather's arm restrained and the next, she managed to get loose."

"I wish we were there," Amy said.

"Did I fail to mention on the phone that she had a gun?" Miranda reminded her.

"Oh, yeah. In that case maybe the boy could've gone."

Eddie balled up a napkin and threw it at her.

Tammy closed one pizza box and opened another. "Are they always like this?"

"Most of the time," Miranda said. "But we adults recognize this form of flirting as the teenage mating ritual."

Amy dropped her half-eaten slice onto her plate. "I just lost my appetite. Thank you very much."

Eddie winked at her. "Shame we're in separate rooms, babe."

"Yeah. Otherwise, I'd puke on you."

"OK, children." Miranda put her hands together in a 'T' formation, signaling a time out. "Please make yourselves seen and not heard so I can get through this today."

With Tammy peering over her shoulder, Miranda read the article in which the reporter-turned-historian shared some of his personal thoughts on the bizarre events that had led to the Vernon family's tragic end.

According to the article, Nancy and Jeff Vernon's children had included a son named Adam and twin daughters, Carla and Natalie. Adam died of a brain tumor in June 1978.

Miranda was reminded of Matt and she wondered if that was yet another connection. She filed the idea in the back of her mind as she continued reading.

One month later, Jeff Vernon killed his daughters in their room with a shotgun before turning it on himself. Nancy Vernon, a German teacher at a local middle school, arrived home from work to find the bodies. One week after the funerals, she committed suicide in her basement. Nancy's body was found later that day, her head in a pool of blood from a self-inflicted gunshot wound. A nickel-plated Smith & Wesson revolver was found beside her. The only fingerprints on the gun were Nancy's.

The house then passed to Nancy's sisters as Jeff Vernon had no living relatives. They paid a contractor to perform minor renovations on the home before putting it on the market. It remained there for two years until a young couple bought it at a reduced price. However, they lived there for less than a year, fleeing the house in terror one night after repeatedly claiming that the place was haunted.

They never returned, nor were they heard from again.

For the next ten years, the house stood abandoned and became a haven for teens looking to get drunk, high, or a cheap thrill from exploring a "haunted" house. Some of them had echoed the last owners' reports of disembodied voices, screams, even the sound of gunfire. Of course, none of these reports had been substantiated, and in April 1989, the township demolished the dilapidated home.

"That's a hell of a story," Tammy said.

"I intend to call Frank Knedlhans in the morning after I read the other articles he wrote," Amy informed them. "Apparently, he published four or five others about the Vernons during the husband's embezzlement trial. I'll schedule an appointment to talk to him. See if I can get more detail."

"If you can, find out why Jeff Vernon killed his daughters," Miranda said. "Now I'm positive they're the girls Matt's been talking to."

"Wait a minute." Tammy snapped her fingers. "Vernon house…"

"What about it?"

"Two of my nurses were talking about a haunted house a few days ago. There was an article in the paper."

Tammy hurried into the living room and came back with a disheveled stack of newspapers. She dropped them onto the dining room table and rifled through them. "I don't know why I bother to subscribe. I never have time to read them. I think it was two weeks ago Thursday." After a moment, she yanked out one of the pages. Sales circulars tumbled to the floor. "This is it." She unfolded the paper and turned it so that her guests could read the article. She pointed to the title, "On Haunted Ground."

"Jackie and Lena told me how they used to explore this abandoned house until one day they heard something that scared them so bad they never went back. Some guy just built a new place on that lot."

The article stated that an art dealer named Elias Gray had just completed construction of a new home on what had been the site of Lancaster's most grisly crime. There wasn't much detail about Elias Gray, but Miranda noted that the date of the home's completion, one week prior to the article's publication, corresponded to the first pair of deaths in the town, Tom and Lori Urban. Gray was quoted in the article as being dismissive of the ghost stories, stating that he hears occasional sounds of settling but that's to be expected.

So why did Miranda feel another surge of pressure in her head?

"Anyone else here think that building a house on that property may have stirred up these ghosts?" Eddie asked.

"I'm sure of it," Miranda agreed. "There are too many pieces falling into place to ignore, but all we can do is speculate. We can't know for sure, unless..."

"Unless?" Amy said.

"We need to get into that house. It's the only way."

"How?" Tammy asked. "We can't just knock on someone's door and say 'Hi, we think your house is haunted by ghosts that are killing people in town. Do you mind if we come in and check it out?'"

IT WAS WELL past one o'clock in the morning by the time everyone retired for the night—all except Miranda. The day's events had left her unnerved and exhausted, but she resisted sleep for fear of her dreams, of watching her brother's final moments before he sped to his death. Instead, Miranda stretched out on a chaise lounge on Tammy's back patio. On the table beside her, a citronella candle provided the only light, other than the innumerable stars that filled the night sky.

That's a view you don't get in the city. As kids, she and Colin had taken comfort in stargazing. Through all of the changes in their young lives, the fabled inhabitants of the heavens had remained constant. Miranda's favorite had always been Pegasus, the winged horse. Perhaps it appealed to Miranda's affinity for myths and legends. Colin, on the other hand, preferred...

"ORION, THE HUNTER."

He pointed up and to the left. "Way over there. He's just becoming visible in the northern sky this time of year."

It was nearly 3:30 on a balmy August morning and he had

been lying on the beach for hours. Worried about his state of mind, Miranda had been unable to sleep, so she grabbed a blanket and joined him.

Since the death of their father over a year ago, Colin had retreated into himself, becoming reclusive and somber. He had focused on his schoolwork to the exclusion of all else and had just graduated second in his class. He had earned an engineering scholarship to MIT. Everything seemed to be falling into place for his future. In a week, Colin would be moving away to start a new chapter in his life, one of independence replete with new opportunities and possibilities.

Yet, Colin didn't give a damn and Miranda knew why. Their father had not been there to witness his son's accomplishments, sending a bright, vibrant young man further into the depths of despondence.

"He needs time, that's all," their mother had said. "Everyone deals with grief in their own way. Some people take longer. Don't you think a part of me died with your father?"

A part of Miranda had died with him, too, yet it seemed to take the heaviest toll on Colin, leaving his spirit broken. Here and now, on a private beach behind a rental house in Rehoboth, Delaware, brother and sister took in the starscape.

"You always considered Orion some sort of protector, didn't you?" Miranda asked.

"We're not kids anymore. The stars are just there to be studied. Hell, if you observed them from any other point in space, they wouldn't even resemble the constellations we know. We have no protectors, Randy. We protect ourselves. That's the way it is."

Miranda sat up on her blanket. "I can't believe that. This gift I have, it's been with me since I was six, and in these past ten years, I've seen things that make me believe there's so much we don't understand. But one thing I know is that we are protected. As much as you looked up to dad, he's looking back at you right now full of pride."

"You said you saw him at my graduation."

"I did, which is how I know what I'm talking about." Miranda found her gaze drawn to a gray backpack tucked under Colin's arm. There was something about it that made her uncomfortable.

"What's in there?"

"Nothing, just some stuff."

Miranda snatched it out from under his arm. "Like what?"

"No!" Colin jumped to his feet. "Dammit, Randy, leave it alone."

Turning away, she reached into the pack and pulled out a small black revolver. "Colin, where did you get this?"

"None of your business."

"Why the hell do you have a friggin' gun?"

"Just put it back in the bag and forget about it."

"What were you planning to do with this?"

Colin looked away toward the tumbling breakers and ran a hand over his face. "I was going to off myself, but I didn't have the guts."

Miranda's shock turned to anger, and Colin withered under her smoldering stare. "How dare you."

"It's my choice."

"Bullshit! Do you think mom could stand to lose both the men in her life? Do you think I could? Did you even consider us when you made your choice? You need help, Colin. Why didn't you come to me? We've told each other everything since we were kids."

"Like I said, we're not kids anymore. My problems are my own."

"Starting right now your problems are mine, too. We're family."

"Randy, you can give someone all the emotional support

you want, but in the end, we fight our battles alone. And I've been alone in this... darkness... for a long time."

"Then let's get the help you need to pull you out of that darkness." Miranda rose to her feet and held up the gun. "And not with this."

She dropped the backpack and trudged toward the surf until the cool water rushed around her ankles. She hurled the gun into the sea. When she returned to Colin, he was sitting cross-legged, head in his hands. His body trembled as he wept.

Miranda wrapped her arms around him. "We're going to get you through this, I swear to God, but you need to promise me that you'll never do anything like this again."

Colin merely stared at the sand.

Miranda put a hand under his chin and raised his head until their gazes met. "Promise me you'll never do anything drastic like this ever again."

"I promise."

CHAPTER 6

DREAMS AND ENCOUNTERS

E lias Gray stared at his outstretched arms as if noticing them for the first time. His shirt was soaked through, his pants drenched and torn. He had also lost a shoe. *How did I manage that?* He recalled that his foot had become caught in something while he was under water and he had to sacrifice his shoe to free himself. *Under water?*

Elias stood at the end of a narrow stone jetty beneath an overcast sky. Waves crashed against weathered rocks far below. *How did I get here?* On either side of him, a vast beach stretched unbroken into the distance. Scattered bodies lay along the sand, but they were not sunbathing. They were fully clothed and motionless.

All of them dead.

Bobbing in the water, bits of debris mingled among crates and flat, rectangular objects. Some of them drifted toward the base of the jetty. Priceless paintings and ancient statues were tossed by waves and smashed against jagged rocks.

Farther out to sea, a jumbo jet's white and blue fuselage tilted sideways and sank into the deep. Within seconds, the ocean had claimed it and the tide carried on its undulating rhythm. From the horizon beyond, a dense fog swirled its way toward land at an impossible speed.

Elias scanned the corpses along the shoreline. He shouted at the top of his lungs, but there was no response. *I can't be the only one. There must be at least a few other survivors.* He dropped to his knees and lowered his head into his hands. *None of this makes sense. I don't even remember getting on a damn plane.*

"Janos!" A voice called from the fog that had by now enveloped the jetty. Elias drew himself up, expecting to find someone running toward him. "Janos!"

No. It came from below. Elias crawled to the edge of the jetty and peered down. "Leland!" His friend had managed to climb halfway up the side. "Hold on. I'm coming to help you."

Elias lowered himself, finding handholds in the crags and crevices as he descended toward Leland. He was nearly within arm's reach of his friend, but there was no way to go any farther. "Leland, if you climb a bit higher, I can pull you up. You can do it, old man."

Leland inched his way closer. Elias grabbed his hand and strained to haul him up. "Dammit, Leland. Push with your legs."

"I'm sorry, Janos." Leland's voice quivered. "I seemed to have misplaced them."

"What?" Elias stretched himself to look past his friend.

Entrails and bone protruded from Leland's severed torso. Elias screamed and lost his grip, sending what was left of his friend plunging into the sea. He pressed his face against the cool damp stone. *Don't panic. Breathe. Just breathe.*

"Lose something?" A voice called from above. Although the man's features were difficult to discern through the fog, the double-barreled shotgun bent over his arm was visible enough.

"Who are you?" Elias asked.

"I'm... all alone among the dead." He loaded two shells into the gun and took aim at Elias. "And so are you."

Both barrels exploded.

"No!" Elias twisted sideways. His free hand slapped something solid in the fog and sent it tumbling to the floor. *Floor?* When Elias awoke, he found himself lying across his bed face down. The room was dark, save for the pale glow of moonlight from the bay window across the room. Spare change, once stacked neatly atop his nightstand, lay scattered about. The sheets in which he'd become entangled clung to his damp skin. Elias examined his hands in the moonlight. They were covered in blood.

He thrashed and kicked at the sheets until he tumbled off the side of the bed. Scrambling to his feet, he dashed into the bathroom, slipping on the cold tile. He flipped the light switch with his elbow. Bloody footprints streaked the floor.

"Christ, what the hell is this?"

In the mirror, his naked body was spattered with blood, but there were no open wounds and he felt no pain. Seconds later, he was in the shower, taking comfort as ruddy water disappeared down the drain—until it didn't. Instead, it began filling the tub, covering his feet, his ankles. Something rubbed against him. Elias leapt out of the water just as a fully clothed body surfaced face down. It was a woman of slim build, her drenched auburn hair matted to her back and shoulders. Elias turned the body over.

The woman's green eyes flashed open. "You're all alone here," she whispered. "Alone among the dead."

Elias awoke with a shout. He tore aside the covers and stormed out of the bedroom, pacing the length of the hallway until his anxiety abated. *They were just dreams. Just dreams. All the talk about ghosts in this house. Need to stop taking this shit seriously.* According to the antique brass clock on the wall, it was nearly ten-thirty in the morning. He'd never slept so late in his life.

He opened the window at the end of the hall and leaned out. The sky was overcast, just as it had been in his dream, but everything else appeared normal. All except for the cellar doors. Directly below, they were wide open.

"What the hell?" They had been closed and locked for the past two days. Had Leland and Hagen returned in the middle of the night to double-cross him? Perhaps they wanted to steal the art back and sell it on their own, cutting Elias out of the deal.

He ran back to his bedroom and slipped into jeans and a polo shirt before retrieving the Luger 9mm hidden behind his bedside table. He crept down to the first floor, but there was no one to be found. In the kitchen, however, the door leading to the basement was open—again.

I'm putting a fucking padlock on this thing. Elias listened for any sounds from below before making his way down. The basement was empty save for the covered paintings and wooden crates along one wall. Convinced that he was alone, Elias tucked his gun into his jeans and made a cursory inspection of his inventory to ensure all pieces were accounted for.

When he was satisfied, he started toward the cellar doors but slipped on the smooth concrete. He raised his right foot. The sole was covered in blood, same with the left.

Behind him, the steps were bleeding.

Like a macabre waterfall, streams of deep red seeped out of each wooden tread and spilled down to the next. Elias drew his gun. He backed away from the steps until something to his right caught his attention. On the wall above his inventory, a word formed.

Verbrecher.

The accusation struck as much fear into Elias as the fact that it was written in blood. The German word for *criminal* remained legible for only a few moments before losing form and dripping down the wall.

The metal doors that led out to the side yard were still wide open. Elias bolted toward them, but no sooner had he reached the second step than one of the doors slammed down on his head, sending him sprawling. His gun fired as it flew from his hand and skittered out of sight somewhere in the shadows of the stairwell.

Pain seared through his skull. Elias cradled his head between his arms. He forced his eyes open and winced at the bright morning sunlight that now pierced the clouds. As if taunting him, the other cellar door remained open. Elias wanted nothing more than to get the hell out of the house but couldn't even push himself up, let alone think through the sharp throbbing.

He heard a voice, a man shouting. Perhaps it was the man from his dream, the one with the shotgun. Before Elias faded out, he wondered where his own gun had gone.

THE PAPERWORK HAD BEEN COMPLETED and the hospice staff briefed. Robert and April were taking their son home to die. They walked beside him as Tammy pushed his wheelchair down the hall. When they reached the elevator, she leaned down to give him a gentle hug.

"The man from the house is coming," Matt whispered. "He's on his way to the hospital in an ambulance."

"Which man?"

"The one with all the paintings."

"You mean the art dealer? Elias Gray?"

Matt nodded as the elevator doors opened and several people filed out.

"What happened to him?" Tammy asked.

"The girls said he lives alone." Matt lowered his voice as his father backed him into the elevator. "Alone among the dead."

April inserted herself between Tammy and her son. "Please, Matt. Not this again."

"I'm sorry, Mrs. Meade. I have no idea what he means."

"Ask Mr. Gray," Matt said. "He'll know."

"I warned you, Doctor." Robert glared at Tammy as the elevator doors closed. "Good riddance."

"HELLO AGAIN." Tammy approached the rear of the ambulance. Its double doors were wide open revealing a familiar face inside.

Mickey regarded her with a grin that made her stomach turn. "Never expected to see you again, Doc. What can I do for you this time?"

"Well, this is going to seem like déjà vu, but I'd like to know about the guy you just brought in."

"Again? Is this a hobby of yours or something?"

Tammy climbed inside the ambulance and sat down opposite Mickey. "I think it might have been someone I know."

"You know some truly unfortunate people."

"Maybe I'm a bad luck charm."

"A femme fatale. I like that."

Tammy raised a disapproving eyebrow.

"I think this one will live. Just took a little bump on the head, probably a concussion. The guy's house is right next to an Amish farm out in Sheba. Cops said the farmer heard a gunshot when he was out in his cornfield and called 911. When they got there, the guy was lying on his basement floor. He was conscious but in a lot of pain. No sign of a gunshot wound. Turns out a cellar door came down on his head. Always guaranteed to leave a mark."

"Mind if I ask his name?"

"Why don't we play the game again where you tell me, and I'll confirm."

"Gray. Elias Gray."

Mickey craned his neck to glance outside before answering. "You're two for two. That's gotta earn me dinner and a movie at least."

"Maybe lunch in the cafeteria."

"Hospital food." Mickey grimaced. "I suppose that's a start."

"Thanks." Tammy hopped out of the ambulance and hurried toward the Emergency Room.

"Oh, hey!" Mickey called after her. "I quit smoking since the last time we talked. Two weeks without a cigarette!"

Without looking back, Tammy extended a thumbs-up just as the doors parted.

"HELLO, I'm Doctor Kurtz, and you are..."

Elias gazed up at the burly physician. The simple act of tilting his head sent an unbearable throbbing through his skull. "Jano-uh, no. Elias, sorry."

"Don't apologize," Kurtz said. "You took a nasty blow to the head. Can you tell me what happened?"

Although the pain made concentration nearly impossible, the memory of the incident rushed back to him. *Verbrecher.* The word written in blood. "It was a metal door," Elias replied. "It slammed closed on me."

"A door closed on your head?"

Elias held up his hand at an angle. "Cellar door that opens up to the outside."

"Ah, gotcha. I'm surprised you weren't out cold. You must have a thick skull."

"So they tell me."

"It's a good sign that you can remember what happened," Kurtz assured him. "Do you feel nauseated?"

"No, but my neck hurts."

"You're not bleeding from the ears or nose. Your eyes look OK. No other bruises than the one on top. I suspect you suffered an uncomplicated concussion, Elias, but I'd like to order a CT scan to be safe. It shouldn't take more than twenty minutes."

Elias nodded and closed his eyes.

"We'll give you some Tylenol for the pain while you're waiting. Is there anyone we should call?"

Elias shook his head, an action he immediately regretted as he winced. "I live alone. No family or friends in the area."

Kurtz thought for a moment. "According to the paperwork, you live in Sheba. Maybe I can find someone on staff who could run you home provided we don't need to keep you here after the CT scan."

"How about a volunteer?"

Both men glanced up at the woman standing in the doorway.

"And you are?" Kurtz asked.

"Doctor Tammy Schell. I'm a pediatric oncologist across the street."

Elias lifted his head for a better view. "Have we met?"

"We're practically neighbors. I live not too far from you in Sheba."

"I'm surrounded by cornfields and woods as far as the eye can see."

Tammy sauntered into the room. "You and me both."

"So we've never met. I'm sure I would have remembered you, concussion notwithstanding. Why are you here?"

"Call it a random act of kindness. I saw the police and ambulance at your house as I drove past and I was concerned."

"Looks like you have a guardian angel, Elias," Kurtz said. "I'll have a nurse bring you some Tylenol while I order that CT scan. Back in a few."

With that, Kurtz was gone, leaving Elias to wonder what this woman was up to.

"So, what road do you live on?" he asked.

"Wagon Wheel," the alleged oncologist replied. "That's about two Amish farms west of you."

He stared at her.

"That was... supposed to be a joke."

Just then, a nurse entered carrying two pills and a cup of water, all of which Elias downed eagerly. He thanked her as she took the empty cup and departed. Tammy closed the door behind her. Elias curled one hand into a fist. Head trauma or not, he would be ready to defend himself should this woman attack.

She stepped close to the bed, her expression tense. "I need to ask you something. Have you ever heard the expression, 'alone among the dead.'"

Long ago, Elias had learned how to maintain a perfect poker face. *How could this stranger know about that phrase?* He would find out soon enough, no doubt. In the meantime, he relaxed his fist and massaged his temples with both hands.

"Here, let me." Dr. Schell, if that was truly her name, took his hands in hers. "Are you familiar with your pressure points?"

"Uh, yes. Specifically, the muscle between the thumb and forefinger. Although, I think this is more than your average headache."

She began massaging his hand and he was careful not to linger too long in her green eyes. Familiar eyes... yet Elias couldn't even think let alone jog his memory. *Who cares, she's—*

"Feel any better yet?"

"Stunning," he breathed. "I mean, it's stunning how adept you are at that. The pain has diminished, yes. Thank you, Doctor."

"Call me Tammy, please."

"Where did you hear that phrase, 'alone among the dead?'"

"Get through your CT scan first, then we'll talk."

———

THREE HOURS LATER, Elias reclined in the passenger seat of Tammy's car. His CT scan had revealed nothing alarming. Before his discharge from the hospital, the pain had reduced to a dull but manageable ache.

"How ya holdin' up over there?" Tammy asked.

"I'm alive, as the throbbing in my skull keeps reminding me."

"Hopefully, you'll be able to get some rest today."

Elias lifted a yellow paper containing a list of instructions from the Emergency Room. "Not if I need to wake up every two hours to ensure that I can be 'roused to consciousness.'"

"Yeah, about that. This is my last night working the grave-yard shift at Irvine. If you'd be willing to give me your number, I could call you every few hours tonight."

Kind as she seemed to be, Tammy was still a stranger. Giving her his number could prove dangerous. Then again, so could the risk of falling into a coma or dying in his sleep. He pulled his phone from his pocket. "What's your number?" She told him and he called her. A muffled buzzing emanated from her purse in the backseat. "To be honest. I could pass out right now, but not before you tell me why you're so keen to help me and where you heard that phrase."

"Let's get you home first."

ELIAS GRAY'S sitting room was long and narrow, with a plush couch facing a stone fireplace. Two easy chairs were positioned at each corner along the far wall. Between them hung a painting of a young gentleman clad in what appeared to be nineteenth-century business attire and clutching a small red book.

Elias returned from the kitchen and handed Tammy a cup of tea. He lowered himself onto the opposite end of the couch and leaned his head back. "I had a dream last night. Two of them, actually, and that phrase was in both. Alone among the dead."

"What were the dreams about, if I may ask?"

He told her. "And as for the woman in my tub, she looked exactly like you."

Heat flushed from Tammy's face. "That's impossible. We never met before today."

"Maybe I'm misremembering the details." Elias waved a hand toward the bandage on his head. "But the green eyes were unmistakable."

Tammy could think of nothing to say. She took a sip of tea.

"I'm sorry," Elias said. "I don't wish to make this any more awkward than it already is. I'm still trying to sort all of this out. You had something to tell me."

"I'm sure you're aware of the strange deaths and suicides in and around town over the past few weeks."

"I've read about them in the paper. Why?"

Tammy imparted all of her experiences so far, starting with Matt's predictions and how he claimed to have learned his information. She told Elias why she had contacted Miranda Lorensen and her team of paranormal investigators and what they had found so far in their research. Finally, she delved into the incident at Heather Marceta's apartment, although she didn't mention Heather or her brother by name.

Elias rubbed his forehead as he absorbed Tammy's story. "Remarkable. I take it that you and your psychic friend think that I've raised the ghosts of the Vernon family by building my house on what was once their land? I'm not completely ignorant of paranormal theories. I've heard many stories of people stirring up spirits after renovating their homes or otherwise disturbing the ground."

"Something like that, yes."

"It might surprise you to know that I've had cause to look into it already." Elias leaned forward. "Ever since I settled in here, there have been voices, shadows, locked doors opening by themselves, or in some cases, *closing* by themselves." Again, he gestured at his wound. "I've had friends here who experienced it, too. So I know I'm not mad. In fact, I doubt my injury was an accident."

Tammy was riveted now. "Sounds like you could use some help with whatever's going on here, especially if you think it's getting dangerous."

"What sort of help?"

Tammy set her cup on the end table. "If you're interested, I could ask Miranda and her team to check out your home some night this week or next. Although it seems to me the sooner the better."

Elias tapped the side of his cup, pondering her offer. "All right, but I have some conditions before I allow it. No media and no camera crew. I don't want to see any footage of my house on YouTube. I value my privacy. All I want to do is get to the bottom of this without drawing attention."

"Absolutely. I'll make sure this stays low key," Tammy assured him.

"Very well. When can this be arranged? Do you think Wednesday night is too soon? That would be optimal for me."

"I'll call Miranda today and ask, although something tells me that'll work out just fine."

Elias clutched his growling stomach. "Sorry. I haven't eaten yet today."

Tammy glanced at her watch. "I don't need to be back at my office for another three hours. You like Chinese? My treat."

TEN MINUTES after Tammy left to pick up dinner, Elias ventured into the basement. No blood flowed down the steps or oozed from the wall. Maybe that was all a dream, too. Which was why he hadn't mentioned any of it to Tammy. No sense scaring off a beautiful woman he'd only just met.

The events of the morning swirled in his throbbing head. Scenes played back in no particular order. Elias pushed them aside as he made a cursory inspection of the artwork that would soon allow him to retire. His main concern right now, however, was his gun. When he'd been knocked to the floor, the weapon fired after flying from his grasp. Its whereabouts remained a mystery. No one had found it earlier—not the Amish farmer who came to his rescue, not the police, and not the ambulance crew who helped him out of the basement.

Elias ducked beneath the wooden steps that led up to the cellar doors, but the pistol was nowhere to be found. He slumped against a wall as fatigue and hunger vied for his attention. Perhaps it would help to take a quick nap before Tammy returned. Wherever the gun was, no doubt it would turn up.

Chapter 7

The House that Elias Built

"Those dreams of his were warnings." At a diner across from Franklin and Marshall College, Miranda switched her phone from one ear to the other and lowered her voice. "And he's either brave or stupid to have spent the night there, but at least he agreed to the investigation."

"It didn't take much convincing," Tammy said. "Only that we promise to keep the whole thing private."

"No worries there," Miranda assured her. "Problem is, we don't have all of our equipment with us, so I'll need to call Marc to see if he's available and have him bring what he can. As much as we appreciate your hospitality, it looks like we're in for an extended stay, so I just made reservations at the Best Western for the next three nights."

"Would you mind if I join you on Wednesday? I've never been on a ghost hunt before."

"That would be great. You'll get to see the team in action. Amy's about to pay a visit to the Historical Society. I'll let you know what she finds out."

As Miranda ended the call, Eddie swallowed the last of his cheeseburger. "I take it this is getting serious now."

"I think it got serious when people started dying," Amy said.

"I just hope we can do something to make sure no one else does," Miranda added. "Elias Gray had a close call this morning. I'm convinced the answer is in that house."

THE LANCASTER HISTORICAL SOCIETY was headquartered in a modest red brick colonial alongside the Wheatland estate of James Buchanan, fifteenth president of the United States. From the Society's website, Amy had learned that Buchanan died in the Wheatland mansion in the summer of 1868. As Miranda pulled into the parking lot behind the Visitor Center, Amy wondered if Buchanan might still be hanging around the property. It was a curiosity she would have indulged under different circumstances, but it was the recently deceased that occupied everyone's attention now.

"It isn't active," Miranda said.

Before opening the passenger door, Amy gazed at her, eyes wide. "What?"

"You were wondering if the mansion was haunted. It isn't. Ol' Buchanan's long gone."

"How did you know I—"

"Psychic."

"Right."

"Call me when you're done. In the meantime, Eddie and I will pack up everything at Tammy's."

Minutes later, in the foyer of the Historical Society, Amy was greeted by a plump, middle-aged woman who led her down a wide corridor past a series of glass display cases, each one filled with a collection of small antiques. Starting with the

1960s, the contents of each display moved backward in time. The next theme was the turn of the century, followed by the antebellum period before the Civil War, and finally, the colonial days when Lancaster was first settled and officially declared a town in 1730 by the governor of Pennsylvania.

Amy had always been fascinated by history and had a fondness for antiques but even in this shrine to years gone by, time was not on her side. Finally, they stopped outside the library door.

"Are you a college student?" the woman asked.

"Yes, ma'am." Amy reached into her attaché bag and produced her student ID from the University of Maryland.

"Great, just show that to the library assistant and she'll waive the five-dollar fee."

Amy thanked her and opened the door. The library was larger than she had expected and the lighting much brighter than the rest of the place. It was also deserted save for a stocky, gray-haired man with bushy eyebrows seated at a table near the center of the room. He didn't glance up from his newspaper as Amy passed him on her way to the main desk. She showed her ID to the young library assistant, a petite, fair-skinned woman with short red hair. Amy surmised that she was a college student working a summer job, judging by her age and amply-filled Franklin and Marshall T-shirt. Amy chided herself mentally. It wasn't that she was jealous of women with larger breasts, but at times it made her self-conscious when she noticed them. In this particular case, the redhead's were hard to ignore.

"I wonder if you could help me," Amy began. "I'm looking for certain newspaper articles from the Intelligencer around the late seventies. Would you happen to have them on microfiche? I wasn't able to find much online."

"Yep. We're in the process of digitizing our archives so there's still a lot on microfiche. I'll show you." The woman stepped out from behind the desk in bare feet and led Amy into a small room at the back of the library. The lights flickered on as soon as they entered, revealing three microfiche scanners on folding tables against one wall. Amy followed the assistant to a row of black metal filing cabinets at the back of the room.

"Let's see." The assistant looked from one cabinet to the next before tapping on one near the middle. "Yeah, this has all the Intell issues from the seventies. Each drawer is about two years' worth of papers including daily and weekend editions. Is there anything in particular you're looking for?"

"There was a series of articles about a family by the name of Vernon. They—"

"Right down there." The assistant pointed at the second drawer from the bottom.

"Are they that popular?"

"You don't grow up in Lancaster without hearing about the Vernons."

"Gotcha. Well, thank you for your help."

"If you need anything else, just let me know. My name is Ginny."

FORTY MINUTES and five articles later, Amy had become so engrossed in the tragic saga of the Vernons that she barely noticed when someone else had entered the room.

"Interesting reading?"

With a start, Amy glanced up at the middle-aged man she had passed in the library earlier.

"Sorry. Didn't mean to startle you. I'm Frank Knedlhans, Director of Archival Services." He nodded at the screen. "Saw the name Vernon on the headline there. Caught my attention."

"You were the reporter who covered the case."

"Guilty as charged." Frank dropped into a neighboring chair and tossed an orange stress ball from one hand to the other as he spoke. "Which is more than I can say for Jeff Vernon. That was like watching a train wreck."

"While I'm here," Amy said. "Any chance I could schedule a meeting with you?"

"We're meeting right now. If you don't mind me sticking my nose into your business, what kind of research are you doing?"

Amy hesitated. "Oh, it's a... psychology paper. That's my major. I'm taking a summer course on... extreme incidents of stress and... how it can affect behavior, you know, as opposed to daily, routine stress."

Frank tilted his head. "Sounds intense."

"You have no idea. Though I'm curious. How did you know I was in here looking up the Vernons? Seems a little more than coincidence."

Frank smiled. "OK, you got me. A little barefoot redhead told me."

"Ginny?"

"She's my daughter."

"Really?"

"Yeah, and I swear to God she has more shoes than my ex-wife and never wears any of them. I don't get it. Thought I left all that free-spirit hippie crap back in the seventies."

The two shared a brief laugh before Amy continued. "Well, before I came here, I read one of your articles online. It was mind-boggling. The Vernons' eight-year old son dies of a brain tumor, then Jeff Vernon is tried for embezzlement and acquitted. After that, he murders his daughters with a shotgun before killing himself, then Nancy Vernon commits suicide two weeks later."

"Yeah, that about sums it up."

"But why would an innocent man not only kill himself but take his kids with him?"

Frank shrugged. "I guess Jeff had a breakdown, considering that he'd just lost his son and his job at what used to be Midlin Paper. He was falsely accused of a serious white-collar crime and was drowning in medical bills. All of that probably pushed over to the edge."

"Did you ever get the chance to interview him?"

"Oh, hell no. Couldn't get anywhere near the guy, but we all descended on their house to get to Nancy. I felt bad for her. She refused to speak to any of us and I don't blame her. We were all looking for dirt on Jeff."

"The last article you wrote was about Roger Matthias, the VP of Finance at Midlin Paper. He made some bad investment decisions using swap loans and tried to cover it up by framing Jeff."

Frank squeezed the stress ball. "Correct. Swap loans had just been introduced by some economics guru from Yale. I'm no financial expert, but Matthias cooked the books to make it seem like the fees that Midlin absorbed in these swaps were lower than what they really were. He skimmed a little off of each department's budget at the start of the fiscal year and dumped the money into an account from which the company paid out charitable donations. Instead, the money went to pay down the excessive swap loans. Somehow, he tried to frame Jeff for it. I don't remember the details but when the dust settled, Matthias spent five years in a country club prison."

"And I read that he died of a heart attack the morning he was scheduled to be released," Amy said. "Then his wife killed herself two weeks later just like Nancy Vernon."

"That coincidence didn't go unnoticed," Frank said. "I was surprised when I learned about Nancy's death. She was a strong woman, a real hard ass. She ripped me a new one when I went to her house to get a statement after she buried her family. In hindsight, I would've done the same. Like I said, the press was relentless."

"Including you?"

Something in Frank's eyes conveyed... remorse? Regret? Amy couldn't determine, but it was obvious that all of this reminiscing triggered long-buried memories for the retired newshound.

"There was a bit of history about Nancy that stuck with me," Frank said, ignoring Amy's question. "Somebody I spoke with back then said that she'd been smuggled out of Germany as a child after her parents were killed by the Nazis. Her grandfather got her out of Europe and brought her to America. They settled here in Lancaster. That was a time when people of the same ethnicity tended to cluster together. It wasn't a stretch when Nancy became a high school German teacher."

Amy typed hasty notes into her tablet. "What about the general manager of the company where Jeff worked, Lori Switzer? She still around?"

Frank resumed tossing his stress ball from hand to hand. "She's a philanthropist now, donates money to all sorts of charities through her foundation. She pops up in the local news now and then. Her late husband left her a fortune. Last I heard, she was living in Adamstown or had an office there or something. I thought this was a psychology paper about extreme stress. Seems our discussion has drifted away from that."

"There have been an excessive number of deaths around here lately," Amy said. "Each one of them followed by the suicide of a family member."

"And?"

"I cross-referenced the names of the recently deceased with some of the witnesses at Jeff's embezzlement trial, specifically, those who testified against him. The names match up except in one case where it was the son of somebody who testified,

Nick Garnell. He was killed in Iraq last week. Did you happen to notice these coincidences?"

Frank leaned forward in his chair. "You're very astute. Yeah, I noticed the pattern, but I didn't connect it to the Vernons until I learned that some art dealer built a house on what used to be their property. All those people started getting killed shortly after he showed up."

Amy was tempted to follow that line of conversation, but Elias Gray had asked to remain out of the public eye. Besides, she had all of the information she needed and time was critical. "That's probably just another coincidence."

Frank smiled. "Yeah, probably."

IT WAS early afternoon by the time Amy left the Historical Society. Frank had wished her luck with her course, although it was obvious he didn't buy her cover story.

Maybe when this is all over, I'll come back and tell him the truth. Then again, he probably wouldn't believe that either.

Back in Miranda's car, Amy turned in the passenger seat to smirk at Eddie, who was sandwiched between the door and a stack of duffle bags and laptop cases. "All packed up, I see. I thought you were riding shotgun?"

"I was saving it for you," he said. "It's easier to cut your seatbelt from back here."

Miranda sighed. "What did you find out in there?"

As Amy imparted the details of her morning's research and her conversation with Frank, she reached back and pretended to adjust her head rest, flipping off Eddie in the process.

"So, from what I'm hearing," Miranda said. "We only have one person left from Jeff Vernon's past who was involved in his embezzlement trial, correct?"

"Right, Lori Switzer, the former general manager of Midlin Paper, now head of The Switzer Foundation."

Eddie leaned forward in the back seat. A laptop bag tumbled down behind him. "Jeff's saving the big shot for last."

"We need to find her," Miranda said. "You said she lives in Adamstown?"

Amy nodded. "Not too far from here, but she travels all over the world working with different causes and charities."

"Eddie, once we're settled in at the hotel, jump online and figure out where she is now."

A FAMILIAR FACE was waiting in the hotel lobby when the trio arrived. After a quick round of handshakes and hugs with Marc, Amy and Eddie began catching him up on their progress while Miranda stepped away to check in at the front desk. She had reserved two adjoining rooms, one for the men and another for the women.

Eddie turned to Marc. "So, how did it go at old lady McCarren's on Tuesday night?"

"Oh, it's extremely active. Squirrels and senility are running rampant through that house. The squirrels found their way into her attic through a hole in the wood fascia, which explained the scratching noises. As for the doors opening and closing on their own, well, let's just say that Mrs. McCarren's senior moments are stretching into hours. When I got there, her front door was wide open, and she thought I was breaking in."

"Oh, no." Amy laughed.

"Took me three tries to convince her that I was the investigator she called. Finally, at the end of the night, I recommended that she get an exterminator in to evict the squirrels and a roofer to fix the fascia."

"How did you explain the doors opening and closing?" Eddie asked.

"Delicately."

"Wish I was there to hear that." Miranda returned to the group and handed out the room keys. "I appreciate you running up here on short notice, Marc."

"You actually did me a favor. My sister, Anna, has been nagging me to get some repairs done on our mom's house. Turns out, Anna's going to the beach for a week and just wants me to take care of mom while she recuperates from surgery. Every time someone in the family needs help, my sister makes other plans."

"Women," Eddie grumbled in mock disgust.

Amy snickered. "Like you would know."

Miranda held up her hands. "OK, before you two get started again, let's get the luggage up to the rooms."

On their way to the elevator, Marc leaned close to Miranda and spoke in a hushed voice. "What the hell's going on in this town? So far, all I've heard about is a string of suicides, a kid in the hospital that sees ghosts, and some possessed woman waving a gun at you."

"Oh, trust me," Miranda said. "There's so much more. By the way, don't think I failed to notice you shaved off your goatee."

Marc ran a hand over his chin as they stepped into the empty elevator. "Yeah, well, it didn't seem too popular with the ladies."

"Ladies?"

"I seem to recall a particular blonde who didn't care for it."

"But I'm only one lady."

"The only one that matters."

In the hallway, Eddie and Amy exchanged glances. "We'll take the steps," they said.

"So, how about dinner with your old man tonight?"

At the Historical Society, Frank Knedlhans leaned against the counter as his daughter logged off of the computer.

"Only if you let me buy this time," Ginny said.

"Call me old-fashioned, but—"

"A man should always buy for a lady. Yeah, yeah."

"I was going to say that fathers like buying things for their daughters."

"Well, daddy's little girl is all grown up now and makes her own money." Ginny leapt up onto the counter and sat lengthwise, leaning back on her hands. She stretched out her legs and wiggled her toes. "So, where do you want to go?"

"Any place that requires shoes."

THE PRESSROOM RESTAURANT was located in the heart of Lancaster in the historic Steinman Hardware Building, constructed in 1866. Since the Steinman family also owned Lancaster Newspaper Group, which included the Intelligencer, it was no surprise that the dining room of their establishment was decked out in a newspaper motif.

On this balmy summer afternoon, Frank and Ginny took a table outside in Steinman Park's inner section where the rush of a twenty-foot waterfall provided ample cover for their conversation—a circumstance that suited Frank just fine.

"I've never eaten here before," Ginny said after a cursory scan of the menu. "And now I see why."

Frank hid a smirk behind his menu. "You sure you can cover the check?"

"Absolutely... the next time we're at Isaac's."

Father and daughter shared a laugh as the waiter arrived to

take their drink order. Frank realized that he hadn't had a Guinness all week, and it was about time to correct that. Ginny opted for a raspberry iced tea.

"Keeping up the façade for your old man, I see."

"What?"

"Ordering iced tea instead of a beer."

"I don't drink."

"Uh-huh."

"I don't," Ginny insisted. "Besides, you don't get free refills with booze. We poor college students need to save as much as we can."

Frank folded his menu and placed it on the edge of the table. "That's funny, an hour ago, you said you had money."

"I didn't say how much. Hey, you think you can get me a raise?"

"Did you figure out what you want?"

"Pasta Primavera. It's the cheapest thing on the menu."

"Well, it sounds like I'm buying."

"New York Strip."

"That's what I thought. Nothing goes better with a Guinness than steak."

"I wouldn't know." Adopting an innocent expression, Ginny glanced up at the waterfall. "Nice try, though."

After the pair had ordered their meals, she leaned over the table. "So, what happened with that girl today, the one who was asking about the Vernons?"

Frank swallowed his beer. "Amy was her name. Nice enough but terrible liar. She was allegedly researching some psychology paper about extreme stress. I could tell it was a cover. She was all over the map with her questions about the Vernons. The reporter in me knows something's going on. Almost all the people who died in the last week knew Jeff Vernon, with one exception, a guy named Nick Garnell. He was just killed in Iraq last week, but his father worked for the same company as Jeff. About six years ago, he was shot and killed by... oh, damn..."

Ginny leaned forward. "Killed by who?"

"Killed by *whom*."

"Whatever."

"By his other son. I don't recall his name now, but he shot his old man multiple times, then hanged himself from a second-story railing in their house. Two deaths, one a suicide."

"Just like what's happening now."

"Every one of them involves at least one suicide, right? Jeff Vernon's son dies of cancer. He goes nuts, murders his daughters then commits suicide. A week later, his wife kills herself. Always a suicide in the mix and that's the coincidence that Amy brought up today. I wonder what that girl's really up to."

While Frank spoke, Ginny's gaze drifted off to her left. "Well, you could ask her since she just sat down two tables back and to your right."

Frank picked up his beer and glanced over his shoulder. "Now that's a motley group. Something tells me they're not psychology students."

"I can see the wheels turning in your head, Dad. What are you going to do?"

"Do?" Frank's brow furrowed as he gazed at Ginny in mock confusion. "What's there to do? A mysterious young lady appears at the library where I work to ask about one of the biggest cases in my career then shows up a few hours later at the same restaurant." He sat back, took another sip of beer and shrugged. "Probably just coincidence."

Ginny tilted her head. "Yeah, probably."

"THE KID in the hospital is like an early warning system."

The dinner conversation was growing lively and alarming

to those at neighboring tables. As Miranda responded to Marc, she lowered her voice and leaned forward. In unison, the rest of her team did the same.

"Exactly. Matt claims he's being visited by twin girls, about eleven or twelve years old, who warn him when their parents are about to kill their next victim. The girls gravitate to him. At first, I wasn't sure why but thanks to Amy, we're starting to put the pieces together."

"You know who this family is, then?" Marc asked.

"Yes, and I think it was the mother who possessed Heather Marceta the other night."

"That's the woman who pulled the gun on you."

"Right, but looking back now, I think that was a ruse to get to me. Nancy Vernon said that Heather was not that important, and she made it way too easy for me to stop her. Although, I doubt her brother would agree, considering the welts on his back."

"But how the hell would this ghost even know who you are?" Marc asked.

"Her daughters told her."

"How did the daughters know?"

"They paid me a brief visit."

"When?"

"The night Tammy called."

"When we were at your house for dinner?"

"Get the hell out," Eddie said. "Why didn't you tell us?"

"At the time, I didn't know what it was all about. I thought it best to wait."

Marc laughed under his breath. "Every time you answer a question, I have two more."

"We're gonna need a program book for this one," Eddie muttered.

"Did the girls actually communicate with you that night?" Marc pressed. "Do you know why they came to you?"

Miranda held up both hands as a signal for everyone to settle down. "It's really very simple. Thanks to Amy's research we know that the Vernon girls were Carla and Natalie. They had a younger brother named Adam who died of cancer at the same age that Matt is now."

"No shit," Eddie blurted, before swallowing a heap of potato filling.

"Don't cuss with your mouth full," Miranda chided before continuing. "The girls gravitate to Matt because he reminds them of Adam. Now, you asked me why the daughters visited me. Think about it. Tammy is Matt's doctor. Carla and Natalie know that. When she called me that night, they knew that, too. They popped in just for a moment, maybe to check me out or warn me to stay away, I don't know which because there was no communication."

"This is unreal." Marc drummed his fingers on the table. "The father makes the first death look natural or accidental and the wife possesses the second person and pushes them to suicide. Their daughters are warning this kid who then tells his doctor and she calls you."

"Some wild shit," Eddie said.

"Do you talk to your parents with that mouth?" Amy asked.

"I avoid my parents like the plague, like they avoid each other."

"What's the point?" Marc asked. "Don't take this the wrong way, but if Jeff Vernon's ghost is getting revenge on people who hurt him thirty-odd years ago, why doesn't he kill them all at once and get it over with? It's not like he needs to hide from the cops after each victim until things cool down. He can strike at will."

"That would take too much energy," Miranda said. "I think Jeff needs to regroup after each killing and gather his strength for the next one, and I think he goes back to the house we're investigating tonight to do that. That's where this all started. When Elias Gray built his new home on the old Vernon property, he stirred them up. I also think Jeff is drawing his energy from Nancy and his daughters and maybe Elias, too."

"If this ghost is that dangerous, how do we know it won't attack us?" Amy asked. "He might see us as intruders, sticking our nose in where we don't belong."

"I don't know how Jeff Vernon will react. So, we'll stay in pairs during the investigation. Safety in numbers, as usual. No one goes anywhere alone. My guess is that Jeff is too focused on the people from his past to waste energy on us."

"By 'guess,' you mean hope," Eddie said.

Marc raised his glass. "Then may all your guesses be right."

———

IT WAS NEARLY sunset by the time Miranda and her team paid the check. As they started back toward The Pressroom, Miranda realized that they were the center of someone's attention. She stopped beside an empty table and scanned as much of the park as she could see, but no one among the milling bodies was even looking in her direction. Those seated on benches or at tables were engaged in eating, chatting, or staring at their phones.

"Hey, you all right?" Marc was beside her. The rest of the team strolled back to join them.

"Yeah, sorry." Miranda nodded. "Would any of you mind if we went out through the park?"

———

THE PEDESTRIAN ARCADE was a covered promenade that bordered one side of Steinman Park. Frank Knedlhans stood a few steps back from one of the four arches that opened to the outside dining area.

After dinner, he had taken Ginny back to her apartment and returned to the park. Hidden in shadow, he watched as the blonde halted on her way out and glanced around as if she knew someone was watching her. Frank filed that observation away as the rest of the group gathered around her. After a moment, they moved off in the opposite direction, toward the flagpole court. After allowing them a five second lead, Frank Knedlhans was on the move.

CHAPTER 8

WHO ARE YOU, LADY?

"You have reached your destination."

Miranda brought her car to a stop in front of a two-story stone home that was just as secluded as Tammy's place.

"So this is where Jeff Vernon took out his kids then offed himself," Eddie said from the backseat.

"It happened on the property, yes, but not in this house," Amy reminded him.

"I wonder if Jeff Vernon knows that."

In the rearview mirror, a second pair of headlights closed in before gliding to the right. Eddie watched through the rear windshield as Marc's SUV rolled to a stop beside Elias Gray's house. "Huh, a driveway. Missed that."

Miranda peered up at a meager blue glow from one of the second-floor windows. Two young girls stared back.

"Randy, what do you see?" Amy slid down in her seat to follow Miranda's gaze. "What's up there?"

In unison, the girls stepped away. Shadows on the ceiling quivered and jumped in the dim light as if cast by the gamboling flames of a candle. Then there were gunshots. Two of them.

Miranda gasped, her body jolting with each explosive burst.

Eddie leaned forward between the front seats. "Whoa, Randy, what happened?"

"Nothing. I'm... I'm fine."

There was a knock on the driver side window. Miranda screamed, sending Eddie reeling into the farthest corner of the back seat.

"You sure about that?" Amy asked.

Miranda glared at Marc as she slapped the button to lower the window.

"Sorry, didn't mean to scare you," he said. "Just wondering if we were waiting for something."

"Nope, not at all."

"You OK?"

"No," Eddie said.

"Yes." Miranda smiled. "I'm fine. We're all fine and we'll be out in a moment."

With that, she closed the window, leaving Marc with a befuddled expression as he wandered off. Miranda leaned her head back and closed her eyes.

"Can you tell us what you saw up there?" Amy asked.

"I suspect we're going to have an eventful night so let's get on it."

———

THE TEAM GATHERED on the front porch. As she rang the doorbell, a growing tightness in Miranda's chest added to her festering anxiety. Within a few seconds, the lights on either side of the storm door flashed on. Elias Gray was waiting for them—and he wasn't alone.

"Hey, gang." Tammy pushed open the storm door and leaned out.

"I didn't see your car out there," Miranda said.

"It's in the driveway."

"We didn't see that either," Eddie muttered.

Tammy stepped aside. "Oh, well, come on in. I'll introduce everyone."

Miranda held open the storm door and waved in the rest of the team ahead of her. Once they were inside, she started to follow, but there was a presence somewhere nearby. It wasn't attached to the house, but it was observing them. She crossed the porch to the railing but could see little in the darkness save for the first few rows of a sprawling cornfield several yards beyond the driveway.

Behind her, the storm door swung open. Marc joined her at the railing. "What's going on?"

"We're being watched."

"Something in the house?"

Miranda shook her head. "Whatever's in the house knows we're here. I sensed that the moment we pulled up. This is different. It's out there somewhere. Same thing I felt at the restaurant."

Marc glanced up and down the street.

"Don't bother. You won't see anything," Miranda said. "One way or another, whoever it is will show themselves in time."

FRANK KNEDLHANS FELT like a reporter again.

It had been far too long since he'd staked out a story, but not so long that he'd forgotten how. He had kept a discreet distance from Amy and her friends during the drive from Steinman Park to the art dealer's house.

What the hell are you people up to? Frank turned off his headlights and rolled to a stop. The street curved to the left about forty yards past Elias Gray's property. Just before the apex of the curve, where Frank had stopped his car, the street intersected with a dirt road that led to an Amish farm about a quarter mile away. Gray's house remained visible for about fifty feet along the dirt road before trees and overgrowth obstructed the view.

Frank marveled at how little had changed in thirty-three years as he put his Jeep in reverse and backed up onto the dry, cracked soil. The last time he'd parked here, he was a twenty-six-year-old reporter for the Intelligencer, clad in an impenetrable armor of callous indifference. In retrospect, Frank realized that he'd been an arrogant, callow prick who had confused objectivity with apathy. People had been nothing more than a job. Their pain, guilt, victories, and losses were mere fodder for the front page.

On that particular occasion, the job had been Nancy Vernon, the last surviving member of a family whose six month ordeal had thrust them into the media spotlight—and just as quickly destroyed them.

Covering Jeff Vernon's embezzlement trial had been standard fare and when the man was acquitted, Frank had moved on to the next assignment. A week later, Jeff returned to the headlines for reasons far more dire than embezzlement and Frank was all over it. According to the police, there had been no suicide note and no indication that Jeff had become mentally unstable in the days before he murdered his daughters and took his own life.

Afterwards, Nancy had become a recluse, refusing to open her door to anyone but family and friends. One day, Frank had learned that she put the house on the market. Refusing to let her slip away without a statement, he'd waited for two hours parked on the same dirt road then as tonight. Frank had never been above stalking. It had proven effective in getting to Nancy before they found her body in the basement the following day.

The porch lights flashed on at Gray's house, bringing Frank's thoughts back to the task at hand. The door opened and the group filed in—all but the blonde. Just as she had at Steinman Park, the woman pulled away from the rest. She stared into the cornfield as if searching for something.

"Who are you, lady?"

"You have some interesting artwork, Mr. Gray," Amy was saying as Marc and Miranda entered the house. "Have you been collecting for a long time?"

"You could say that. I'm opening a gallery in town. It was always an ambition of mine to become immersed in art."

Amy examined a painting on the wall across the room. It was a portrait of a young man formally dressed in an elegant suit complete with a gray vest and black coat. He held a small red book in his left hand.

"That's called 'Portrait of...'" the art dealer trailed off for a moment before raising a hand to his bandaged head. "Sorry, still a little hazy. That's called 'Portrait of a Gentleman' by Sturtevant Hamblin, circa 1845. He was a somewhat obscure American folk artist. That's just a print, of course, the original is in the National Gallery of Art in D.C."

Miranda didn't find it particularly appealing. The colors were drab, and the style primitive, almost cartoonish. Still, there was something compelling about the image that held her attention far longer than it should have. *What are you trying to tell me?* The pressure behind her eyes intensified the more she stared at it. Tunnel vision began closing in, blurring everything at the edges until the painting was all that remained clear.

There was movement beside her. People were shaking hands. "And these are our fearless leaders," Tammy said. "Randy?"

Miranda tore her gaze away from the mysterious painting and forced a smile. "Sorry, long day."

"Do you need to sit down?" Elias offered, gesturing toward one of the easy chairs.

"No, thank you, I'm fine. Just more exhausted than I thought. It's nice to meet you."

"Tammy tells me you're a sensitive," Elias said as they shook hands.

"Yes."

"I understand that spirits have been known to drain one's energy when trying to communicate. Perhaps that's what you're feeling?"

"That can happen." Miranda was amazed at his insightfulness. "Best thing to do would be to familiarize myself with the environment, see if I 'pick up any vibes' as Tammy would say."

"Can you tell us what you've been experiencing, Elias?" Marc asked.

"Most of the activity has been in the basement and kitchen. The door to the basement opens and closes on its own almost daily. I've heard voices in both areas, as did a few guests who were here recently. I've also heard footsteps and what sounds like whispering on the second floor in one of the spare rooms I've converted to an office."

"Furthest window on the left?" Miranda asked.

"Yes. How did you know?"

"Sensitive."

Elias smiled. "Right."

"Welcome to our world," Eddie said.

"I can only imagine. Should we take the nickel tour?"

"Before we do that," Miranda held up a hand. "I'd like to discuss the history of the property, if you don't mind. Obviously, you're well aware of the Vernon family and the deaths that occurred in the previous house that was here."

"Of course," Elias said. "Unfathomable tragedy."

"Were you told about any of that *before* you bought the land?"

"Not officially. Pennsylvania has a 'don't ask, don't tell' policy about such things. It wasn't until construction started that I heard about Jeff Vernon. Some of the builders were Amish. One of them also works at the adjacent farm. In fact, it was his father who called the police when he heard my cellar door slam shut. It was so loud he thought it was a gunshot.

"They're wonderful people, but when I asked them about the Vernons they were tightlipped. I didn't press them. In fact, I dismissed the entire thing as superstition."

"Yet here we are," Miranda said.

"Wait." Eddie held up a hand. "The Amish don't have phones so how did he call the police?"

"Times have changed," Amy replied. "Even though the Amish reject house phones, some now carry smart phones."

Eddie frowned. "What's this world coming to?"

MIRANDA WANDERED around the basement with Marc standing just a few feet away. Elias had thought it best to start the tour at the bottom and work their way up. Despite the presence of the two men, she felt profound solitude, but it didn't trigger the same reaction as the painting had earlier. This was subtle, restrained, as if someone were grieving in silence after losing everyone they had loved. That someone was Nancy Vernon, no doubt. They had found her body in the basement—but not *this* basement. Then again, the

Vernons may not even realize, or care, that this was not their house.

Miranda surveyed the room—beige stucco walls, small vinyl windows, concrete floor—all brand new. Her gaze came to rest on the metal doors that led outside. She started toward them when a surge of vertigo overtook her. She reached out to steady herself against the nearest wall, but her hand met empty air. Miranda stumbled forward until she collided with the water heater in the corner. "Marc?"

There was no reply. She took a few deep breaths to regain her composure. Outside, wind driven rain pelted filthy wood-framed windows. Against the back wall, where Marc and Elias once stood, sat a slate gray oil tank. Elias did not have oil heat. One of the first things Miranda had noticed when she arrived was the electric baseboard radiators. *Where the hell am I?*

She found her answer in the body that lay on the floor beneath the worn wooden stairs. Blood pooled around the woman's head, matting her hair to the concrete floor. Miranda crept toward the prone form of Nancy Vernon until she caught sight of a metallic glint just beyond the shadow of the staircase. She crouched down for a closer look at the silver revolver.

"This is where we had our first bizarre experience," Elias said.

Miranda spun at the sound of his voice, realizing that she had never physically moved. Neither Marc nor Elias had noticed anything out of the ordinary. With a forced calm, Miranda joined them at the bottom of the stairs.

"I'd just settled in a few days before," Elias continued. "And was giving some friends a tour when one of them heard what sounded like a woman sobbing on the other side of the steps." He pointed toward the water heater situated against the wall under one of the windows. "We all stopped to listen when those cellar doors slammed shut. Needless to say, it got the blood pumping."

"I'll bet," Marc said. "Do you think the sobbing could have come from outside?"

"Possibly. In fact, we were about to shrug off the entire thing until we heard a distinct male voice from the kitchen."

"How distinct?" Miranda asked. "Could you make out what it said?"

The color drained from their host's face. "Alone among the dead."

Marc shot a sidelong glance at Miranda. "Say again?"

"I didn't catch it at the time, but now that I think about it, that was the phrase we heard when my guests were here."

"Just like in your dreams," Miranda said.

"Correct." Elias made his way up the steps. "Well, shall we continue the tour?"

Marc motioned for Miranda to wait. "'Alone among the dead?' Something you forgot to tell us?"

"All I know is that according to Tammy, Elias said he had a dream in which someone used that phrase."

"So he heard it first—or thought he did—it scared him, and he dreamt about it later. Well, that's not evidence so I can see why you didn't mention it." Marc started after Elias.

"Uh, yeah, slight wrinkle there," Miranda said. "Do you remember Matt? The boy in the hospital? He used that exact phrase when he was talking to Tammy about Elias. He knew when Elias had been injured and was on his way to the hospital."

Marc sighed. "OK, I'll tell you what, if we capture that phrase as an EVP, we'll include it as evidence but until then, it's just coincidence."

"That's one hell of a coincidence."

"That we can't substantiate unless we capture it on audio."

Hardly a productive case passed without this debate in one version or another. At times, it had become tedious, even infuriating. If only Marc could have witnessed Heather Marceta's possession or talked with Matthew Meade, he would be convinced. Still, she couldn't argue with his bottom-line reasoning. Without hard evidence, they had nothing to show the client.

"I know the drill."

Marc's expression softened. He was a sucker for Miranda's pout, and she knew it. He crouched down on the steps to bring himself at eye level with her. "Look, you know I'm not trying to be a hard-ass. I believe in your experiences. What happened upstairs? It looked like you were transfixed by that painting."

"I wish I could tell you. There's definitely something germane about it but I didn't get anything specific, only that I was meant to pay attention to it. Sometimes the answer presents itself later. A lot of paranormal investigation is patience."

Marc smiled. "I know the drill. What about down here?"

"For about ten seconds while Elias was talking, it was as if I was in another basement in a different house. I'm pretty sure it was the Vernons' place."

"Did you see any of them?"

"You could say that."

Miranda and Marc caught up with Elias in his sitting room, where the team was busy unpacking and setting up equipment.

"Where to next?" she asked.

Elias led them upstairs to his home office. Even as they approached the room, the blue glow was visible in the doorway just as Miranda had observed it from her car when she arrived. As Elias flipped the lights on, she noticed rippling waves of a calm ocean under a clear sky—the screen saver on the art dealer's computer monitor.

"I sometimes hear children's voices in here," Elias began. "A conversation of whispers, indiscernible. The first time, I thought it was a group of Amish kids passing by but when I peeked through the window, there was no one about.

"Then last night, I had a more direct experience. To be honest, it could've been a result of this bump on the head. I was in here working until sometime after three in the morning, and I had to reboot my laptop. While the screen was dark, I caught the reflection of two young girls standing over there." Elias pointed to the opposite wall where a cherry wood filing cabinet was flanked on either side by matching bookcases. "But when I turned to look—"

"They were gone," Miranda and Elias finished in unison.

"Can you describe them?" Marc asked.

"Maybe ten or so years old, judging by their height. The floor lamp in the corner was behind them. They were more silhouettes than anything."

"They were identical twins," Miranda said.

She could see them across the room, the same girls that had appeared in her kitchen two days ago. Now, however, they each lay peacefully tucked in their beds. As it had in the basement, the scene transformed around her. Marc and Elias disappeared. A small mint green lamp with a yellow shade sat atop a square table between the girls' beds. Above their headboards, their names were spelled out in multi-colored construction paper, undoubtedly from a classroom art project. To Miranda's right, Elias's desk had been replaced by a painted dresser that matched the lamp in color. A full-length mirror hung on the wall beside it.

Miranda parted the orange curtains. To her surprise, she looked directly out into the woods. Cornsilk Drive was off to her left. Elias had built his house perpendicular to the

Vernon's. Miranda filed that away in the back of her mind and turned her attention to the girls.

According to the clock on the wall, it was almost four-thirty in the afternoon. She thought it odd that they would be asleep so early. As she approached, Miranda noticed that their eyes were open—lifeless eyes that stared up at the ceiling, oblivious to her intrusion. She called out their names, but they didn't flinch. Miranda leaned over Carla and lifted her blanket. She covered her mouth to stifle a cry at the sight of the girl's blood-soaked midsection—or what remained of it. She dared not disturb Natalie.

Miranda had seen nothing but death since she arrived. Before their investigation began, the team needed to be warned. She turned to hurry from the room and collided with Marc.

He reached out to steady her. "Randy, slow down. What's wrong?"

"Get everyone together." Her words came out in a rush. "Jeff Vernon is here, and he's made it clear that we're not welcome."

"He told you this?" Elias asked.

"No, he showed me."

IT WAS time for a closer look. Frank skulked toward the house along the edge of the cornfield that stopped about six yards from the art dealer's driveway. Late summer corn was tall, and Frank ducked for cover behind the first row. A blue SUV, belonging to one of the visitors, was parked in the driveway. From his car, Frank had watched them unload several dark cases and carry them into the house.

Drugs? Weapons? Counterfeiting plates?

Frank turned at a rustling sound close by in the cornfield.

It was pitch black and the stalks were dense. It was impossible to see anything. He waited for several minutes but heard nothing more. He dismissed it as a deer or other wild animal. *Just hope it isn't a skunk.*

"Leave me alone!"

Frank reeled back and stumbled to the ground. As he lay there, he winced up at a cloudless blue sky. *What the—?*

"But Mrs. Vernon, if your husband was innocent, why did he kill your daughters and take his own life?"

Mrs. Vernon? Frank rolled onto his side and peeked out through the stalks.

"Because people like you destroyed him. You dragged his name through the dirt just as much as those liars who falsely accused him. You pried into our personal life, harassed me and my kids everywhere I went, just like you're doing right now."

Oh, shit. This can't be happening. Frank scrambled to his feet and crept to the edge of the cornfield for a better look. The reporter's back was turned to him, but it didn't matter. He knew who the man was.

"Now I have nothing left." Tears streamed down Nancy's face. "All of my children are dead. My husband is dead. I'm about to lose my house. What more do you people want from me? Do you want me dead, too? Will that make you happy, you fucking bastard?"

"I'm sorry for your losses, Mrs. Vernon," the man said without an ounce of sympathy. "I'm just doing my job."

Nancy gazed into his eyes with a hatred that had burned into Frank's memory. Seeing it again now made him cringe.

"You already did your job. Now get the fuck off my property before I call the cops." With that, she stormed into the house and slammed the door.

The man ambled back to his car, parked along the dirt road around the curve from the Vernons' house.

Frank lowered his head. "God forgive me for being such a heartless fuck back then."

"God may forgive you," a voice said from behind him. "But I won't."

Frank spun to find himself eye to eye with the impossible. "How can you—"

His words ended in a gurgle as a fist slammed into his chest. His legs buckled yet he remained standing, impaled on the arm of his assailant. The hand was inside of him, crushing his heart. Frank let out a strangled gasp and began to convulse. His vision blurred.

"You should've let it go back then, Frank. Just like you should've let it go tonight. Bad idea to come back here. You weren't on my list, so I consider this a bonus, but don't worry, Frank. You won't be lonely. Your daughter will be joining you soon."

The world tilted and the ground rose up to meet him. It was night once more. Clouds gathered above, lined in stark, pale moonlight. Cornstalks swayed in the breeze. Frank found a strange comfort from it all before the world faded away.

CHAPTER 9

THE FATE OF THE VERNONS

"I'm almost afraid to ask, but how could two dead girls end up neatly tucked in their beds?" After turning off the lights, Amy sat against the edge of Elias's desk and leveled her IR camera at the opposite end of the room where Miranda had seen the Vernon girls lying in bloody repose.

From the comfort of the suede office chair, Miranda shrugged. "I have no idea."

"It's interesting that you had visions in specific rooms, as if what happened back then occurred in this house."

"Well, anywhere we go here, we're in the vicinity of those events," Miranda said. "For example, the basement in my vision wasn't laid out like what's down there now. It was the Vernons' basement. At least part of this house occupies the same space as theirs did. From what I saw, their house was perpendicular to this one. It faced the woods, not the street, but there was still a second-story room right about where we're sitting."

"Maybe Eddie was right earlier," Amy said. "Maybe Jeff Vernon doesn't know that this isn't his house."

Miranda held up her digital voice recorder. "Now would be a good time to ask him."

"Ask me what, ladies?"

She jolted at the new voice, which should have sent her rolling backward if the chair still had casters instead of worn wooden legs. She slid from the orange vinyl seat and backed into what should have been Elias's desk, but it was gone—as was Amy. The mint green dressers had returned.

Miranda dragged the chair toward her, a protective barricade between herself and the murderer in the doorway. Jeff Vernon didn't acknowledge her at all but smiled at his daughters sitting on the floor, books strewn about.

Yellow walls were aglow with daylight from open windows. A warm breeze rustled mint green curtains as Jeff entered the room. Heat flared in Miranda's face, as one might experience when turning a corner and nearly colliding with a sworn enemy. Rubbing his bloodshot brown eyes, Jeff joined his daughters on the floor.

"It's the last week of summer reading club," one of the girls said. "And we're learning the planets, but Natalie's having a hard time keeping them in order."

"You didn't get it right either," her sister cried.

Jeff held up his hands. "OK. Settle down. Did Mrs. Prembel teach you a trick to memorizing the order of the planets?"

"Yes," Natalie said. "It goes like this, 'My Very Excellent Memory Just Served Up Nine Planets.'"

"Right, so what are they?"

"Um, Mars, Venus, Earth, Mercury, Jupiter, Saturn, Uranus, Neptune, Pluto."

"Almost right," Jeff said. "You just need to swap Mercury and Mars. Mercury is closest to the sun. Think of it like this. When you're sick and we take your temperature, you know that silver stuff in the thermometer? That's called mercury.

When you have a fever, the mercury rises because of the heat. So when you think of mercury, think of heat." He raised a hand toward the windows. "The sun is hot, and the planet Mercury is closest to it."

It occurred to Miranda that all she knew of Jeff Vernon came from tragic newspaper articles and a cryptic warning from his wife's ghost. Here and now, Jeff was a human being, a caring father. He was also a broken man with slumped posture that signified resignation to the suffering that life had inflicted upon him. Long sideburns extended from an unkempt mane of chestnut hair and ended in dense stubble. His gray shirt sagged from his gaunt frame while the waistline of his navy blue pants was bunched up under a white belt. Rapid weight loss from the stress of the embezzlement trial and despair at the loss of his son, no doubt. Miranda sensed his detachment from the world and knew he was no longer engaged in living, which could only mean one thing.

This was the day.

"You know, girls, I've been thinking a lot about Adam," Jeff said. "I miss him and I know you do, too." Tears welled up in his eyes. "I, uh... I was thinking maybe there was a way we could be with him again. Would you like that?"

"Adam was sick, Daddy," Carla said. "You and Mommy said so."

"They took him from me. From us." Jeff struggled to catch his breath. "I wasn't there when he died because they lied about me. People I trusted for nine years turned on me and because of them, my son died alone. They destroyed my family."

By this time, he was mumbling to himself. Everyone else was frozen in place, staring at him, including Miranda. Jeff wiped his eyes. "Someday, they'll get theirs, but I know a way we can be together again with Adam."

"What about Mommy?" Natalie asked.

"She'll join us later."

"What do we need to do?"

Jeff pulled himself to his feet. "Just close your eyes."

Miranda shrank into the corner and slid to the floor. "No, please. Don't make me watch this. I know what happened. I don't need to see it." The twins exchanged confused glanced before shutting their eyes. "If only I could grab you both and run away from here."

That was impossible, of course. The history that played out before her was immutable, a permanent scar on the land. It was no different than what she had experienced at the Emery Zoo a few days ago and a hundred places before that. Miranda had long since become inured to glimpses of violence in her visions, but never to the horror of watching children die.

While birds sang and curtains fluttered in a summer breeze, two ten-year-old girls sat on the floor, oblivious to their fate.

In the doorway, their father reached around for the pump-action shotgun.

THE FIRST FLOOR of Elias Gray's house was immersed in darkness, save for the meager glow from the monitor in the sitting room. From there, Elias and Eddie could view almost the entire kitchen in frame, as Marc had positioned the IR camera atop the refrigerator. According to Eddie, if the door should open on its own, they might capture an apparition otherwise invisible to the naked eye.

Earlier in the evening, before the team dispersed to begin the investigation, a distressed Miranda had informed them of "dangerous visions" she had experienced during her tour of the house. She had urged against going anywhere alone. Now, however, her fears seemed unfounded if not melodramatic. Elias checked the time in the lower right corner of the screen. It was just after midnight. Three hours had passed without incident.

Behind them, Tammy had long since dozed off in one of the easy chairs. Elias gazed at her, able to do so now without inhibition. Here in this absurd situation where strangers roamed his house in search of a nefarious *geist*, waiting anxiously for a door to swing open or the call of a disembodied voice, Elias took the time to admire this woman. Even in bleak gray light, she was gorgeous.

"Some people just don't have the stamina for this," the boy said.

Elias glanced at the monitor. The kitchen door remained closed. "Unfortunately, some of us don't have the patience for it either." He rose from his seat. "If you'll excuse me, I'm going to step outside and stretch my legs. If anything exciting happens, give a shout."

THERE WAS blood on the curtains.

Jeff Vernon lifted the limp form of his daughter and placed her gently onto the bed. Just as he had with Natalie, he positioned Carla's arms at her side and lovingly smoothed the covers over her body. "Don't worry about the mess, I'll clean it up." Jeff kissed her on the forehead. "You just sleep and dream of Adam as I often do, and I'll be with you soon."

Huddled in the corner, Miranda trembled as an insane man's depravity played out before her. Jeff hurried from the room, hands and shirt spattered in dark red. From somewhere down the hall, the hiss of running water was followed by fading footsteps. Across the room, Natalie and Carla lay beneath their covers just as Miranda had seen them earlier, but this time there was blood on the wall, the floor, and the foot rail of the nearest bed. It was even on the books.

Miranda choked down the bile that burned her throat.

The shotgun lay atop a wooden toy chest just inside the door. Jeff hurried back into the room carrying a bucket of soapy water and rags. He knelt down and scrubbed the floor.

"Yeah, that's good. Don't want to leave a mess for Mom. You know how she gets about that."

Miranda gripped the back of the chair to steady herself as she stood. She wanted to run, but her legs refused to move.

"Much better." Jeff Vernon retrieved the shotgun from the toy chest. He turned as if to leave but instead he came to a stop before Miranda. She reeled back, slamming into one of the dressers. Jeff showed no reaction as he lifted the chair with one hand and carried it across the room. He placed it between the girls' beds and took a seat, letting the weapon slide through his hands until the butt touched the floor. With one last look at his daughters, Jeff rested his chin on the barrel and reached down for the trigger.

A moment later, there was blood on the ceiling.

ON THE PORCH, Elias peeled the front of his polo shirt from his damp chest. Even at this hour, the humidity was intolerable. He strolled to the top of the steps and stifled a yawn as he took in his surroundings. The nocturnal song of crickets was all that broke the eerie silence of the rural night. In the starless sky above, drifting clouds revealed a full moon before obscuring it once more.

In his peripheral vision, something fluttered in midair. It darted out from beyond the roof of the house and flew in a wide, erratic circle above the neighboring cornfield before disappearing into the night. Fascinated, Elias kept his gaze fixed on the sky. He recalled the Amish farmers talking about the brown bats that hovered over their fields, feeding on crop pests.

Elias dropped onto the maple wood bench he had purchased from an Amish shop in Intercourse and leaned his head back against the wall of the house. He chuckled to himself at the thought of full moons, bats, and strange noises in the night. All the while, people scrambled about his house chasing phantoms.

Elias wondered what Leland would think of it all. "*Wahnsinn!*" would likely be the first word out of his mouth and he might be right. This investigation could be nothing more than an exercise in lunacy. Had there truly been a voice in the kitchen that night just after the cellar doors slammed shut? Or a woman sobbing? Perhaps the doors had not been fully propped open. Perhaps the mysterious noises were simply from the house settling, or the central air turning on, or a loud radio from a passing car. Even out here in the sticks, the latter happened from time to time.

But what of the disturbing phrase in his dreams that was later repeated by a terminally ill child Elias had never met? And the bleeding steps? The word on the basement wall? *Verbrecher*. Criminal. Were these things also part of his dream?

The screen door opened and Tammy ambled out to the porch. She pushed auburn locks out of her eyes and stretched her arms above her head.

Elias admired the view. "Back among the living, I see."

Tammy smiled and slid onto the bench beside him. She massaged her temples as she spoke. "Sorry for nodding off."

"No need to apologize, especially at this hour. What roused the fair maiden from her slumber? A disembodied voice, perhaps? Did your chair levitate?"

Tammy chuckled and shook her head. "Nothing so exciting. It's still dead in there, pardon the pun. I apologize in advance if this turns out to be a waste of time."

"Not at all. I can't think of anyone else I'd rather spend the night with," Elias said. "In a matter of speaking."

Tammy gave him a look of mock indignation, but the stark glow of the porch lights revealed the crimson flush of her cheeks. "You men are all alike. I just came out to see if you were all right."

"Of course I am."

"Really? You suffered a severe head injury after having not one, but two nightmares in which an eerie phrase was uttered and later repeated by one of my cancer patients in direct reference to you. Your house has been overrun by strangers looking for a ghost, and you were out here pacing like a caged tiger a minute ago, which is what woke me up by the way."

"Sorry, I was merely stretching my legs."

Tammy leaned toward him. "You know, you can tell me what's wrong. I am a doctor."

His pulse throbbed as he took what he hoped was his cue. "Well, in that case, I do have a minor problem."

"Maybe I can help."

"I think so."

Their lips met and Elias closed his eyes, dismissing the danger of what he was doing. It felt right. That's all that mattered. Tammy's arm slid across his shoulders, and her supple leg brushed against his.

The front door burst open.

"You guys need to see—oh, uh..."

Tammy pulled away and Elias pondered how best to murder the boy.

"Something happen, Eddie?" Tammy asked.

"Whaaa-yeah, uh, the door just flew open."

"So it did," Elias grumbled.

"No, the *kitchen* door. It opened on its own."

MIRANDA SAT HUDDLED in the corner of the pink bathroom, knees drawn up in front of her chest, fingers furiously twirling a lock of her hair. She rested her head against the vanity and gazed up at shimmering sunlight reflecting off the frosted panes of a small jalousie window. The bathroom was at the rear of the house, opposite the girls' room. It would have taken maybe two hours for the sun to traverse that much sky, yet for Miranda perhaps ten minutes had passed since she fled the domestic carnage.

Time was unreliable in her visions, but this one should have ended by now. *Why am I still here? I saw what I needed to, unless...*

Miranda came here to confirm her theory that Elias had unwittingly awakened the dormant, vengeful spirit of Jeff Vernon. Though all she had seen thus far were imprints of events past, she sensed that Jeff—or someone—was orchestrating them, putting on a show for her. Perhaps this was merely the first act.

Beyond the closed bathroom door, the eerie silence that pervaded the Vernon house was shattered as someone screamed—repeatedly. It was the primal shriek of a mother who had found her children slaughtered.

Nancy Vernon was home.

Miranda could not imagine the woman's shock, the knife piercing her heart. *Not now*, Miranda reminded herself. *All of this happened thirty years ago.* Yet, it was something she feared every moment her own children were an ocean away. She'd give anything to be with them right now. Miranda pushed the thought aside and in her mind's eye, envisioned the scene playing out down the hall. Nancy would see her husband first, the top of his head obliterated. It would take maybe five or ten seconds before her gaze shifted to either side of him, before she pulled back the covers off one of her daughters and realized the fate of both.

The screaming stopped. There was a crash followed by running footsteps. The bathroom door burst open. Miranda's tried to fold her legs back, but it didn't matter. Nancy Vernon's feet passed right through them as she dropped to her knees before the toilet and vomited.

ELIAS STARED at the monitor as Eddie replayed the footage. "I've never been present when the kitchen door opens. It always happens after I've locked it and retired for the evening."

All heads turned at the sound of footsteps on the stairs. After a moment, Miranda came into view with Amy on her heels.

Eddie waved them over. "Randy, the kitchen door just—"

"She can't hear you," Amy whispered. "She's having a vision."

Without acknowledging anyone, Miranda turned into the dining room and stopped. Amy and Eddie aimed their flashlights at her but kept their distance. Perhaps they wished to avoid disturbing the medium, although Elias couldn't help but question her veracity. Was this a bit of playacting conjured up by Miranda and her young friend while they were upstairs?

Amy lifted her radio and spoke in a hushed tone. "Marc, where are you?"

"In the basement."

"Alone? Seriously, you of all people."

"Yeah, yeah. I know. It's been quiet down here. What's going on?"

"Randy's having a vision. She's in some sort of trance. We were chatting on the second floor when she went quiet for about ten minutes, got up, and wandered downstairs. Creeped me out. We're in the dining room now."

"On my way."

Ever the physician, Tammy snatched a small flashlight from Eddie's table and aimed the light into Miranda's eyes, first the right, then the left. "Randy, can you hear me?" After a moment, Tammy lowered the flashlight. "It's like she's in shock."

"This isn't the first time she's been like this," Amy said. "It happened last week on another case."

"What were you two doing just before she fell into this trance?"

"Just talking about the house, then about Jeff Vernon. That's when it started."

Tammy placed a hand on Miranda's bare forearm, then to the side of her face. "Her skin is cold. I don't like this. If she doesn't come out of it soon, I'm taking action, even if that means getting her to the hospital."

She peered into Miranda's eyes once more. "Where are you, lady?"

IN THE DINING ROOM, boxes were labeled, taped, and stacked haphazardly against the walls. On the table, signed paperwork lay beside a stack of brochures listing the home's selling points. Nancy was clearing out.

Miranda searched the first floor before climbing the steps in search of Nancy, but there was no one to be found. In the master bedroom, more boxes were stacked in the corner while clothes—mostly Jeff's by the look of them—were stuffed in a congeries of shopping bags atop the bed.

She soon found herself at the door to the girls' bedroom. After a moment's hesitation, she gripped the knob—but it wouldn't turn. The door was locked. No surprise. Nancy probably hadn't stepped foot in there since that terrible day.

Miranda returned to the dining room just in time to hear shouting from somewhere outside. She hurried through the kitchen and out to the rear patio. They were in the driveway, Nancy Vernon and a young man with long black hair and a thick mustache. He was carrying a notepad and pen.

"Because people like you destroyed him," Nancy said. "You dragged his name through the dirt just as much as those liars who falsely accused him. You pried into our personal life, harassed me and my kids everywhere I went, just like you're doing right now."

From that, Miranda gathered that the man was a reporter. She wondered if he was the same one Amy had spoken with at the Historical Society a few days ago. *What was his name again?*

"Now I have nothing left," Nancy continued, tears streaming down her face. "All of my children are dead. My husband is dead. I'm about to lose my house. What more do you fucking people want from me? Do you want me dead, too? Will that make you happy, you fucking bastard?"

"I'm sorry for your losses, Mrs. Vernon," the reporter replied, in a tone that belied his words. "I'm just doing my job."

"You already did your job. Now get the fuck off of my property before I call the cops." With that, Nancy marched into the house and slammed the door while the man sauntered off.

Nancy tossed two grocery bags onto the kitchen table and fell into one of the chairs, head in her hands. She broke down into quiet sobbing. Tears dripped from her face onto the table. Nancy ran her fingers through the drops as if counting them. One tear for each life extinguished from her world.

The doorbell rang. "Please just leave me the hell alone."

Nancy trudged to the kitchen sink, splashed cold water on her face, and dried off with a paper towel. The doorbell rang again. Miranda followed her into the living room, wishing she could wrap her arms around this woman.

Nancy opened the front door. It was the realtor. Her name was Anita. Miranda had seen her picture on the paperwork earlier. She was a burly, middle-aged woman with sunglasses that covered the entire upper half of her face.

"How are you holding up, Nancy?"

"About as good as can be expected."

"Well, I just wanted to tell you that I'm here to put the 'For Sale' sign out on the lawn before this storm hits in a few hours."

"Sounds good. Thank you."

"Are we still on for the open house this Saturday?"

"Yes, but just so you know, this'll be my last night here. My sister and her husband are coming to move me to their place in Cape May, so the house will be all yours this weekend. In fact, it's all yours until you sell it. I won't be back until then."

"Well, Cape May will be nice for you, I'm sure." Anita gave her a sympathetic smile. "If there's anything else I can do, anything at all, just let me know. Oh, by the way, when I pulled up, I noticed your cellar doors were open out back. I didn't want you to leave without closing them. Don't want a flood down there before the open house."

"Right. I'm just airing out the basement, it tends to get musty in humid weather. I'll make sure they're closed before it rains. Thanks for all of your help, Anita."

With that, the realtor hurried off. Miranda remained inside the house as Nancy stepped out onto the porch. She leaned against the rail and watched as Anita hammered the wood-and-metal sign into the ground beside the end of the driveway.

Miranda glanced around the living room. *Why am I still*

here? It's not as if I can console this poor woman. What's left for me to see?

There was a shuffling noise from the dining room. The documents that had been stacked neatly atop the table moments ago were now scattered all over the floor.

"What the hell happened here?" Nancy returned from the porch and breezed past Miranda. With a sigh, she knelt down to collect the paperwork. The air turned frigid. She folded her arms against the chill.

"Mom, why are you leaving us?"

The familiar voice called out from everywhere at once. Nancy gaped in Miranda's direction, backing away until she collided with the boxes along the wall.

That's impossible! There's no way she can see me. It took a moment for Miranda to realize that Nancy was staring at something behind her. Natalie and Carla stood side by side, their forms undulating. They were dressed exactly as when they had appeared in Miranda's kitchen—and as when they were murdered. Each mirrored the other's perplexed expression as they started forward toward their mother. Miranda sidled to her left, but not before Carla passed right through her. Goosebumps erupted along Miranda's arms. This was unlike any vision she had ever experienced. Physical sensation was rare.

"Why are you scared, Mom?" Natalie asked.

Nancy shook her head, eyes wide with fear. "No, no, no..."

The twins stopped at the dining room table. At first, Miranda expected them to pass through it to get to their mother but to Carla and Natalie, the table was a part of their lives and judging from their demeanor, they didn't realize their non-corporeal state.

Carla sidestepped the table. "Mom, why won't you say anything?"

With a shriek, Nancy made for the stairs, boxes toppling

over in her wake. On the third step, she halted and screamed again. Miranda followed her gaze. *Oh, shit.*

"Hello, Nancy." Jeff Vernon sat on the top step, leaning forward and smiling down at her. "We all miss you, especially the girls. They really wanted to see their mom."

Nancy staggered back, missing all three steps. Miranda reached out to catch her but realized the futility as Nancy crashed to the floor in a crumpled heap. She yelped in pain, clutching her shoulder.

Jeff descended the stairs. "Are you all right, sweetie? This is such an old house. These damn steps are so steep. I always meant to do something about that."

Nancy's eyes darted from Jeff to her approaching daughters. Hunters closing in on their prey.

"Honey, I only want us to be a family again, all of us together." He extended a hand. "Come with us. You'll see, it's better than being alone here. Alone among the dead."

Nancy Vernon, a quivering wreck on the verge of hyperventilating, scrambled on all fours past her daughters. Midway through the dining room, she found her legs and dashed through the kitchen to the back door but it refused to open. Nancy turned the knob and yanked on the door but it wouldn't budge.

"Nancy, please." Jeff stood in the kitchen doorway flanked by Carla and Natalie. "I'm not here to hurt you. I just want to take you with us."

Bracing herself, Miranda barged through Jeff, repressing another shiver. At that moment, Nancy propelled herself across the kitchen and through the open basement door. Her heavy footfalls faded down the bare wood steps.

Jeff crouched down between his daughters. "I need to speak to your mom alone. Why don't you play in your room for a while?" The girls vanished, followed by Jeff.

If these were Nancy Vernon's final moments, it was clear

that she was resourceful enough to have worked out her escape rather than surrender to fear. This was not a woman about to commit suicide—not voluntarily.

What if I don't go down to the basement? What if I stay here? I already know how this ends. No, Miranda couldn't avoid the inevitable. The truth of the Vernons' fate was unraveling for her and the final revelation was yet to come. Against her better instincts, she descended into the basement.

WHILE HER TEAM LOOKED ON, Miranda halted again, this time in the kitchen. Her gaze panned across the room and settled on the open basement door.

"It's as if she's sleepwalking," Tammy said.

Beside her, Marc shook his head. "Her visions don't normally last this long."

"The one she had at the zoo took a while," Amy chimed in from behind them.

Tammy's eyebrows shot up. "She had an episode like this at a zoo in broad daylight?"

"No, we were investigating at night. This zoo was haunted by two boys who died on the land back when it was a farm. At one point, Miranda ended up locked inside the reptile house for several minutes. When she came out, she told me exactly how the boys died. She watched it happen like you and I watch a movie."

"She once compared it to being a ghost in their world," Marc added.

In the dining room, Elias sat at the table and took in the conversation. Although he wasn't convinced of the clairvoyant's performance, he was intrigued to see how this demonstration would end.

But his true attention was on Tammy.

Their all too brief interlude on the front porch had jarred Elias out of his mounting fatigue. She was beautiful, intelligent, compassionate. He wished everyone would leave so he could be alone with her.

Elias marveled at the impeccable timing of their encounter. The final shipment of art, a batch of paintings confiscated during the Nazi occupation of Peterhof Palace in Russia, was due in on Tuesday. His customers would arrive in town two days later to inspect their new acquisitions and pay the final balance. Within one week, Janos Skorzeny, aka Elias Gray and five other aliases, will have reached his goal of 200 million dollars.

Then, he could relax. No more running, no more counterfeit documents, no more surgical disguises. And if luck were in fact a lady, Elias hoped he was looking at her right now.

"Who's watching the IR feed?" Marc called.

"I'm on it," Eddie replied from the sitting room. "I'm not seeing anything in the kitchen."

"So who or what is she chasing?" Amy asked.

No sooner had she spoken than Miranda was on the move again, this time taking cautious steps toward the basement door.

"Let's follow her down." Marc switched on his flashlight, as did Amy. They had turned them off earlier to conserve the batteries.

"*Alone among the dead.*"

It was a whisper, inches from Elias's ear. He leapt from his chair and spun around just as something in the kitchen slammed. The women yelped.

"What the fuck!" Eddie shouted.

"Dammit, it won't open," Marc said.

Elias dashed into the kitchen and switched on the light, IR cameras be damned. "What happened?"

"As soon as Randy stepped through, the door slammed shut," Tammy said. "We can't open it and it isn't even locked."

"It's like someone's holding it closed from the other side." Marc gave the handle a prolonged pull to no avail.

Amy shook her head. "There's no way Randy could be doing that. It's not giving an inch."

"Maybe she's not the one holding it," Eddie said from the kitchen doorway.

Marc looked at Elias. "What about the Bilco doors?"

"Locked. I haven't used them since this." Elias pointed to the bandage on his head.

"Her radio is still clipped to her pocket." Amy lifted hers and pressed the side button. "Amy to Randy. You there? Talk to me." There was no response. Amy tried once more to no avail. The kitchen went dark. "Eddie!"

"I didn't touch anything." He was already hurrying back to the sitting room. "Fuck. Even the laptop lost power."

"How's that possible?" Tammy asked. "It has a battery."

"So does my flashlight and it's dead," Amy said. "Along with my radio. This is exactly what happened at the zoo just before Randy walked into the reptile house. The lampposts went out at the same time as our equipment. The power wasn't restored until she came back out."

"God knows when that'll happen." Marc sighed. "Mr. Gray, I want to make it clear that the safety of the team is always our top priority. Having said that, if I have to break this door down to get to her, I will."

THE RUSH OF WIND.

The smell of impending summer rain.

The sight of Nancy lying prone on the basement floor.

As she descended the steps, Miranda looked around for

Jeff or the girls, but they were nowhere to be found. Judging from her position, Nancy must have stumbled down the last few steps. The woman dragged herself across the floor to a utility sink situated beside a washing machine. She gripped the edge of the sink and pulled herself to her feet. On unsteady legs, Nancy hobbled toward her escape route, favoring her right knee.

The open metal doors rocked in place but held steady. Beyond them in the distance, swaying stalks of corn relented to the wind's fury under a threatening sky. Nancy's hair danced about her head as she neared the short stairwell.

"Nancy..."

The whisper was little more than a sigh carried on the angry breeze. Beside Miranda, Jeff coalesced out of nothing. This time, there was no fear in Nancy's eyes, no trembling. She gritted her teeth, lips pulled back like a feral animal.

"Nancy, please don't leave."

"You murdered my children! What do I have left here?"

"No, I freed them from a miserable world of lies and treachery and incurable diseases. I did it to bring us together as a family."

"You did it because you were weak. You couldn't cope. You were acquitted of the charges. You could have gotten a new job anywhere. We could have left this fucking place and started a new life somewhere else. You could have moved on. *We* could have moved on together."

"Our son—"

"Don't you dare use Adam to justify your actions. I loved him, too, damn you." Nancy broke down into tears. "Why didn't you talk to me? You always kept everything bottled up."

"You knew what I was going through. You saw my suffering. Did it need to be said? You pushed me away after I was arrested, as if you were convinced I was guilty."

"No..." Nancy shook her head.

"Don't lie to me." Jeff scowled. "I can see right through you."

Nancy drew herself to her full height. "I loved you, Jeff, but unlike you, I have the will to move on. Give the children my love." With that, she proceeded up the stairs.

Above her, one of the metal doors unlatched and slammed closed on her head. Miranda cringed as the woman collapsed to the floor. What had happened to Elias was no accident.

"You can tell them yourself soon enough," Jeff said.

As Nancy lay whimpering on the floor, cradling her head, Jeff ambled over to a small gray metal locker in the corner. It opened on its own as he approached. "You didn't sell off my guns yet. Let's see here. Ah, yes. This one will do."

A silver revolver leapt from the locker and spun across the floor, stopping within Nancy's reach. It was the same gun that Miranda had seen earlier lying next to the woman's lifeless body beneath the stairs just a few feet away. Which meant that Nancy had mere moments to live. *She's been dead for over thirty years. This is not happening now.* That truth was of little comfort to Miranda. So why did she feel a disturbing mélange of fear and relief? Fear of being forced to witness the last brutal death in this house, yet relieved to know that this series of unspeakable nightmares would soon end.

Jeff crouched beside her. "Pick it up."

When Nancy refused, he yanked her arm close. She yelped as he forced the revolver into the palm of her hand and clasped his fingers over hers. He pushed her arm down, bending it until the barrel was inches from Nancy's head. She writhed and kicked at him in vain.

"Get away from me!" Nancy's voice was raspy and guttural as she strained against him. She managed to do little more than push herself across the smooth concrete floor until she reached the steps. Jeff's grip remained firm. After a few seconds, her resistance languished either as a result of a concussion or Jeff's enervating presence, or both. It was a common belief that spirits can drain the energy of people near them. Most of the time, their motives were an innocent attempt to communicate or manifest. On the rarest occasions, their intent was malicious.

"Please, Jeff, don't do this." Nancy's defenses were depleted.

Jeff paused as he pressed the muzzle against her temple. "I need you to help me find Adam."

Miranda retreated to the opposite side of the basement, placing the stairs between her and the heinous scene.

"When we find our son," Jeff continued. "You'll thank me."

Nancy screamed. Miranda covered her ears.

For nearly a full minute after the blast, she couldn't bring herself to move. Finally, Miranda returned to the dead body of Nancy Vernon. Blood pooled around the woman's head, matting her hair to the concrete floor. The gun lay to Nancy's right just beyond the shadow of the stairs. Ahead of Miranda, the cellar doors were wide open. Without looking back, she climbed the steps. A torrent of rain and wind assaulted her.

A flash of lightning lit up Amy's face. "Randy?"

"He hasn't found Adam yet," Miranda muttered.

"Randy, are you okay?"

"Even now, he still hasn't found his son." Jeff Vernon wouldn't rest until he was reunited with Adam, but why was he killing people and forcing his wife to do the same? *I wasn't there when he died because they lied about me,* Jeff had said. *My son died alone.*

Miranda stumbled ahead. Exhausted. Drained. Amy grabbed her shoulders and guided her as they trudged around the house to the front porch.

"Amy, tell Marc to pack it in. I've seen enough."

CHAPTER 10

VICTIMS

She felt like an invalid. Concerned faces surrounded her on all sides of the bed—except for Eddie. He was channel surfing.

"Don't you think I've been through this before?" Miranda said. "All I need is a good night's sleep."

Marc sat at the foot of the bed. "We're just concerned because we've never seen you so drained."

"It's been stressful since we got here. The visions were the final straw."

"Why don't we pick this up in the morning?" Amy sat on the other bed, staring at her laptop screen. After a moment, she closed the lid and pushed it away. "We're all tired."

"Not me, I'm totally amped up," Eddie said. "That was some wild shit tonight. Hey, they get BBC America at this hotel."

Marc shut off the TV and Eddie took the hint. The men said goodnight and left through the door to the adjoining room.

"I don't pretend to understand what you went through tonight," Tammy said. "But it freaked me out. From what little you told us so far, it sounded traumatic. Call me tomorrow if you don't feel any better or if you need anything."

"Will do." Miranda piled another pillow atop the stack behind her and laid her head back. "Thanks for being there. I know it wasn't really your thing."

"If nothing else, it was a night I'll never forget."

"So I heard," Amy said with a wry grin.

Tammy blushed.

Miranda frowned. "What did I miss?"

"You're the psychic."

"I'm a tired psychic. What happened?"

"It can wait until tomorrow," Tammy said. "Goodnight, ladies."

Once she was gone, Miranda slid under the covers and let out a moan. Everything ached. "If I snore, just throw a pillow at me or something."

Amy slid her laptop onto the bedside table and turned off the lights. After a few moments, she whispered. "Randy?"

"Mmm."

"Can I ask you a question?"

"Sure."

"What's Eddie's deal?"

"His deal?"

"Ever since I've known him, he's been so snarky. Is that just his personality or—"

"A defense mechanism."

Amy propped herself up on her elbow. "What do you mean?"

"Marc and I met Eddie three years ago at a ghost hunt in Fell's Point. It was Halloween night. He proceeded to detail everything that was wrong with our website. In fact, he told us it sucked, which didn't sit well with Marc since he created it. I asked him if he could do better and a few days later, Eddie created a sample website that was pretty damn impressive. It took some convincing, but I finally got Marc to let Eddie be our webmaster. Shortly after, he started coming along on investigations."

"What about this defense mechanism?"

Miranda hesitated. "Can you keep this conversation between us?"

"Absolutely."

"Eddie opened up to me on the way to a case in Virginia last winter, which was when I learned he had two sisters that were much older. I think the younger of the two has ten years on Eddie. Problem was, by the time he was born, his parents were tired of raising kids. His dad was on the road a lot and his mom worked two jobs. The task of raising Eddie fell to his sisters, who resented it and left him alone most of the time until they moved out."

"That sucks. I have a close family so I can't imagine that. We have our problems, but we always support each other."

"You also make friends easily. Not so much with Eddie. He once told me that if you got more friends than you can count on one hand, you got too many friends. I think that's where his smart-ass veneer comes from. He's been a lone wolf all his life, but since we've known him, he seems to be outgrowing it. I'd like to think he's found a family with us. He's a sweet guy who just needs a chance to mature a bit and let people in. He'll get there."

"I was just curious. Well, I guess we should get some sleep."

Minutes of silence passed in the darkness. Normally, the steady hum of the air conditioner would send Miranda off to sleep within minutes, but there was something nagging at the back of her mind.

"Amy?"

"Mmm?"

"Can I ask you a question?"

"Sure."

"While we were investigating tonight, Tammy was making out with Elias, wasn't she?"

"How did you know?"

"Psychic."

"Right."

"Goodnight."

MIRANDA STOOD over Colin at his dining room table as he folded his suicide note and placed it in an envelope addressed to his wife, Rebecca. With a trembling hand, he leaned the envelope against a clear blue vase filled with a bouquet of carnations and roses. It was Rebecca's usual place at the table.

Sunlight shone through the windshield of Colin's car as he pulled out of the garage, stopping for a wild rabbit that darted across the driveway. He followed it with his eyes until it disappeared beneath a lavender plant in the neighbor's front yard. He turned onto the street. Miranda called his name, pleaded with him to stop and listen but, as usual, the effort was futile. *I need to find a way to get through to you.*

He took the final turn and slowed to a stop. Miranda followed his gaze to the bottom of the hill where four concrete abutments supported the highway bridge that ran above the road. Colin unbuckled his seatbelt. The instrument panel chimed softly in time with the blinking warning light.

Miranda was shaking now. Her stomach ached. She twirled her hair. Behind them, the driver of a pickup truck leaned on his horn. Same one as always. Tires screeched and she was pressed against her seat. Colin turned the wheel to the right, putting the car in line with the nearest abutment.

Ahead, a pedestrian strolled into the street and stopped directly in the car's path. *That's new. Where did he come from?*

Colin didn't react. He continued at full speed. As they bore down on the lunatic, Miranda awoke with a gasp and screamed at the placid face of Jeff Vernon hovering over her.

"Come with me."

MIRANDA SQUINTED against the fluorescent light that materialized in the ceiling directly above her. She looked over at Amy's bed only to find a beige wall inches from her face and another one about six feet to her left. Voices, the chime of an arriving elevator, light laughter muffled behind doors. Another vision. *Dammit! I've had enough for one day. God, please let me sleep. Can't we do this tomorrow?*

"I wish I had better news," a man said in the distance. His voice faded. A door closed.

Miranda propped herself up on her elbows and peered down the long hallway. She glanced behind her—and over the edge of the gurney that had been a hotel bed just moments before. With a groan, she sat up as an orderly stepped out from a nearby room and began pushing the gurney down the hall. She leapt off. The young man continued on until he disappeared around a corner.

People milled about, mostly nurses. The occasional doctor or visitor meandered in and out. Judging by the clothes, hairstyles, and obsolete technology, Miranda placed the scene in the late seventies. Those who passed by didn't acknowledge her and Miranda had never been more relieved to be invisible. She felt almost naked in a tank top and running shorts.

She twirled a lock of her disheveled hair and darted down the corridor to the nurses' station looking for a sign, a placard, a business card, anything that would tell her which hospital this was. Barely three seconds passed when one of the nurses answered a phone call and identified the place as Saint Joseph Hospital.

Where the hell is that?

Someone was crying. Miranda followed the sound to a room just a few doors away from where she had awakened on the gurney. She stood outside and watched as a nurse drew a sheet over the still form of a little girl. She couldn't have been more than nine years old. At the foot of the bed, the girl's mother sobbed, wrapped in her husband's arms. Young, all three of them, far too young.

A doctor entered the room and whispered to the nurse. He was burly, middle-aged, with receding hair and squared mustache. The nurse nodded in reply to his orders. He turned to the couple and spoke soft words of consolation. After a few moments, the mother regained her composure and allowed herself to be ushered out. She clung to her husband as they accompanied the doctor.

Miranda watched them for a moment until her gaze came to rest on Jeff Vernon at the far end of the corridor. He, too, stared at the couple as they passed. The father cast a fleeting look over his shoulder and shook his head. Jeff's shoulders slumped. He closed his eyes and took a deep breath before weaving his way through people and equipment. A large stuffed animal was tucked under each arm and he carried a small orange box in one hand.

Miranda leaned against the wall as he approached, but Jeff merely hung his head as he marched past. At that moment, a nurse stepped out of the little girl's room and scurried down the hall. As the door closed, Jeff stopped it with his foot and slipped inside. He emerged a second later, minus one stuffed animal, and disappeared into the neighboring room. Miranda started after him.

"They were on sale," a voice announced behind her. "Buy one get one free."

The spirit of Jeff Vernon strolled toward her, dressed exactly as when she had last seen him. "I bought the yellow bunny specifically for Pamela. That was her name, the girl who just died. Even though she was gone, I still wanted her parents to have it. I didn't know how else to express my condolences. I wanted to do... something... for them."

Miranda stood her ground, curling her right hand into a fist. Her posture didn't go unnoticed.

"You must think I'm a monster."

That's putting it mildly. "I try not to judge," she said instead. "So... why are we here?"

"Miranda, please relax. Should I call you Miranda? I know your friends call you Randy, but I didn't want to presume."

So, you were *at the house tonight.* "Miranda's fine."

"I'm not out to hurt you."

"I've had a long night, Jeff. Can we get to the point?"

"This was my son's room." Jeff stepped around her and gestured toward the door. "His name was Adam, but of course you knew that already."

He motioned for her to join him, but Miranda didn't budge. Physical harm during a vision was rare, but she didn't trust him.

"Oh, come on, he's a wonderful kid," Jeff urged. "I promise he won't bite, and neither will I."

"No, you just..." *Gunned down your family.*

Jeff craned his neck and peered into the room. "This is where we open the cards." With that, he bounded through the door.

Miranda rocked back and forth on the balls of her feet. *Fine. Let's just get this over with so I can get back to sleep.* With a deep breath, she marched once more into the killer's world.

"THIS WAS the last time I saw my son alive."

With his upper body at a slight incline, Adam Vernon rolled his head to one side to peer at his father seated beside him on the bed. It was no wonder that his older sisters, Natalie and Carla, now gravitated to Matthew Meade.

Adam's gaze fell on the small orange box that his father had brought with him. Inside were packs of trading cards from the movie, *Star Wars*. Mr. Vernon placed one in Adam's hand. In her mind, Miranda decided to call him Mr. Vernon while the man that spoke to her—the ghost standing across the room—was merely Jeff.

"If you flip them over, some of them are puzzle pieces," Mr. Vernon said. "Other ones have facts about the movie. Do you want me to read them to you?"

"Yeah." Adam's voice was barely louder than a whisper. "Where's Mom?"

"She's picking up your sisters from school. They'll be here soon."

Mr. Vernon read from the back of each trading card before handing it to Adam.

"Do you think they'll make another movie?" the boy asked.

"I'm sure they will."

"Can we go see it?"

Mr. Vernon paused for a moment before nodding. "Count on it."

Jeff, the killer, sauntered over to the bed and stood opposite his reflection. It was a bizarre sight.

"I took the kids to see *Star Wars* months before this," he told Miranda. "They were enthralled by it, like all of us. Adam loved the trading cards. I bought them by the box.

"As a parent, you expect to watch your kids grow into the people you hope they'll turn out to be, and you do your best to guide them. You take it for granted that you'll have decades with them. By this time, we were counting the days."

Miranda didn't know what to say. Everything that came to mind seemed cliché or trite. It occurred to her that she had become so wrapped up in this family that she had neglected her own over the past two days. She had not kept track of her children's trek through Europe. She made a mental note to rectify that as soon as she had a moment's peace.

"There were some good times, though," Jeff continued. "Would you mind if I shared some of them with you?"

Do I have a choice? Miranda chided herself for the thought. Fatigue was getting the best of her. Still, there was nothing this man could show her that would justify the murder of his wife and daughters. For now, though, she would give him his due. "It's your show."

The room dissolved around them. Ceiling transformed into blue sky, partially obscured by a lush canopy of green. Tiled floor melted into dirt and stones. Trees replaced walls.

And Adam was walking.

He strolled past Miranda in jeans and a T-shirt. Plastic binoculars hung around his neck while a red water gun bounced off his leg in its brown vinyl holster. Miranda glanced over her shoulder beyond the trees at the Vernons' house with its freshly cut lawn and manicured flower beds.

Happier times...

"Dad!" Adam called out. Jeff was nowhere to be found. She followed the boy into the woods until they came upon a small clearing with a miniature wooden fort at its center. Standing about four feet tall and trapezoid in shape, two square windows had been cut into the front wall and a small door opened in the back. There was enough room inside for three children of Adam's size. It reminded her of the plastic and wood castle that her ex-husband had built for their twin boys when they were Adam's age.

"Pretty nice, huh?" From across the clearing, Jeff sauntered through the walls of the fort and joined Miranda. "I built this for him the summer before he was diagnosed. I don't remember what happened to it after..." He trailed off and cleared his throat. "At first, we set it up in the backyard and Adam would stay in there so long he'd sometimes fall asleep reading comic books or playing with his *G.I. Joe* figures. He called it his hideout. There was one time when Adam wanted to camouflage the fort, so we piled leaves around it and then..." Jeff's voice cracked as tears rolled down his face. "Then I tied a string to the nearest tree, and we ran it through one of the windows in the fort. I cut a small piece of copper pipe that slid down the string with one of his *G.I. Joe* figures on it. He loved to see it crash through the leaves and into the window."

Jeff choked out a laugh. "It was all Adam's idea. God, he had such an..." He broke down and turned his face away, shoulders trembling under the weight of his grief.

"Imagination," Miranda said. Her trepidation toward this man melted into pity, not only for the depth of his loss but for what he had become as a result.

Jeff caught his breath and for several minutes merely stared at his past self enjoying brighter times with his son. "Thank you, Miranda. I'm sorry for that."

"Don't be. I can relate to what you're going through, in a way."

"You lost a child?"

"A brother."

Jeff waved toward Adam. "I exist here, in these days. I try to reach out to him, to communicate with him. I know he can't see or hear me. These are just scenes from our past playing over and over, but these moments are all I have. You'd think by now, I'd stop trying."

Yeah. Me, too. "You love him too much to stop."

"Exactly. You know, it occurs to me that if people knew I was in the woods with a scantily clad blonde, they might talk."

"Hey, you're the one who pulled me out of a sound sleep."

"Actually, I pulled you out of a speeding car. What was that all about, by the way?"

"None of your business." Miranda held up her hands. "Sorry. Didn't mean to snap. I'm exhausted and I've seen a lot today that I need to process. As for you and me, we both know that no one can see or hear us in this... realm."

"Well, in that case." Jeff held out a hand. "How about a party?"

FAINT MUSIC ECHOED through the trees as the pair made their way along the path out of the woods. Adults conversed and laughed as children darted back and forth. The aroma of the grill, swaying balloons of every color, covered picnic tables, and a Happy Birthday banner spanning the front porch columns.

"Let me guess," Miranda said as they came to a stop. "Adam."

"His last birthday."

Nancy pulled bottled drinks from a cooler while her husband tended to burgers and hot dogs. Others milled about while Adam and several friends kicked a soccer ball around the yard. As Miranda started forward, the ball cut through her mid-section on its flight path.

She put a hand to her stomach. "That doesn't happen every day."

"You'd make a terrible goalie."

Miranda and Jeff took up a position on the far end of the porch from which they could observe the festivities.

"I'd give you a tour of the house, but I think you had that

already," he said. "You might be interested to know who some of these people are." He pointed toward the small round tabletop grill. "The guy standing next to me there is Tom Urban and the two nerds over there at the table are Arnold Weiss and Mike Leigh, all former co-workers... and former friends. The rest are family and some people we knew from church."

Miranda recognized the names, but it took a moment to make the connection. She leaned over the rail and peered at all three of the men and recalled the phone conversation with Tammy that brought her here in the first place. *All three of these guys have been killed in the past two weeks!*

"This was a combination Labor Day and birthday party," Jeff continued. "And also the day we realized something was wrong."

"What do you mean?"

"You'll see right about... *now*."

Adam stumbled toward his mother, but never made it. He rubbed his head before collapsing to his knees. Nancy helped him to a nearby chair.

"What's wrong, sweetie?"

"My head hurts again."

Nancy glanced at Mr. Vernon standing beside the grill. "Let's get him inside."

"I'll do it." He handed the tongs to Tom Urban and hurried over.

"Everything OK?" Another woman asked.

"He's just tired," Nancy said as her husband carried their son away. He crossed the porch and disappeared into the house.

The other woman folded her arms across her chest. She was the same height as Nancy with a similar build and hair color. Her eyes were concealed behind large sunglasses. "Another headache?"

Nancy didn't meet her gaze but fussed with a stack of paper plates. "He'll be fine, Sherri. He's just tired."

Sherri gripped Nancy's arm. "Hey, this is your sister you're talking to. Let me in."

Nancy sighed and dropped the plates onto the table. "We don't know what's wrong. That's his third headache this week. I'm calling the doctor tomorrow."

"Maybe he's developing allergies."

Mr. Vernon returned a moment later. "OK, folks, there will be a slight delay on the cake. Our birthday boy needs a short nap."

Beside Miranda, Jeff fell back against the wall of the house. "If only that was all he needed. God knows, I would have traded places with him in a heartbeat. Then I wouldn't have gone insane and the rest of my family would still be alive."

Miranda remained silent, her gaze fixed on the party.

"Hey, this is it," Jeff said.

"What?"

"One of my favorite songs. Nancy and I used to dance to this."

Miranda had paid little attention to the music as the drama unfolded around her but now, she recognized Joe Cocker's "You Are So Beautiful." Jeff pushed off the wall and extended a hand.

"Dance with me."

"What?"

"Come on, one dance."

"Jeff, I told you I'm exhausted."

"It's a slow dance."

"Look, I get the point. I know you loved your son and you're still in pain. What do you want from me?"

"Just one dance in the sun." He held out a hand. "Please? It's been so long for me."

Miranda snickered. "Oh, what the hell."

She took his hand and he led her from the porch into the middle of the yard. He smiled as they danced. It was a disarming smile. Under other circumstances...

"Ever danced with anyone in this—what did you call it—*realm*?"

Miranda shook her head, unable to tear her gaze from his. "No, I usually can't interact at all."

"First time for everything."

Something had troubled Miranda ever since Jeff appeared to her in the hospital. She knew it would ruin the moment, but the question nagged at her. "Why weren't you there when Adam died?"

The song ended. Jeff pulled away.

Beside them, a pair of weathered picnic tables, lined up end to end, melded into one long polished mahogany surface. Benches separated into sections each transforming into high-backed leather chairs. The outdoors became indoors as wood-paneled walls formed around them. Plush green lawn flattened into a coarse rust and orange carpet.

Miranda and Jeff stood at the windows of a spacious conference room. According to the gaudy wall clock across the room, with its tarnished brass face and wooden tines resembling the points of a star, it was nearly nine o'clock at night. Outside, a ribbon of dark blue ran across the horizon beyond an empty field. The early summer sun had just set.

Late meeting. Miranda studied the faces of those seated around the table. The men from the picnic were there, Tom Urban, Mike Leigh, and Arnold Weiss. There were two others but Miranda didn't recognize them. At the head of the table, separated from the rest, sat a thin woman in her early forties with jet black hair. She was impeccably dressed, posture rigid.

Lori Switzer, no doubt. "Who's the guy next to her?" Miranda asked.

"Roger Matthias, VP of Finance for our division.

and Roger were screwing around."

Matthias appeared to have ten years on Lori. He had a long face that was starting to show jowls. His dirty blonde hair, gelled to a shine, was gray at the temples. His choice of dark blue shirt, white tie, and white suit jacket embroidered with small blue anchors screamed seventies.

Miranda turned to Jeff. "You weren't at this meeting?"

"Watch and listen." He leaned against the window, chin resting between thumb and forefinger as Lori Switzer began speaking.

"You all know we have a problem, gentlemen." She glanced at Tom, Mike, and Arnold in turn. "The swap loans that each of you researched and Roger approved six months ago cost us one-point-three million in fees from the bank and investment advisors. That was far more than we'd budgeted for. We're being audited next week by the corporate office. Let me be clear that heads will roll unless we fix this."

"You approved the swaps," Tom spoke up.

"Based on your recommendations."

Roger held up both hands. "This is not about assigning blame. This is about keeping our jobs."

"Shouldn't Jeff be here?" Arnold asked. "He is the head of Accounts Payable, after all."

Lori shook her head. "Jeff is tending to his family's needs and I don't want to disturb him. The doctors have given his son two weeks at most. It could be any day now."

"What do you propose we do about the one-point-three mil?" Mike asked.

"Roger presented a solution earlier this afternoon that I feel will work, although it requires a bit of 'cooking the books,' as they say."

"The cost of backing out of the swaps is prohibitive," Roger began. "Far more than one-point-three million. On the books, we're going to reduce the bank and advisors' fees by half, but we'll pay the full amount to avoid any litigation. We're going to skim some money from each department's budget to cover the fees. Since revenues were below plan for this past year, they'll accept a budget cut, and no one will be the wiser."

"Putting aside the fact that we'd be lying," Tom said. "If corporate digs deep enough, they'll find out. If they learn that we slashed the departments' budgets to pay the fees, even half of the one-point-three million, they'll want to know where the rest of the money went."

"And here... we... go," Jeff muttered.

"Perhaps it went missing." Lori leaned back in her chair and steepled her fingers. "You'll pardon the cliché, but this is where we separate the men from the boys. We need a scapegoat."

Tom's expression turned rigid. "You're talking about embezzlement."

"Merely the appearance of such."

Miranda felt the heat rise in her face. *I can see now how this bitch got where she is.*

Arnold shot to his feet. "This is bullshit. I'm not listening to any more of this."

"Sit down, boy," Lori snapped. "Anyone who leaves this meeting before I've dismissed them will make our search for a fall guy that much easier."

Arnold dropped into his chair. Chastened, he folded his hands atop the table and never took his eyes off of them for the remainder of the meeting.

"So, who shall it be, men?"

"Somehow, I think you already knew," Jeff said.

"Fine, I'll start then." Lori rotated her chair as she considered her own question. "What about Nick Garnell? He's new. No one knows him."

"The summer intern?" Mike was appalled. "No one would buy that. He's a kid, he barely knows our systems, and he's part-time."

"Emily, then."

"From Data Processing? She knows the mainframe and she oversees the backup of our data, but she has no access to change financial records or move money around."

"So what you're telling me, Mike, is that we need to pin this on someone with the ability to both transfer money across cost centers *and* manipulate computer records."

"I didn't say we should pin this one anyone. Those are your words."

Lori leaned forward. "Yes, and my word is law here. I believe Jeff is the one who worked with Data Processing to implement the new mainframe system a few years ago, just like he's working with them now to test the new magnetic disk upgrade."

The room fell silent. Lori peered from face to face around the table. Arnold still refused to lift his gaze. "Jeff and his family are drowning in medical bills not entirely covered by insurance. He might be so desperate to find a way to pay them that he starts embezzling."

Jeff turned to Miranda. "Get the idea?"

THEY WERE ONCE AGAIN in Adam's hospital room—without Adam. An empty bed filled the space between Miranda and Jeff.

"Nancy and I were all set to visit Adam here. It was near the end. We knew it. Just before we left the house, the doorbell rang. Four cops stood there. They had a warrant for my arrest on charges of fraud and embezzlement. Two of them took me away while the other two searched my house.

"I tried to tell them my son was dying but it was a waste of breath. Nancy lost it. I had a hell of time calming her down. She stayed home while they searched the place for God-knows-what but when they were nearly done, Nancy got the call. The end came sooner than anyone expected.

"I was arraigned a few hours later and the prosecutor said they had enough evidence against me for a trial. I pled not guilty. I had no idea what the hell they were talking about. We couldn't afford bail, so Nancy called a bondsman. The trial started two weeks after we buried Adam. It lasted for all of five days. The company's case unraveled fast.

"They tried to use a set of punch cards to program our mainframe to transfer money from specific accounts into one that didn't exist on the books. They made it seem like I created the account and was gradually diverting funds to it over the course of a few months. They created false reports and almost had a tight case."

"Almost?"

Jeff smiled. "Well, there was one obvious problem. Where was the money? I sure as hell didn't have it. There were discrepancies found when their reports didn't match up with all of the computer records. I think they were hoping no one would bother to comb through thousands of pages of computer logs that showed these transactions were made when I wasn't in the office. Luckily, I had a great lawyer.

"The judge dismissed the case after five days. He actually apologized to me. Small consolation. When it was all over, I had nothing. My son was dead, my marriage was in shambles, and I was out of work. Deep down, Nancy suspected I might've taken the money and hidden it away somewhere so I could run out on her. We started falling apart well before the trial. That was just the final straw."

"I can only imagine what you went through."

"No, you can't," Jeff said. "But don't be concerned with

me. I didn't show you all of this for your pity. I know what I did to my wife and daughters was unspeakable. I also know I'm being punished now. Until you came along, I didn't expect to see my son again. I won't rest until I do."

"There's something else," Miranda said. "I met your wife a few days ago."

Jeff's eyes flashed wide. "Where?"

"Before I get into that, I have to tell you ... all the guys you pointed out to me earlier, Tom, Arnold, Mike, they're all dead. Each of them were killed within days of each other as well as Nick Garnell, Jr. I believe his father was the summer intern?"

"Yeah, but he was never involved in the trial. What does any of this have to do with my wife?"

"Shortly after each of those men died, someone in their families committed suicide. Much like when Roger Matthias died on his last day in jail and his wife killed herself a week later."

"I didn't know that."

"After Nick Garnell, Jr. was killed, I happened to be there when his fiancée tried to take her own life. When I stopped her, Nancy appeared to me."

Jeff dropped into the chair beside the empty bed. "What was she doing there?"

"She said you were forcing her to push those people to suicide."

"What? Why would I do that?'

"You tell me."

"Did she really say that?"

"Not in so many words."

"What, then?"

"She said you've been forcing her to kill and you won't let her be at peace until they're all dead. Jeff, tell me the truth. Did you kill those men out of revenge?"

"I can't even leave my house!" Jeff replied. "Something is

keeping me there. I don't know what it is but even if I could get out, I don't want to kill anyone. I'd be out looking for my son. As for Nancy, I haven't seen her since... Why would she tell you that?"

"If you can't leave, then how were you able to appear in my dream? How can we be here right now?"

"I reached out to you and brought you into my past. These are just visions, where I exist in my head, but I can never stay for long. They drain me. Look, I knew you were at my house earlier and I know what you saw. I wanted to show you that I wasn't a psycho."

"Why? I suspect it was for more than just a dance in the sun."

Jeff rose from his seat and stood at the foot of the bed. "You obviously have a certain ability to communicate with people like me. I want you to help me find Adam... please."

"Is that all?" Miranda yawned. "My abilities don't work that way. How, um..." Her vision blurred. It became difficult to concentrate—or stand. She put a hand on the bed to steady herself. "How do you expect me to do that?"

"You'll figure it out." Jeff helped her onto the bed. "I know you're tired. Why don't you sleep on it?"

Miranda pushed her head up onto the pillow. "What about Nancy?"

THERE WAS no answer in the darkness of the hotel room, only the hum of the air conditioner—and snoring from the other bed. As her eyes adjusted to the dim amber glow from the courtyard light outside, she tried to wrap her mind around the night's events. Sleep was out of the question now.

With a glance at the alarm clock, her shoulders slumped. Sunrise was an hour away. Miranda slid out of bed and crept over to the sliding glass door. She pushed it aside and stepped out onto the cool concrete of the small balcony. She leaned on the worn iron rail, cool metal against her forearms. In the courtyard below, spotlights along the winding brick walkway illuminated a thick oak tree nearly as tall as the hotel itself. During the day, the oak's voluminous crown provided shade for several park benches. Miranda fixed her gaze on the its thick branches and inhaled deeply of the clement pre-dawn air.

"Don't let go," she whispered.

"I SAID, DON'T LET GO!"

Randy dangled in her older brother's grip as he lowered her to the next branch.

"I can't hold you forever. You need to climb down."

She pressed herself against the oak's immense trunk and shook her head. "It's too small. It won't hold me. Pull me back up to the big branch."

Above her, Colin sighed. "This branch can't hold both of us for too long. I thought you wanted to learn how to climb trees."

"I do, but—"

"Well, there's a little bit of danger involved." Colin's voice strained. "That's what makes it fun. Now, you need to trust me. That branch down there will hold you. You only weigh, what, thirty-five pounds? You're the smallest girl in your class. Just keep close to the trunk."

Randy stretched her legs until her feet met the branch. She released Colin's hand and hugged the ancient oak for dear life. Her heart racing, she risked a glance at the ground below and squealed. It seemed so far away.

"I'm gonna die." Frozen in place, she shifted her gaze to

Colin—but he was gone. There was movement elsewhere in the tree. Randy gasped as the oak shuddered for a moment. There was a distant thud. "Now what are you doing?"

Colin called up to her. "You can jump from there."

"No."

"I just did."

When Randy refused to budge, he folded his arms across his chest. "I'm not coming up to get you."

After a moment, Randy muttered. "Then I'll just stay here."

"Really? How long?" Colin asked. "Until you're big enough to jump? Until you get tired? Hungry? I don't think Mom and Dad will go for that."

"Go get Dad."

"No, you need to do this, Randy. Just sit down on the branch first, then slide off. You're close enough to the ground."

Randy bent her knees and straddled the branch, one leg dangling on either side, her back against the trunk. Her palms were sweaty, and her entire body trembled from fear and fatigue.

"Now jump."

Randy shook her head, although Colin didn't seem all that far down. He raised his arms. "I'll catch you."

"Promise?"

"Promise."

"If you don't, and I get killed, I'll come back and haunt you."

"Yeah, that's what I need. My whiny little sister's ghost hanging around."

"I am not whiny, you're—whoa!"

She slid from the branch, screaming all the way into Colin's arms.

They fell to the ground in a tangle of limbs. Despite her earlier fear, Randy laughed.

"See? You did it," Colin said. "I told you I'd catch you. When did I ever let my little sister down?"

"NEVER," Miranda whispered. "I wish I could say the same about my big brother."

She found herself twirling tangled locks of her hair again. Miranda forced her thoughts back to the task at hand. After stretching for a few seconds, she slumped in one of the green plastic chairs and peered up at the fading stars. *What the hell have I gotten us into? Someone's lying. Charming or not, Jeff is a murderer. He forced his wife to kill herself. It wouldn't be a stretch to think he could force her to kill others if he had power over her. Does he? Why would Jeff be trapped in that house but not his wife or daughters?*

There were more questions than answers and far more than Miranda could sort out in her hazy head.

"Hey." Amy emerged onto the balcony and took the other seat. She was tall enough to rest her heels atop the railing with ease.

"Sorry if I woke you," Miranda said.

"No, it's OK. You all right?"

"I'm always all right."

"Is that your way of saying you're not really all right?"

"Just a... bad dream. One that I have a few nights a week."

"About your brother?"

"Now who's the psychic?"

"Lucky guess," Amy said. "I didn't know you six months ago. If you don't mind my asking, why did he take his life?"

"Depression. Colin was diagnosed after our dad died. He was eighteen, I was sixteen. He would have bouts that lasted for weeks then he'd bounce back. Rinse and repeat every so often. It wasn't until it affected his marriage in recent years that he did something about it. They put him on meds and that helped... for a while. The problem was exacerbated when Colin became a workaholic prone to burnout. He would run himself into the ground just to keep his mind out of that dark place, but it only made it worse."

Amy swatted at something on her leg as Miranda went on.

"He told me years ago that he was walking through life 'like an automaton, going through the motions of living but no longer feeling anything.' He functioned like that for years, withdrawn from the world. It eroded his marriage, but his wife stayed with him, God bless her. She deserved better and their kids needed their father. Two months before he died, Colin stopped taking his meds.

"I came home from work exhausted that day. After classes were over, I stayed around to meet with the parents of a problem student. The conversation got heated because their kid could do no wrong. By the time I got home, I didn't want to deal with anyone. I asked my daughter to watch the boys while I took a nap. I didn't make it ten minutes before my mom called to tell me that Colin had killed himself. He drove into a bridge abutment three blocks from his house. The car exploded. Police said he died in a fireball."

"I'm so sorry," Amy said. "And I feel terrible for asking."

Miranda's voice quivered as she fought back tears. "If I'd known what was happening, I guarantee you he'd still be alive."

"You can't be at someone's side twenty-four hours a day. You have a job, three kids to raise. You can't blame yourself. It wasn't your fault."

Miranda wiped her eyes. To the east, the night sky began its surrender to daylight. She wished she could go back to sleep, but she knew the dream would only start again. "This ability of mine lets me help so many strangers, but it failed me when it came to my own brother. I can't change that, but I'll be damned if I'm letting the Vernons take one more life in this town."

SOMEONE WAS HOVERING beside his bed. He shuddered at the harsh chill that passed over him. "Mom?" Matt opened his eyes. Though his vision had deteriorated, he could discern two silhouettes in the meager yellow glow from the night light across the room.

"Oh," he whispered. "Hey, you never told me your names."

"I'm Carla," the girl on the left said. She pointed across the bed. "That's Natalie."

"Matt, listen," Natalie said. "You have to tell them about the barefoot girl. Her name is Jenny. She has short red hair and—"

"No, her name's Ginny," Carla chimed in. "Not Jenny."

"Who?" Matt's head was starting to throb again.

"The girl," Natalie insisted. "She has short red hair and goes barefoot. Her father's name was Frank." She looked to her sister for confirmation. "He's dead. They'll find him in the cornfield next to our house. His daughter is next."

Where's mom? She was just here. So cold. Need another blanket.

"He's fading away like Adam did."

"Once he's with us, he'll feel better."

"Yeah, but I don't think he can help anymore."

"We know someone who can. Come on."

All was quiet. Someone was hovering over him again. "Matt?"

He opened his eyes to another silhouette. He wasn't so cold anymore. "Mom."

She brushed his hair aside. "Who were you talking to just now?"

"The girls," he whispered.

His mother remained silent for a long moment. Matt began to drift off again.

"The same girls from the hospital?"

"Yeah."

"Maybe you were just dreaming, baby."

"No, they were here."

"Well, what did they want?"

"Ginny."

"Who's Ginny?"

But Matt was fast asleep.

CHAPTER 11

SUSPICIONS RAISED

P hone calls at odd hours were nothing new to Denny Teelko. After eleven years as a detective in the Red Rose City, he'd become accustomed to the occasional wakeup call in the dead of night. He was a light sleeper anyway, unlike his wife who couldn't be roused from slumber if a plane crashed on their lawn. For Denny, this was a good thing. It spared him from complaints of beauty sleep interrupted whenever his phone buzzed on his nightstand.

While the late-night call hadn't disturbed him, the location did. This was Amish country. Nothing much happened out here beyond the occasional speeder or gang of teens looking for a dark place to get high or wasted. Neither of those warranted four patrol cars and an ambulance.

But a body in a cornfield on the other hand...

One of the uniforms greeted him as he rounded the front of his car. It was Conroy, a five-year veteran. He was a head taller than Denny with thick ginger hair trimmed to a buzz cut. "You're not gonna like this. Amish farmer found him about forty minutes ago at the edge of his cornfield."

"Murdered?" Denny asked as they started walking.

"So far no blood or marks on the head. Clothes are intact, not even a tear. No indication that the body was dragged into the field and only one set of footprints in the dirt. That's as much as we could see without moving the body."

"Did anyone knock on their door yet?" Denny pointed to the house beside the field.

"Not yet, and no one's come out either."

A camera flashed. Beams of light bobbed along the stalks accompanying a murmur of solemn voices. Denny pointed at another patrol car up the road. "What's going on there?"

"We found the victim's Jeep parked along that dirt road. Looks like he backed up out of sight then walked down here."

"And how do we know for certain it belongs to the victim?"

Conroy lifted the caution tape tied across the row of corn. "You're really not gonna like this."

Denny held the man's gaze for a moment before ducking under the tape. Two officers with flashlights backed away from the body. Denny moved in for a closer look. He lowered himself to one knee. Someone aimed a flashlight at the dead man's face.

"Oh, fuck no."

Elias Gray sat on the throne of Charlemagne.

Elsewhere in Germany's Aachen Cathedral, the great emperor himself had been entombed almost twelve centuries ago. Distant church bells pierced the night air with a simple two-tone melody. There was something unusual about their chime, but his perplexity vanished as Elias turned his gaze to the floor. He grinned in approval at the priceless artwork strewn around him—plunder, every bit of it.

And all of it for him.

He felt no shame or guilt, for it had not been by his hand that these treasures were stolen. All that mattered to Elias was his own financial empire. Truth be told, he didn't give a damn about the Nazis or the trail of bodies they had left in their march across Europe. Such were the prejudices and sins of the small minded. Blood on the hands of a previous generation.

Here and now, in Aachen Cathedral, impenetrable darkness loomed beyond towering stained-glass windows. Elias slouched against the cool marble on which over thirty Roman emperors had been coronated during the Middle Ages. Above him, gamboling flames in hanging alabaster lamps cast dancing shadows across ancient walls.

He closed his eyes, felt himself drifting to sleep, secure in his plans for prosperity. Within minutes, the crack of metal against wood jarred him awake. He leapt from the throne and spun. Behind him, past a small marble altar, lay three pine caskets.

Where did they come from?

Elias descended the stairs to the marble floor. The paintings and sculptures had disappeared. The heat of anger burned in his face—until he toppled the lid from the first casket. His stomach turned at the sight of Leland, his lower half missing. Elias backed away only to collide with the middle coffin. Inside lay young Hagen, his face awash in blood from a bullet hole in his forehead. As if moved by a force beyond his own volition, Elias approached the third casket and trembled at the sight of Tammy, drenched auburn locks matted around her face.

"No..." Elias wept as he reached in and pushed her hair aside.

Tammy's eyes shot open. Her hands clutched his wrists. Elias screamed and reeled back, pulling her to a sitting position. "What have you done to me, Elias?"

"Nothing." He writhed, but her grip was absolute. "Let me go."

Tammy's face twisted and distorted until it transformed into the visage of another woman. Green eyes turned to hazel, auburn hair to brown. "You're all alone among the dead here, *verbrecher*."

Elias tore his arms free of her grasp.

"*Du kannst nicht entkommen*." Holding him in her gaze, the woman lowered herself back into the casket, crossed her arms over her chest, and closed her eyes. *You cannot escape*, she had said in flawless German. But who was she?

Someone started hammering. Elias snapped his head up. A man stood over Hagen's coffin. He lined up another nail on the lid and pounded it into the pine. "Don't just stand there." He waved at the other caskets. "Finish what you started."

They stared at one another over the middle casket—Elias Gray and a man who had ceased to exist nearly twenty-five years ago. Elias gaped at the sandy blonde hair, grey eyes, and dimpled face that had once been his before the plastic surgeries, the aliases, the narrow escapes from justice.

The face of Janos Skorzeny.

"How can you be here?" Elias whispered.

His younger self merely smiled. "*Wir sind der Anfang und das Ende, du und ich.*"

We are the beginning and the end, you and I. What the hell does that mean?

Janos hammered the final nail in Leland's coffin before turning his attention to Hagen. "*Willst du das nicht beant-worten?*" he asked.

Answer what?

The flickering golden glow of the alabaster lamps changed to flashing red and blue. The two-tone chime of the church bells grew louder until it seemed that Elias was standing beside them in the belfry. The crack of the hammer against wood exploded in his head.

Elias covered his ears against the unbearable din and called out to Janos. "*Hilf mir!*"

Janos flashed a genial smile just before burying the claw end of his hammer into Elias's scalp.

He yelped as he tumbled out of bed and hit the floor with a thud. With a groan, Elias turned over and lay on his back. Blue and red lights splashed across his bedroom ceiling. The two-tone chime mixed with an incessant pounding.

The doorbell!

Elias was on his feet, peering through the blinds. Four police cars were parked near the cornfield. Cops milled about. Elias calmed himself. If they were after him, wouldn't they have parked in front of his house? In his driveway? It must be something else. Just in case, he reached beneath his bedside table, but his hand found only empty floor. *Shit*. The gun that had been there was still lost somewhere in the basement. *I need to find that damn thing*.

Elias pulled on a T-shirt and jeans before running down the steps to the sitting room. He considered going for the gun tucked away behind the easy chair on which Tammy had fallen asleep earlier, but the clamor at the front door was becoming intolerable.

"*Halt die Klappe!*" he muttered while unlatching the deadbolt and turning on the porch lights. He opened the door. "Yes, can I help you?"

"Sorry to wake you, sir." The man looked as haggard as Elias felt. It was an easy deduction that he had also been roused in the middle of the night. Two uniformed officers stood behind him. He held up a badge. "I'm Lieutenant Teelko. Did you hear or see anything unusual in the last five to six hours?"

If only you knew. "Uh, no. It's been quiet, like any other night. Plus, I'm a sound sleeper."

"Wish I could say the same. Can I get your name, sir?"

"Gray. Elias Gray. May I ask what this is about?"

"Your neighbor, Mr. Zook, found a body in his cornfield about an hour ago. Just at the edge, not too far from your property line in fact."

Elias looked at him. Was that an insinuation? Names instantly came to mind. Leland? Hagen? Tammy? He thought of three pine caskets. "Who was it?"

"Can't divulge that until the family's been notified." The detective produced a business card from his back pocket and thrust it at Elias. "If you recall anything you might've seen or heard—raised voices, a suspicious car, anything at all—please call me."

Elias accepted the card and nodded. "Certainly, sir."

Teelko wished him a good night and stalked off. A man and woman wheeled a stretcher out of the cornfield, the gray body bag visible under the interior lights of a waiting ambulance.

He closed the door and dashed upstairs. It would be about 10:30 in the morning in Cádiz, where Leland and his nephew Hagen were supposed to be loading the last of the artwork on a private cargo plane bound for New Jersey.

But what if they had returned earlier than planned? What if one of them killed the other and planted the body to frame him? The survivor could sell the artwork and vanish forever. Elias wouldn't put it past either of them. Leland may have been a lifelong friend, but that didn't mean they trusted one another.

It was time to make a long-distance call.

DENNY LEANED against the patrol car and rubbed the bridge of his nose as the ambulance pulled away. *Stay focused. Get the job done. Mourn later.*

"You all right?" It was Conroy.

"I'm called out to an Amish farm in the middle of the night to find the dead body of one of my best friends. Other than that, I'm fuckin' great. How about you?" Denny nodded toward Elias Gray's house. *Something Frank said about—* "That used to be the Vernon property."

"Yep. Some of the guys were just talkin' about that. Why?"

"Back in the seventies, Frank covered the Vernon case for the paper. I had lunch with him about a week ago and he thought there was something suspicious about that guy, Elias Gray. Frank said he drove by here after that house was built. It was after midnight and these guys were unloading stuff out of a van."

"No laws against that. The guy was probably still moving in."

"This is Frank we're talking about. Everything's cloak and dagger. Anyway, he said he drove by a few more times late at night and saw the same guys unloading stuff from the same van, so he got suspicious."

"Last I checked, that's called stalking."

"He was a bored old newshound," Denny said. "I told him to back off. Obviously, he didn't listen. He must have seen something more to make him walk right up to the place."

"Tow truck's on the way for the victim—" Conroy caught his gaffe as Denny glared at him. "For Frank's car. You think something shady was going down and Frank got caught snoopin' around? Wouldn't make sense. If the art dealer killed him, why leave the body out in the open twenty feet from his house?"

"I'm not pointing fingers. We got nothing to go on right now. Just talking out loud. This conversation stays between us. I want to play this close to the vest."

"Understood."

Denny pushed off the car. "I'm going to talk to Frank's

daughter. I'll be back in about in a few hours when the sun's up. Keep a car here until then."

"I can stay."

"Thanks. While you're at it, keep a lookout for Mr. Gray over there. I have a feeling we're not done with him."

"Where's Marc?"

"Out getting breakfast for all of us," Eddie muttered as Amy closed the door between the adjoining rooms. "Where's Randy?"

"Sleeping late. She had a rough night. So, whatcha up to?" Amy dropped beside him on his bed, their backs against the headboard. She rested her chin on his shoulder and gazed at the image on his laptop screen. Wet hair brushed against his face and arm.

What the hell is happening right now? Eddie stole a furtive glance at her. He couldn't help but notice that she wore no bra under her mint green tank top. He cleared his throat. "Uh, I'm just reviewing some of the IR footage from last night, specifically when that door in the kitchen slammed shut."

"I thought we were supposed to do that as a team."

"Hey, ain't my fault we menfolk can get up earlier than you."

"For the record, Randy and I were up at four-thirty."

"Was that you I heard out there?"

"Yep."

He felt her breath on his neck. Heat rose in his face.

"If you heard us, why didn't you come outside?" Amy asked.

"I was trying to sleep."

"We were naked."

He caught the laptop before it slid off his outstretched

legs. Their lips were not more than an inch apart. "Well, let me know next time and I'll get the cameras ready."

She gave him a broad smile. "You wish. Actually, I just came over to use your hair dryer." She leapt off the bed and made her way to the bathroom.

"What's the matter with the one in your room?"

"I don't want to wake Randy."

Eddie hated being teased, but was there a hint of sincerity in her eyes? He knew better than to read too much into it. *Who am I kiddin'? I don't have a chance in hell with her.* The click of the door lock shook Eddie out of his reverie.

Marc shot a surprised look at Amy as he passed the bathroom. "Where's Randy?"

"Sleeping. She had a rough night."

"Well, I have eggs, bacon, pancakes, muffins, biscuits, and fruit cups," Marc said.

"Did you get extra syrup?" Miranda asked from the doorway to the adjoining room.

"The blonde is finally up."

She perused the food that Marc was laying out on the desk, a buffet in styrofoam.

"I claim three pancakes," Miranda announced. "And a biscuit."

"How can you eat like that and stay so, you know..."

Miranda peered up at Marc. "No, I don't know. Tell me."

Marc crammed a muffin into his mouth and uttered something that sounded like "hot." Randy twisted her mouth into a wry grin.

"It's like watching your parents flirt," Amy said.

"That makes one of us," Eddie said. "Hey, Randy, since you're here, can you tell us what happened with that painting at Gray's house last night? When we got there, you were almost mesmerized by it."

Miranda shrugged. "Not sure. When I looked at it, there

was this surge of pressure in my head, like what I feel when there's a presence nearby. It only lasted a few seconds, but I saw a younger man with a completely different face, different eye color, different hair. It wasn't Jeff Vernon. Not sure who it was. I still need to collect my thoughts about everything that happened last night—after breakfast and a shower."

"Did anyone else notice his hesitation when Amy asked him about it? I found it a little odd that an art dealer forgot the name of a painting hanging in his own house, so I Googled it." Eddie turned the laptop around to face his team members. "He said the painting was called 'Portrait of a Gentleman' by Sturtevant Hamblin. This is it."

Marc frowned. "That ain't the painting we saw."

"Sure isn't," Miranda agreed.

"No, but..." Eddie swiveled the laptop and clicked on another image to enlarge it. "This is."

Miranda leaned in close. "Portrait of... Elias Gray."

"Get the hell out." Amy rushed over.

"Have a look." Eddie slid the laptop across the bed. "My first thought was that maybe his parents named him after the painting and Gray was just too embarrassed to talk about it or is sick of telling people about it. My mom is a total Edgar Allan Poe freak. Believe me, school would've been a lot smoother if my name wasn't Edgar."

"If the guy was embarrassed," Marc said. "He wouldn't have it on display in his home. What do you think, Randy?"

Miranda remained silent as she gazed at the image.

"Uh, is it happening again?" Eddie asked.

"Randy?" Marc repeated.

"He's hiding behind it," she whispered. "Another face, another scheme. There's more to him than meets the eye."

"Such as?"

"He profits from man's inhumanity to man." Miranda closed her eyes and staggered back onto the other bed.

Marc was at her side. "Randy, you all right?"

"Yeah," she sighed. "I just need to eat and get my head straight."

"What about Elias Gray?" Eddie asked.

"He's outside our scope," Miranda replied. "This situation is complicated enough. Whatever Gray is into, it's not our concern. We need to focus on the tasks at hand."

"Tasks?" Amy asked. "I thought our only task was to determine if this string of suicides has a paranormal cause, and I think we proved that the moment you saw Nancy Vernon at that girl's apartment the other day. What other task is there?"

"I had a visit last night from Jeff Vernon."

The color drained from Amy's face. "In our room? You didn't mention that on the balcony earlier."

"You're just full of surprises, lady," Eddie quipped.

Miranda held up both hands. "Jeff wasn't in the room. He came to me in the middle of a dream about my brother and took me on a brief tour of his life around the time his son died. I saw Adam Vernon. He was a wonderful little boy. Jeff loved him very much."

"What else?" Marc asked.

"Jeff's co-workers tried to frame him for embezzlement. Adam died alone in the hospital while the cops arrested Jeff and searched his house. You'd think that would play right into our theory that Jeff is getting revenge on the people who framed him, but he insisted that he couldn't have killed anyone because he's trapped in the house."

"Elias's house?"

"I don't think Jeff realizes that Elias is there. Jeff still sees the house as he knew it in the seventies. I told him about my encounter with his wife at Heather Marceta's apartment. He seemed genuinely shocked. He claimed that he hadn't seen Nancy since he... killed her."

"Is that what you witnessed at the house last night?" Marc asked.

"That and much more. When I was in the basement, I saw Jeff's spirit force Nancy to shoot herself. She tried to escape through the Bilco doors. They were wide open, but Jeff made them slam down on her head."

"No shit," Eddie said. "Just like what happened to Gray."

"That could be nothing but coincidence," Marc asserted. "We can't jump to conclusions."

"Jeff's a murderer. That's a fact," Amy reminded them. "He killed his daughters and his wife. Do you really believe he's not out there killing again right now?"

Miranda cradled her head in her hands. "Right now, I don't know what to believe."

"What did Jeff Vernon want from you?" Marc asked.

She looked up at him with weary, red eyes. "He wants me to find his son. But first, I need pancakes."

FORTY MINUTES LATER, Miranda stood with her back to the shower head. She had turned it to the massage setting and allowed the narrow, hot torrents to work on her shoulders and upper back. In the adjacent room, the team was hunkering down for what would be at least six hours of evidence review from Elias Gray's house. Once they were finished, Marc would head home.

It didn't take a psychic to notice his feelings for her. His once subtle hints had become more overt as of late, nearly to the point of tripping over his own heart. Miranda found him adorable but, like her ex-husband, he had yet to fully accept her abilities. At least Marc had shown a willingness to keep an open mind, which is more than Brian ever did.

She pushed that train of thought aside as she stepped out

of the shower and dried off. A welcome rush of cool air greeted her as she opened the bathroom door and didn't bother to wrap herself in a towel. She strode across the room to the desk and opened her laptop. She looked forward to the daily photos from Europe that Brian and the kids posted online.

Let's see where you are today.

"That would be Ireland."

Miranda gasped as she dropped into the office chair, crossed her legs, and covered herself with the open laptop. She stared wide-eyed at her father, seated at the foot of Amy's bed.

"They're kissing the Blarney Stone at this very minute."

"Dad, oh my God, you scared the hell out of me."

"Can't I drop in to see how my Miranda Panda's doing?"

"How about waiting until your Miranda Panda has some clothes on."

"Sweetheart, your mother and I saw you in your birthday suit long before you learned to be embarrassed by it."

"Yeah, well, a lot has changed since those days, thank you very much. What are you doing here?"

"I'm concerned that you're in over your head on this. This isn't mysterious footsteps or disembodied voices. People are dying."

"Not since I got here."

"You sure about that?"

Miranda waited for him to elaborate. Instead, he said, "I watched you interact with that Jeff Vernon fellow. As much sympathy as you have for him, I don't trust him."

"I can handle it."

"How, by dancing with him?"

"No, Dad, by helping him find his son if the boy's spirit is still here."

"And you have a plan for that."

Miranda hesitated. "Not yet, but I suspect that if I can

reunite Jeff and his son, they'll both move on and if we're lucky, Nancy will, too."

"If you're lucky," her father repeated. "Let me get this straight. Your first theory was that Jeff Vernon has been murdering everyone who tried to frame him for embezzlement and then coercing his wife to push one of their family members to suicide."

Miranda nodded.

"Now, just because Jeff claims he's trapped in the house, you think Nancy might be doing all of this on her own?"

"Possibly."

"If so, what makes you think Nancy's spirit will move on just because Jeff and Adam do?"

"Because it's all I got, Dad."

"I see." Her father nodded. "Either one of them could be lying, and if you interfere, there's nothing stopping them from coming after you or your friends. Jeff and Nancy are already damned for their sins. They have nothing to lose by killing you. So you tell me, who do you trust?"

"I trust Adam. He's the key, if I can find him."

"He seemed like an adorable kid. Reminds me of your brother at that age."

Miranda lowered her gaze. She wanted to mention that she'd dreamt of Colin again last night but thought better of it.

"You know, Adam really liked playing in that fort out in the woods, didn't he?" her father said.

"Yeah, he sure..." She peered up at thin air. "did."

DURING THE DRIVE to Ginny's apartment, Denny had steeled himself for the worst. Delivering the news of a loved one's death was an onerous task, one that he'd performed far too often in his career. Years ago, he had learned to detach himself from the inevitable breakdowns of the families he visited. He offered sympathy and apologies and sometimes a hug, but for the sake of his own sanity, kept his emotions walled. *They're strangers*, he'd told himself time and again. *They need to deal with the grief, not me. I can walk away.* But this was his best friend's daughter. There would be no walls where she was concerned and he couldn't simply walk away from her pain, or his own.

As they sat on the floor where Ginny had collapsed, Denny held her until her tears were spent. Her body trembled as she struggled to breathe. "I want to see him. I want to see my dad. Where is he now?"

"By now, he's... at the morgue." Denny helped her to the sofa. "Whatever you need, you know Liz and I are here for you, but I have to ask. Do you know why your dad would have gone to Elias Gray's house?"

Ginny shrugged. "I don't know. He didn't say anything to me, but..."

"Take your time."

"This girl showed up at the library two days ago. She was asking a lot of questions about the Vernons. My dad talked to her for a little while, then she left. But later that night, she showed up at The Pressroom with some other people. They sat a few tables away and my dad was really curious about them. He started talking about the recent suicides, and how all the people were connected to the Vernons somehow. He thought there was more to this girl than met the eye."

"Did you happen to get her name?"

"I think it was Amy or something. Tall, skinny, about my age." Ginny frowned. "You don't think she was involved with..."

"I don't know, but I'll do my damndest to find out."

CHAPTER 12

A PARANORMAL CUSTODY BATTLE

It was late afternoon by the time the team packed up the equipment that would be returning to Baltimore with Marc. After reviewing the audio and video footage from the previous night, everyone had agreed that Elias Gray's house provided the most exhilarating investigation to date.

"So in summary," Marc began. "We not only have the footage of the kitchen door opening and closing but also two audio clips. The first is a woman sobbing in the basement before Randy went down there, and the other one is a male voice saying 'alone among the dead.' Amy picked that up on her digital voice recorder in the dining room."

"That was Jeff's voice," Miranda said. "Those were his words to Nancy before he killed her. I saw it in my vision which, by the way, I intend to share with Elias."

"You absolutely should."

She narrowed her eyes. "Who are you and what have you done with Marc?"

"We have more than enough evidence and personal experiences to confirm not only a haunting but that it's damn likely to be the Vernons."

Miranda turned to Amy and Eddie. "You both heard that right? Amy, check outside and see if it's snowing."

"You know, despite our occasional debates," Marc said. "I've told you more than once I believe in you."

"It's all good, Marc. I'm just teasing."

He glanced at his watch. "Well, I need to hit the road. My mom goes in for hip surgery tomorrow morning at six."

"We'll all help with the equipment," Miranda said.

In the parking lot a few minutes later, they were assaulted by the blistering mid-afternoon sun. Amy and Eddie loaded the gear into Marc's SUV while he took Miranda aside.

"Look, even though we proved that the Vernons are hanging around that house, there's still the question of exactly who or what is causing these suicides. Even if it is Jeff Vernon, what can you do about it?"

"I'll think of something," she said.

"That's the thing. Just like Elias Gray's secrets are out of our scope, I think these suicides are, too. They're not your problem."

"They're the whole reason why Tammy called me here."

"I know, but I'm worried about the three of you. This is a dangerous situation."

"We can handle it."

Marc sighed. "If you say so. Any idea who's next?"

"A woman named Lori Switzer. I think she's the last target. She was the president of the company that Jeff worked for and one of the people who tried to frame him for embezzlement. I had Eddie track her down."

"Randy Lorensen saves the world."

"Not the world, just one person."

"That one person is gone and it's hard, I know, but there's nothing you can do about that."

Miranda folded her arms. "Who are we talking about here?"

Marc held her gaze for a moment before opening his car door. "Just be careful. That goes for all of you."

The team waved as he drove away.

"Now what?" Eddie asked.

"Three calls," Miranda said as they made their way back to the room. "First, let's see if Elias can spare us ten minutes to show him what we got. Eddie and I can handle that. Amy, would you mind hanging back and calling Lori Switzer's office? Try to get an appointment for tomorrow. The earlier the better."

"What if she's booked?"

"Mention Jeff Vernon. Tell whomever you talk to that Mrs. Switzer will understand."

"Who's the third person you want to call?"

"Tammy. See if she'll be home tonight. I'm sure she's dying for an update, and don't think I've forgotten about her little interlude with Elias. I want details."

ELIAS GRAY WAS INDEED available and anxious for the results of last night's "spectacle" as he had called it on the phone.

"Doesn't look so menacing in daylight," Eddie remarked as Miranda pulled into the driveway.

"They usually don't."

"Hey, that wasn't there last night, was it?" Eddie pointed toward the cornfield where yellow caution tape flapped in the warm breeze. It had been weaved around several stalks near the perimeter.

"I don't think so." Miranda climbed out of the car. "Let's take a look."

"Careful. There's a cop parked up the road."

Perhaps a hundred meters beyond Elias Gray's house, the front half of a patrol car was visible at the end of a dirt road.

"What the hell happened?" Eddie muttered.

A dull ache started in her temples as Miranda stared at the black and yellow tape. She felt herself swaying but held her balance. Tunnel vision set in until only the word "CAUTION" was clear. It danced and fluttered before her.

The yellow tape peeled away. The cornstalks parted. A man's corpse lay supine, eyes wide in shock. Somehow, Miranda knew he was the one who had spied on her yesterday at Steinman Park and again outside Elias Gray's house. A name flashed in her mind, Frank Knedlhans— the man that Amy had spoken with at the Historical Society.

The malicious absurdity of it. He had been nearly within arm's reach last night, hiding behind a row of corn.

People are dying.

Not since I got here.

You sure about that?

Her father's words sliced into her heart.

How could I be so arrogant?

"Can you help us?"

Frank's body was gone. In its place stood Natalie and Carla Vernon dressed alike as usual. Miranda crouched down, bringing herself at eye level with them. She wished she could tell them apart. "Help you how?"

"We tried to warn Matt, but he can't hear us anymore."

"He's really sick," the other girl said. "Like Adam was."

This could be the turn of luck Miranda had been waiting for. "I know. I feel terrible for him. What can I do?"

The girl on the left spoke first. "The man who was here, he has a daughter."

"The barefoot girl," her sister added. "I think her name's Jenny."

"No, it's Ginny. I told you before."

"We'll figure that out." Miranda was reminded of her twin boys who often corrected each other. "What about the barefoot girl?"

"She's in trouble. You have to save her."

"Save her from what?" Miranda knew the answer, but it was time for a bit of strategy. "Is someone going to hurt her? Maybe... your mom?"

The twins exchanged nervous glances but remained silent.

I'll take that as a yes. Now for the million-dollar question. "Can you tell me who killed Ginny's dad?"

"We can't say anymore. Our mom doesn't like it when we tell people about our family problems. We should go before we get in trouble."

"Please wait." Miranda shot to her feet as the girls vanished into the cornfield. She took a step forward to follow but her vision blurred. She lost her balance and stumbled backward into Eddie's arms. After a few deep breaths, her vision cleared. "I'm good now, thanks."

Eddie released her. "This case is really putting you through it. What did you see in there?"

"Another victim." Miranda steered him toward the art dealer's house. "I'll explain back at the hotel. I don't want that cop up there getting suspicious. Let's get this over with."

MIRANDA SAT opposite Elias in his dining room while, at the head of the table, Eddie prepared to present their evidence. Dressed in jeans and a rumpled black T-shirt, Elias looked on with puffy, bloodshot eyes that seemed to be held open by sheer willpower.

Miranda sympathized. In this town, she'd experienced

some of the most powerful visions since her abilities mani-fested at the tender age of six. Each one had drained her, espe-cially the experiences in this house. Yet here and now, she felt nothing. Miranda wasn't sure whether to be grateful or wary.

"I'm going to venture a guess that you had a sleepless night as well?" Elias asked.

"Is it that obvious?"

He imparted the details of his early morning wake-up call. "Naturally, I mentioned nothing of our activities to the police, but it disturbs me that a dead body may have been lying out there the entire time."

"Who was it?" Eddie asked.

Elias shrugged. "No idea. Check the news tonight."

"That wouldn't explain the police car parked up the road, unless they consider it a crime scene."

"That occurred to me too," Elias grumbled. Then, to Miranda, "I'm sorry to rush you, but my gallery opens tomor-row, and I have some final preparations this afternoon. What do you have for me?"

"Just three brief pieces," Miranda replied. "One video clip of your kitchen door opening then slamming closed just after I went down into the basement and two audio clips."

Ten minutes later, after reviewing the evidence, Elias slumped back in his chair. "Remarkable. You captured the phrase I've been hearing."

"'Alone among the dead.'" Miranda replayed the male voice from the EVP, or electronic voice phenomenon. "That was caught on Amy's digital voice recorder in this room. She left it on the table after she and I came down from the second floor, or so I'm told."

"Yes, you were in a trance and you stopped in here for a short time," Elias said. "Tammy was concerned. You were non-responsive. Tell me, what happened to you? You departed so abruptly last night, and Tammy said only that you were troubled by your visions."

"I apologize for leaving that way. If you remember, we talked about the family who lived on this land back in the seventies."

"The Vernons, yes, but as I said I don't know much about them beyond what little the locals told me."

"I watched them die."

That shook Elias out of his fatigue. "Unless it's too disturbing for you, what did you see?"

Miranda recounted her experiences throughout the house. The bloody details were irrelevant. She divulged only what was necessary—the fact that Jeff Vernon had killed his daughters, then himself and came back after his funeral to murder his wife. As she waited for Elias to respond, Miranda realized that even abridged, the story was incredible.

Eddie packed away his laptop then slid a USB thumb drive across the table. "This is a copy of the evidence we just showed you."

"Is it always like this for you?" Elias asked Miranda. "Are your visions always so clear?"

"No. Many times I get nothing, or just a feeling," Miranda explained. "What happened last night was rare."

"I see. So, what's your conclusion?"

"If we'd only captured audio, I'd call it a residual haunting, which is simply a playback of past events with no intelligence behind it. It doesn't even know you're here. However, the fact that the kitchen door slammed shut and the power cut out after I entered the basement tells me it's more than that."

"Especially since all battery-operated devices shut down, too," Eddie added.

"There's something else," Miranda said. "Before Jeff Vernon's ghost murdered his wife in the basement, she tried to escape to the outside through the cellar doors. They were wide open, but when she started up the steps, the doors slammed closed on her head."

Elias raised an eyebrow as she continued.

"Of course, at the time there was a storm approaching and the winds were fierce. The doors could have simply blown shut."

"There are few coincidences in life, my dear. I suspect the afterlife to be no different."

"Even less so." Miranda's mounting anxiety over what she had yet to reveal must have shown on her face.

"I sense there's more," Elias said.

"The completion of your new house coincides with a series of unusual deaths in and around town. I'm sure you've heard about the recent suicides."

"Yes. Go on."

"There's a consistent pattern to them. First, someone dies of what seems like a natural or accidental cause. Then, a few days after their funeral, a family member takes their own life. This has happened four times so far. There would have been a fifth had I not intervened."

"I admit that's bizarre, but I fail to see the connection to my house."

"Multiple murders and suicides occurred on this land thirty-three years ago. It lay mostly undisturbed since then, until you came along. Among those in my field, it's an accepted theory that dormant spirits are roused by changes to a building or land they inhabit. That's the most viable explanation for your problem, and also why almost every person who died in the past two weeks was not only a former coworker of Jeff Vernon's, but also testified against him at his embezzlement trial.

"In short, the Vernons have been exacting revenge on those who they feel destroyed their lives thirty-three years ago."

Elias's expression changed from engrossed to incredulous. "You say that with such conviction. Are you sure of your facts?"

"We did our research," Eddie replied.

"And who else have you told about this?"

"No one outside our group," Miranda assured him. "You asked us to keep the results private and we respect that."

"If even a rumor of this gets out, it could draw unwanted attention."

"Understood. We've had many clients express a desire to remain anonymous. The last thing we want is to disrupt your life or jeopardize your business."

"Thank you. This is all rather overwhelming. In your estimation, am I in danger here?"

It was the one question that had been foremost on Miranda's mind since leaving his house last night. She had no conclusive answer and told him so. "It's your home. If you feel threatened, you should take a stand. It may feel strange doing this but try talking to them. Tell them that you just want to live in peace and if they can't understand that, ask them to leave. If all else fails, many people reach out to a priest or other clergy for help. To maintain your privacy, you can simply ask for a blessing of your new home without mentioning anything about a haunting."

"Will that also stop the killings out there?"

"I'm working on that."

FIVE MINUTES LATER, Miranda backed her car out of Elias's driveway and coasted by his house. There was something more to be done here, a nagging task she couldn't remember.

"That cop is gone," Eddie said. "Shouldn't we be going the other way out of here?"

Miranda heard him, knew he was looking at her, but found her attention drawn to the dense trees that bordered the other side of the art dealer's property. Her father's words came back to her. *You know, Adam really liked playing with that fort in the woods, didn't he?*

"So, dude was pretty freaked out. Do you think he'll really call a priest?"

"I don't know," Miranda answered.

"Do you think it would help?"

"I don't know."

"Did I ever mention my idea of doing a nude ghost hunt?"

"Sounds good, Eddie."

"Yeah, you ain't hearin' a word I'm sayin'."

"What? Oh, I'm sorry, sweetie." Miranda pulled off the road onto the grass. "Are you up for a walk in the woods?"

"Uh, why?"

"To find Adam Vernon."

Eddie's eyes widened. "No frickin' way."

"Way. Well, maybe way. Grab the bug repellant from the glove compartment and let's go."

"GREAT, now my arms smell like citronella."

"If Amy were here, she'd tell you to man up." Miranda sprayed her bare legs with repellent. "At least you're wearing jeans and sneakers." Then again, she'd never known him to wear anything else, no matter the season.

"Where was that psychic ability when you were getting dressed this morning?" Eddie teased.

Miranda pointed toward the trees. "Start walkin', kid."

They strode along a path overgrown with weeds, honey-suckle, and the occasional thorn bush. Along the way, they dodged more than one spider web and a nest of bees at the base of a pine tree.

"Are you sure about this?" Eddie lifted the hem of his t-shirt to wipe sweat from his brow. "You don't expect to see this kid's ghost just standing around the woods waiting for you."

"Probably not."

"Then what are we looking for?"

They came upon a clearing, if that was the proper term for it. Like the path, it bore little resemblance to what Miranda had seen upon her first visit here with Jeff Vernon, but then again that was a vision from over three decades ago. Crushed beer and soda cans, half buried and caked with dirt, lay strewn about along with random articles of clothing—a grimy white sock, black t-shirt, two different flip-flops, even underwear.

"Nice place," Eddie said.

"It used to be." Something near the center of the clearing caught Miranda's eye. "That's it."

She hurried toward a broken tree that had toppled across the center of the clearing. Miranda estimated its bole to be no more than two feet in diameter. It rocked slightly as she pushed it with the sole of her sandal. There was something beneath it. It looked like plywood.

"Help me move this."

"Am I allowed to ask why?"

"The answer is underneath."

Eddie planted a foot firmly on the trunk and together, they rocked the tree back and forth before leaning into it. Finally, it rolled away to reveal several scattering insects and writhing worms covering a sheet of crushed, damp plywood. One rusted hinge was still attached.

"I don't get it," he said. "You're looking for rotted wood?"

"It's not just wood. It's a kid's hideout—or what's left of

it. Jeff Vernon built it for his son. He used to play in it right here." A chill sent Miranda into shivers. "Did you feel that?"

But Eddie was gone, along with the fallen tree and litter. Adam's hideout stood erect before her, as if fresh from Jeff Vernon's workbench. It was surrounded by leaves of red and gold.

"Who are you?"

Miranda spun to face the little boy. "Hello, Adam." *Thank you, Dad. You were right again.*

"How do you know my name?"

"I'm a... friend of your father's."

"You know my dad? Where is he? I haven't seen him in a long time." Miranda crouched down and smiled. "Your dad's at home." She nodded in the direction of the house. "If you want, I can take you to him."

"Mom says dad left. Someone else lives there now."

"Is your mom around?"

"I've been here for quite some time."

Miranda glanced around the clearing but there was no one to be found. Still, the voice was unmistakable. Goosebumps rippled down her arms and legs. The air was once again frigid. "Nancy?"

"Jeff always did have a roving eye."

Miranda started as the woman materialized directly beside her. "Especially for blondes. Hello, again."

Miranda backed away to stand beside Adam.

"Let me guess," Nancy continued. "My husband sent you here to find our son."

"How did you know?"

"Why else would you be in these woods?"

"When we first met, you said that Jeff was forcing you to kill."

Nancy leaned forward to address Adam. "Sweetie, why don't you play in your hideout while I talk with the lady?"

With that, the boy trudged off.

"I might've misspoken," Nancy said. "I'm forced to take action thanks to Jeff's cowardice."

Miranda closed the ground between them. The fact that this woman could easily take her life paled in comparison to the rage boiling inside her. "You lied to me. You're the murderer."

"I call it retribution. A wife killed by her husband. Daughters shot to death by their father. Who the hell are you to judge me? Do you have any idea what I can do to you?" Nancy sidestepped Miranda and began circling her. "Next time you see Jeff, please tell him that he'll never see his son again and as for you—"

Miranda yelped as Nancy grabbed a handful of hair and jerked her head back. The dead woman put her lips close to Miranda's ear, yet she felt no breath. "I'm not yet finished with the people in this town, but thanks to you, I'm forced to accelerate things. If you think you can stop me, bitch, give it your best shot, but don't think I don't know who called you here in the first place. I can get to her just as easily as anyone else. Unless, of course, you leave *now*."

"Did you kill Frank Knedlhans?" Miranda asked.

"He was more like a bonus. I suppose I would've gotten around to him eventually but you led him right to me. Only two to go now."

"Then what?"

Nancy released her with a violent shove that sent Miranda stumbling forward into Eddie's arms.

"It's not often I have women throwing themselves at me," he said. "But twice in one day? I'm almost afraid to ask what happened this time."

Miranda winced as she rubbed the back of her head. "Let's get moving."

When they were out of the woods and back in the car,

Miranda turned up the air conditioning. She closed her eyes and sat back in the driver's seat, damp shirt pressing against her back and shoulders. "Well, the good news is that I found Adam and I know who our killer is. The bad news is that I planted myself firmly in the middle of a paranormal custody battle."

CHAPTER 13

BLOOD & WATER

One hour and two respective showers later, Miranda and Eddie sat with Amy and recounted their experiences of the afternoon, from learning about Frank's murder to Miranda's confrontation with Nancy Vernon in the woods.

"How the hell do we handle this?" Amy asked. "She can kill anyone at any time. You could have ended up like Frank."

Miranda slipped a reassuring arm around her shoulders. "But I didn't, and I think I know why. She didn't have the strength. Nancy had just murdered Frank the night before. Each time she kills, she must expend a great deal of energy, especially if she manifests visibly as she did with me. All of that would drain her."

"Which could explain why it takes almost a week between each set of victims," Eddie observed.

"But we can't rely on that anymore," Miranda said. "Now she's going to 'accelerate things' because we're screwing up her plans, and that's exactly what we need—a plan. I think I'm starting to put the pieces together."

"I don't know." Amy lowered her gaze. "Maybe Marc was

PHIL GIUNTA

right. We proved the Vernons are still here. Our job is done. We can't stop them. Frank died last night because of us."

"How's that our fault?" Eddie asked.

"If I hadn't met with Frank, he wouldn't have been any wiser about us. He wouldn't have followed us to that house, and he wouldn't be dead right now."

"Nancy would have killed him eventually. She made that clear to me," Miranda reminded her. "And thanks to your meeting with Frank, we know who his daughter is and have a better chance of keeping her alive. We'll figure this out and put an end to it, I promise."

"You can't promise anything," Amy said. "You're driven by guilt over someone you couldn't save. What happened to your brother wasn't your fault, any more than what's going on in this town and nothing you do here will bring him back. I'm sorry if that crossed a line, but this isn't just about your loss or your need for redemption. Ginny's father was taken from her and all you can say is 'Nancy would have killed him eventually?' I expect that kind of callousness from Eddie, but not from you. Now, if you want to kick me out of the group, that's fine but—"

Miranda held up a hand. "Nothing could be further from my mind. Don't think for one second that I lack sympathy for Ginny. I know exactly what she's going through right now. You struck a nerve, which I didn't appreciate, but you might have a point about my motivations." She leaned toward Eddie. "Our newest member is a real tiger."

"Does that mean she'll be a cougar by the time she's your age?"

"You might end up riding home on the roof after all, smart ass. Now, let's figure out how to get to Frank's daughter before Nancy does."

"On it." Eddie rolled his chair to the desk and opened his laptop. "How do you spell Ginny's last name?"

Amy handed him Frank's business card.

"Did you get hold of Tammy?" Miranda asked.

"Oh, yeah. She said we could stop by at eight-thirty. I also called Lori Switzer and talked with her assistant, Maggie. She said she'd try to get us a few minutes, but she didn't sound hopeful. I'm expecting a call back. Mrs. Switzer is flying to Spain the day after tomorrow. She'll be gone for about four days."

"I wonder if that will put her out of harm's way until we resolve this mess."

"YES, MA'AM."

"Oh, and make sure that there's a half apple or something for the reverend to stand on so he can reach the microphones and be seen behind the lectern. God bless him, he's shorter than my third husband."

Sitting back in the leather chair behind her desk, Lori Switzer pushed a lock of silver hair behind her ear. There were few things that made Lori anxious anymore and it was out of character for her to be concerned with such trivial details of the many charity events sponsored by her foundation. Yet lately, she found herself focusing on anything that would distract her from the fear that had invaded her life over the past few weeks.

"I'm sorry," her assistant said. "Half apple?"

Lori waved her hands in the shape of a square. "It's a stage term. Half apple is a wooden box that's used to prop something up. Sometimes actors stand on it to make themselves taller. We're definitely going to need one for Father Federico, trust me."

"OK. I'll arrange that. Is there anything else?"

"Not from me. I don't want to hold you up on a Friday unless you have something more."

"How's your grandson?"

Lori tilted her head back, feeling every bit the little old lady instead of the jet-setting philanthropist she portrayed. "Not well, which is why I've cut this trip from a week to four days."

"Are you sure you don't want to cancel?"

"If this were any other event, I would've bailed out in a heartbeat, but I promised Father Federico my support. He's doing God's work and we're funding it—substantially. I explained it to my daughter yesterday. She wasn't happy with me but then, we've never seen eye to eye on a great many things. Whatever. I don't want to turn this into a kvetching session. We'll be here all night."

"No worries... oh." Maggie pulled a slip of blue paper from beneath her notepad. "I do have one more item for you. A woman named Amy Healy called a few minutes ago asking to meet with you. Do you know her?"

"Doesn't ring a bell."

"She wanted to talk to you about someone named Jeff Vernon."

Lori's gaze drifted to the pile of newspapers on her conference table. She had saved each one that reported the death of a former co-worker and the inevitable suicide of a loved one. "Would you please shut the door?"

After doing so, Maggie returned to her seat, pen and paper at the ready.

"You won't need to take notes." Lori drummed her fingers on her desk, manicured nails clicking a slow, thoughtful rhythm on its mahogany surface. "I'm thinking of retiring."

Maggie slid her notepad and pen onto the cushion beside her. "Wow. Those are words I never thought I'd hear from you."

Lori gave her a thin smile before rising from her chair to

stand by the window. She opened the dark green mini blinds to let in the afternoon sunlight and fixed her gaze on the parking lot of a large antique mall at the bottom of the hill.

"Mrs. Switzer, is there something I should know?"

"I opened an office in Adamstown because of my fondness for antiques," Lori began. "In fact, when I was younger, I wanted to retire well before now and open my own shop along the strip. Here I am at seventy-four and I'm finally starting to feel like an antique."

"You've always been in fantastic shape," Maggie said. "You have more energy than some people half your age, speaking as someone who has to keep up with you."

"And exactly how long have you been with me now?"

"Going on seven years."

"Seven years. Funny how you can spend almost every day with someone and certain topics never come up in conversation."

"Such as?"

"Do you believe in karma?" Lori asked.

"I know it can be a real bitch sometimes."

"In this case, it's a bastard, and he's working his way up to me."

Maggie shook her head. "Sorry, you lost me."

Lori joined her on the couch. "You've indulged my… eccentricities from the beginning, and I appreciate that, but I need you to indulge me one more time."

"Sure, anything."

"What about ghosts? Do you believe in them?"

"Ghosts," Maggie repeated. "Well, I've always been on the fence about the supernatural. Where is this going, ma'am?"

Lori smiled. "To Spain, dear." *Where I'll be out of Jeff Vernon's reach.* "Go make those arrangements. I'm heading home to pack."

Maggie held up the slip of paper. "What about this Amy Healy?"

Lori extended a hand and Maggie relinquished the note. "I'll take care of it personally. See you Sunday morning?"

"Six o'clock. Your flight is at eight-thirty, provided it isn't delayed by the storm."

"They say it should clear out by Saturday night."

"Let's hope so."

"Thank you, Maggie. Enjoy your weekend."

"You, too, Mrs. Switzer."

Lori waited until Maggie closed the door behind her before balling up the paper and dropping it into the wastebasket.

ACROSS THE TWO-LANE ROAD, the sun was beginning its descent behind a distant corn silo as they arrived at Tammy's house.

Miranda parked her car in the driveway, but there was no answer to the doorbell a few seconds later. She called Tammy, but it went to voicemail after four rings. She didn't bother to leave a message. "That's odd. She knew we were coming."

"Maybe she's out back," Eddie said. "I'll go check."

He returned a moment later and shook his head. "But there's a light on the second floor, last room on the left."

Miranda rang the doorbell once more to no avail. She motioned for Eddie and Amy to precede her back toward the car. No sooner had they stepped off the small porch than Miranda was overcome with panic.

Don't think I don't know who called you here in the first place. I can get to her just as easily as anyone else.

Though Miranda sensed no presence here, malevolent or

otherwise, she tried the front door. It was unlocked. She pushed it open.

"What are you doing?" Eddie asked.

Miranda held up a hand for silence. "Tammy?" she called. When no one appeared, she flipped the light switch just inside the door. The house was silent save for the hum of the window air conditioner in the dining room. She made her way through the first floor, stopping in the kitchen. Tammy was nowhere to be found.

Despite her mounting worry, Miranda still felt nothing out of the ordinary, aside from a measure of discomfort at traipsing through someone's house when they weren't around. She made her way back to the living room and waved the others inside. "Amy, would you mind staying down here in case Tammy shows up while Eddie and I check upstairs?"

"Sure."

Miranda jogged up the steps with a reluctant Eddie in tow. To their left, a strip of light shone from beneath a closed door. It was the bathroom.

"Eddie, check the bedrooms."

"But she's probably in there."

"Do it," she snapped.

"Yes, ma'am." Eddie backed away and started down the dark hallway while Miranda opened the bathroom door.

The first thing she noticed was the crimson water. What had probably been a bubble bath a few hours earlier was nothing more than thin, dissipating islands of suds floating above Tammy's naked, still form. Her eyes were closed, head tilted to one side.

"Oh, no, no, no." Miranda dropped to her knees beside the tub and pressed her fingers against the side of Tammy's neck. There was a pulse. "Tammy, wake up."

"Mmmm?"

"Thank God. We thought you might be dead."

"What?" Tammy opened her eyes and winced against the light. "Randy? Why am I all... whoa." She kicked her legs, splashing ruddy water everywhere.

"Tammy, it's OK. Relax. It's just me."

The door flew open. "What's going—oh my God." Eddie's face darkened, nearly matching Tammy's bathwater. He backed out of the room and closed the door. "I didn't see anything, I swear."

Tammy burst into laughter. Miranda couldn't help but to do the same.

"Did you see his face?" Tammy said as she caught her breath. "Oh, it's a good thing I'm not shy." She held out her arms. "Yuck. So much for my bubble bath."

"I damn near had a heart attack. It looked like you were bleeding out."

Tammy reached under her right leg and retrieved an empty plastic bottle. "And so much for my cranberry juice. It must have taken a dive after I fell asleep. I pulled a twelve-hour shift and the water was so warm. I told myself twenty minutes, tops. I must have dozed off. Sorry for the scare."

"No worries. Should I get you a towel?"

Tammy stood up and pulled up the drain stop. "In a second. Let me rinse off under the shower first."

"I'll meet you downstairs."

"This will only take a second." Tammy closed the shower curtain and turned on the water. "Like I said, I'm not shy. In my line of work, I've seen everything there is to see, believe me. Besides, we're girls. We have the same parts."

"Yeah, but your parts are nicer than mine," Miranda muttered.

"What's that?"

Miranda raised her voice. "Tell me about Elias."

"Not much to tell. I'm going out with him tomorrow

night. Dinner and then a private tour of his gallery before it opens to the public."

"What happened to Heather Marceta's brother, what's his name?"

"Kyle. Yeah, he's a real player. Every girl who walks into his gym is a target."

"I know the type," Miranda said. After a pause, she continued. "You know when you asked me if I get a 'vibe' about things?"

"Yep."

"Well, I got one about Elias."

Tammy turned off the shower and slid the curtain aside. Miranda handed her a towel.

"What do you mean?" Tammy asked as she dried off.

"I'm not sure, but I have a bad feeling that he isn't what he seems."

"Of course not, he's a guy. They're all like that."

"I just think you should be careful."

Tammy smiled. "Always am."

***

AFTER SERVING A ROUND OF COFFEE, Tammy dropped onto the sofa wearing running shorts and a powder blue t-shirt. Her wet auburn hair was combed straight back. To her right, Eddie pressed himself against the armrest and focused on his phone.

Tammy stifled a giggle that would only embarrass the poor kid further. Instead, she addressed him with a sympathetic tilt of her head. "Sorry if I alarmed anyone."

Eddie refused eye contact as his face reddened again. "Just glad you're OK."

"Why wouldn't I be?" Tammy turned to Miranda. "What made you think I'd be dead when you got here?"

Miranda swallowed a sip of coffee. "You've been marked by Nancy Vernon."

"Excuse me?"

"You might want to start with the dead guy in the cornfield," Eddie suggested. "Oh, but then we have some interesting video and audio to show you from last night."

"Dead guy?" Amy glared at him.

Eddie held up his hands. "Right, sorry, that was callous of me."

"Mother of Christ," Tammy said. "What the hell have I gotten us into?"

ELIAS OPENED THE BASEMENT DOORS, locking them in place and shaking them until he was satisfied they were secure. As he emerged onto the patio, and the tranquility of a sultry summer night, he turned his gaze to the star-dappled sky. It had been far too long since Elias took pause to admire the heavens. *There once was a time...*

He'd had a different name then, a different face. Over the decades since, most of his nocturnal activities had been far less innocent. *Never thought I'd live long enough to say I'm getting too old for this shit.* Elias closed his eyes and drew in a slow, deep breath, taking in the scent of freshly cut grass, the sound of branches rustling in the warm breeze. He was one transaction and $70 million away from retirement. *This is the first night of the rest of my life...*

Yet death still surrounded him.

Did I really unleash a serial killer from the other side by building this house? The suicides, the dead man in the cornfield —more blood on my hands? Will Tammy be next?

Will I?

Elias turned his gaze to the metal doors.

Verbrecher.

A word in German written in blood on his basement wall, a fact he'd concealed from Tammy and her psychic friend. It would have raised too many questions. Elias had been marked. *Verbrecher.* Criminal. It was an accusation and his injury was punishment. The Vernons had declared war on him.

After Miranda and Eddie had departed earlier in the day, Elias called Heart of Christ Church and scheduled a blessing of his home for next week. A bible, a crucifix, and an aspergillum were not his usual weapons of choice. He'd become accustomed to facing his adversaries down the barrel of a gun or the blade of a knife. Sometimes he'd walked away unscathed, other times within inches of his life, but he was still here. They weren't. Elias was a survivor, and no fucking *geist* would change that. *You'll leave this house before I do if I have to burn it to the ground. I could fake my own death and go anywhere in the world. Wouldn't be the first time.*

A red glow appeared in his peripheral vision. It grew brighter as it glided across the cornstalks. He crossed the patio and stood at the edge of his driveway as the white cargo van backed in and came to a stop within arm's reach. Elias wasted no time in opening the rear doors.

"In a hurry tonight, are we?" Hagen climbed out of the passenger seat. "This is it, our last—what happened to your head?"

"Flesh wound. Let's get this stuff inside."

"We just drove three hours," Leland grumbled as he rounded the back of the van. "The least you could do is offer —what the hell happened to your head?"

"Flesh wound," Hagen said.

Elias climbed into the van for a cursory inspection of the inventory. Though this final shipment of Nazi stolen art— direct from Otto Skorzeny's personal collection—was the least in terms of volume, it contained the most precious pieces. Six paintings were to be purchased tomorrow morning by one unnamed buyer. Anonymity in such transactions was common. Third-party contacts were always employed to complete the deal.

These six paintings had been concealed among a dozen works from contemporary artists. The latter were slated for sale in the art gallery and had been purchased by Elias and Leland during the Portugal Arts Festival a month ago. As usual, each framed painting was wrapped in lint-free cloth under a layer of bubble wrap.

"I was going to say, I'd like to get a drink first," Leland said. "If you don't mind."

"Get this one down to the basement." Elias reached for the largest one, nearly five feet wide, and slid it across the floor of the van. "Then feel free to indulge yourself. You know where the kitchen is."

"Is there a problem, Janos?"

"Just tired, that's all."

Hagen lifted on end of the painting. "Ghosts keeping you awake?"

"Don't start that shit again." Leland grabbed the other end.

"How do you explain all that activity the last time we were here?"

"The only activity was in your head. Now get moving."

There was no doubt where Leland's share of the money would be invested. His wife had died young at forty-four, killed by a bullet intended for him. Leland's second marriage had been to the bottle and they'd been inseparable since.

Footsteps approached the van and without turning, Elias pushed several of the smaller paintings behind him toward the open doors. "We'll wait for Leland before we take anymore big ones in. Just grab those for now."

When nothing moved after several seconds, Elias glanced over his shoulder. "Hagen, I said take those—"

The woman gazed at him, blood trickling from a bullet hole in her temple.

Elias had never been one to panic. In this case, however, he blurted the only words his mind could muster. "Nancy Vernon." She was the woman from his dream, the one in the casket.

"You bring the blood of millions into my home." Her voice quivered with a simmering rage matched only by the venom in her glare.

And then the paintings bled. All of them. Streams of thick crimson seeped across the floor of the van—all flowing toward Elias. He pressed himself against the back of the driver's seat. "This is not your house. It hasn't been for thirty-three years. You need to move on."

Nancy raised her other hand, leveling a gun at him. It was the Luger he'd lost in the basement on the day of his injury. He snatched up one of the smaller paintings and hurled it at her. The gun fired. Elias threw himself to the floor.

"What the fuck?"

An irritated Hagen stood where Nancy had been. "Quit throwing shit at me. I'm working as fast as I can. You should throw something at Leland. All he does is drink and bitch about everything."

The blood was gone. All was normal.

Elias scrambled out of the van. "Sorry."

"Christ, you look like you just saw a ghost. Did you?"

Without a word, Elias brushed past him.

"Where are you going?"

"To get a drink."

CHAPTER 14

GINNY

The main door of the two-story townhouse was wide open when they arrived, but there was no one in sight as Miranda peeked through the glass of the storm door. She rang the bell.

"This is going to be awkward," Amy said in a nervous, sing-song voice.

"Just let me start and we'll be fine."

A rotund woman in navy slacks and a teal blouse hurried toward the door. Jaw-length salt-and-pepper hair framed her round face. She adjusted her glasses as she leaned out. "Yes?"

"I'm very sorry to disturb you at this difficult time, Mrs. Knedlhans," Miranda began before introducing herself and Amy. "We were hoping that Ginny was home?"

"No." The woman frowned. "Can I help you?"

"We just wanted to express our condolences on your loss, Mrs. Knedlhans, and we have some infor—"

"My name isn't Mrs. Knedlhans, that's my maiden name. I'm Frank's sister, Bonnie. Did you know my brother?"

"I did, ma'am," Amy spoke up in a doleful voice. "Ginny and I were classmates this past year. I was hoping to see her before I leave for vacation. I'm transferring to a different college in the fall and this may be my last chance to tell her how sorry I am. Her father was very kind to me. I was just talking to him a few days ago at the Historical Society. I can't believe he's gone. I asked my mom to bring me here. I left messages on Ginny's phone, but she probably doesn't want to talk to anyone right now." Amy lowered her glistening eyes.

Bonnie's expression softened. "Well, Ginny doesn't live here. She has an apartment near the college. Hold on, I'll get you her address." She closed the door and disappeared into the house.

Behind the women, Eddie leaned forward. "What the hell just happened?"

Miranda put a hand under Amy's chin and gently raised her head. "Since when did you major in theatre, young lady?"

"You know what they say about desperate times." Amy jutted out her lower lip in a mock pout.

"No wonder you get along so well with my oldest." Miranda tapped Amy's chin playfully. "You and Andrea know how to turn on the water works."

Bonnie returned to the door with an index card. She handed it to Amy. "Here you go, honey, although I called her just before you arrived. She said she wanted to take a walk to clear her head. Ginny's no wilting flower, mind you, but she and Frank were as close as any father and daughter could be. This is going to hurt for a long time."

"I know the feeling," Miranda nodded. "Thank you, ma'am."

On their way back to the car, Miranda shook her head. "This doesn't feel right. If Ginny's out alone, it would be an opportunity for Nancy to take her."

BEYOND THE GLASS doors of the foyer, the last rays of the late morning sun faded behind encroaching storm clouds. Inside, Amy scanned the apartment's directory. Finding Ginny's name, she punched in the number on the keypad.

"She's on the tenth floor?" Eddie observed. "Posh."

"These are student apartments," Miranda said. "Don't expect a penthouse at the top."

"If Ginny's not here, we'll have to wait for her," Amy said when there was no response from the intercom. Lightning flickered through the clouds, answered by a deep rumble of thunder. "With this storm coming, hopefully she won't be out for long."

"Unless she stopped somewhere," Miranda suggested.

"Like a bar," Eddie said. When both women looked at him askance, he added, "What? That's how some people clear their head, by making it numb."

"She could've gone to the campus or the gym or a friend's place," Amy suggested.

Miranda crossed her arms and leaned against the wall. "If you're right and she gets trashed, it'll be that much easier for Nancy to take advantage of her. Amy, try again. We're speculating on her whereabouts and she could be in the shower or taking a nap for all we know."

Amy tapped in the number once more, but again, there was no response. "Now what?"

Miranda let out a moan as a rush of vertigo overtook her. *She's up there. Try again.* The words pushed themselves into her mind. "Dial her one more time."

Amy hesitated.

"Trust me."

She complied and instantly, the lock clicked.

Eddie pulled the handle. "No shit." He stood aside, holding the door open. "Ladies first."

Amy cocked her head at Miranda. "I won't even ask."

Thanks, Dad. Miranda pushed off the wall, her dizzy spell abating. She led the way through the lobby. A few minutes later, the trio stepped off the elevator into a sweltering tenth-floor hallway. The distinct aroma of latex paint permeated the air.

Eddie pulled the collar of his T-shirt up over his nose. "Ugh. It's miserable up here."

"With most of the students gone for the summer," Amy said. "It's the best time to renovate."

"We're looking for ten-thirteen." Miranda started down the hall to the right. The apartment numbers were increasing. Before turning the corner, they passed an open door. Eddie stopped at the threshold and peered inside. The empty apartment reeked of fresh paint—classic yet monotonous off-white. Rollers in half-empty paint trays lay on a carpet covered with stained plastic tarps and canvas drop cloths. Eddie lifted his head, allowing the collar of his shirt to fall back into place.

Across the room, wind-driven rain tapped a steady beat on a section of plastic tarp beneath an open casement window. Eddie made his way across the room and cranked the handle, leaving the window ajar to allow ventilation while obstructing the rain.

If I had an apartment like this, I could get the hell away from my fucked-up family, maybe find a girlfriend, and—

"Ahem." Amy appeared in the doorway, arms folded. "What are you doing in here?" She waved away the question. "Never mind. We found Ginny's place."

"Is she there?" Eddie asked as they started off together.

"No one answered the door, but it was unlocked. Miranda opened it and called Ginny's name, but no one answered."

"Creepy. Are we going in?"

They stopped outside apartment ten-thirteen. The door was wide open, but Miranda was nowhere in sight.

"Apparently, we are." Eddie gestured for Amy to precede him.

"Randy!" she called, but her voice was drowned by a roar of thunder that shook the building.

The layout was nearly a mirror image of the empty apartment down the hall. In the center of the living room, several paperback books lay strewn across a glass top coffee table. To the right, throw blankets covered the back of a light blue sofa. Folded laundry had been left neatly stacked on the middle cushion, topped with two strapless bras. Their cup sizes raised Eddie's eyebrows.

"I don't think you'll find her under there, sport."

Eddie held up a hand. "Wait, do you hear that?"

"What?"

"Rain."

"You just noticed that now?"

"No, it sounds as if..." He started down the narrow hall and peeked into the bedroom. After a moment, he motioned for Amy to join him. He pointed to an open window that led to a fire escape.

"Nancy, let this one go... *please.*"

"You heard that, right?" Eddie asked.

"That was Randy. Is she on the roof?"

In unison, the pair hurried to the window.

"Wasn't it enough to take her father?" Miranda shouted over a blast of thunder. "What's the point of killing this girl?"

Another voice responded but was too far away to comprehend.

"Shit, we're too late," Eddie said. "She's trying to talk Ginny off the roof which means Nancy got in her head." He leaned through the open window and craned his neck to peer up, squinting against the relentless downpour.

"Can you see them?"

Eddie ducked back inside and wiped his face with his shirt

sleeve. "No, but it's only a few steps up the fire escape then a short ladder to the roof. Let's go."

"What? No way." Amy shook her head. "If you want to climb on metal in a lightning storm, be my guest."

"Randy did it and she may need our help."

Amy shifted her nervous gaze to the fire escape. "I can't do steps with open risers and I'm not good with heights."

"That's strange coming from an amazon."

"Shut up."

"Fine, stay here. I'm going."

Eddie climbed out onto the black metal grating and ascended the short flight of steps to the ladder. Gripping the first rung, he risked a glance at the parking lot ten stories below. To his left, a bolt of lightning turned gray sky white. He pressed himself against the ladder, bracing for thunder's angry retort. "Christ, you call this ghost hunting?"

"Eddie, be careful." At the open window, Amy ducked back inside before extending a perfectly toned leg out into the rain. A moment later, she unfolded gracefully onto the fire escape. "Screw it. I'm coming with."

Admiring her sudden courage—and denim mini shorts—Eddie pushed his sodden hair away from his eyes and continued up the ladder to the roof. Amy was beside him seconds later.

"I'm not leaving without Ginny." Randy stood about twenty feet away, her attention riveted on the barefoot redhead at the far end. Ginny, in grey shorts and a maroon tank top, leaned against a wrought iron rail that bordered the entire roof. In order to jump, she would need to climb over it.

So why haven't you? Eddie wondered. Was Ginny still in there, fighting for her life, or was Nancy Vernon in total control? If so, why hadn't she sent Ginny plunging to her death by now? Could Miranda be getting through, eroding

Nancy's resolve? Eddie hoped so. From what he could see of Ginny, it would suck if Nancy succeeded.

Thunder rumbled overhead. To his left, a large wood deck was furnished in green plastic patio furniture. Approximately ten feet in front of that, and only five steps to Miranda's right, stood the stairwell access. It was the size of a small storage shed and the perfect cover that would put both Ginny and Miranda within reach.

"Let's move."

Eddie and Amy crept over to the far side of the stairwell access and peeked out. At this angle, they were positioned just behind Miranda to her left. Ginny was directly ahead near the corner of the roof.

Amy pulled Eddie back behind the wall. "My turn now."

"What do you have in mind?"

"We have the element of surprise. I can easily cover that distance and take Ginny down before she can get over that rail."

"Are you sure?"

"Dude, I'm a sprinter. Trust me. I can end this right now."

"You're beautiful when you're determined—and drenched."

Amy grinned. "And you're still a dork, but a brave dork. Stay here until I have her pinned down."

———

"NANCY!" Miranda called. "None of this is going to bring back the life you had or the children you lost. Ginny never did anything to you. She's innocent." What had started as a dull ache in her shoulders and upper back was now unbearable. She wanted to collapse on a soft bed in dry pajamas. *Lord, please. I'm getting too old for this. Help me out here.*

Ginny spun, her eyes filled with rage. The eyes of Nancy Vernon. "So were my children."

"Then why take another child's life? I won't allow it. Give Ginny to me, now!"

"You can't stop me." Ginny swung a leg over the rail. "You can't win."

Amy bolted from the stairwell on a dead run. She lunged, wrapping one arm around Ginny's midsection. The girl screamed and slid several inches along the slick rail before Amy's weight brought her down to the asphalt roof in a crumpled heap. Ginny cried out, wincing in pain. For a few moments, she remained still, her mouth hanging open. Her chest heaved as she breathed in spasms. Beside her, Amy pushed herself to her knees and swept a veil of drenched hair from her face. Scrapes and scratches on her hand and arm were just beginning to bleed.

"How's that for being stopped, bitch?"

Miranda hurried toward them. "Are you okay?"

Amy nodded just as Ginny rolled onto her side with a strangled moan and drew her knees up to her chest. Amy slipped her arm from the girl's waist and laid a gentle hand on her shoulder. "I'm sorry, Ginny."

"Don't be. She may be hurt, but you saved her life." Miranda crouched down and grasped Ginny's ankles. "We need to be careful now. Hold her down. If Nancy's still—"

"Get away from her right now!"

A tall, husky middle-aged man approached from the fire escape. His black jeans and dark blue polo shirt were already soaked. A police badge was clipped to his belt.

And his semi-automatic was leveled at Miranda.

She lifted her hands, palms out. "Sir, we're not armed."

"I don't care. Move away now."

"Denny!" Ginny cried. "These are the people I told you about, the ones from the library and the restaurant. They forced me up here and tried to throw me off." Her body trembled as she sobbed. "Help me, please."

Taking one hand off the gun, the cop pointed toward the stairwell access. "I'm going to tell you this only once. Both of you will release Ms. Knedlhans and get over there on your knees, hands on your heads, right now."

Miranda refused to budge. "If we let Ginny go, she'll jump. She was already up here when we arrived. Now, you can shoot us, but I guarantee you'll be scraping her off the street. All we want is to get her safely back inside. Then I'll explain everything."

"I don't think so, blondie," Ginny scoffed, but it was Nancy Vernon who met Miranda's gaze. She shot a sidelong glance at the cop. "I'm so sorry, Denny. I know how much she meant to you."

Denny took a step forward. "Ginny, what are you—"

The girl swung her fist upward and backhanded Amy, sending her stumbling into the railing. Miranda leaned over Ginny to pin her arms to her side, but Nancy anticipated her. She slammed both feet into Miranda's midsection, knocking the wind out of her. Ginny pushed herself up and reached for the rail.

Denny lowered his gun and bolted forward. "Ginny, stop!"

Miranda charged forward, grasping for the girl with both hands. By the time she stopped moving, Miranda was bent over the rail with a bird's eye view of the parking lot. The fleeting memory of dangling high in an oak tree flashed through her mind. *Don't let go...* Amy's arms wrapped around her legs, providing ballast.

"A little help. I can't hold her." Miranda strained to breathe against the pressure of the railing against her stomach. With one hand, she held Ginny's left forearm while in the other, a wad of stretched maroon tank top was beginning to tear.

Denny climbed over the rail. Hooking his feet under it, he held on with one hand and reached down, fingers brushing Ginny's shoulder. "Grab my hand, sweetie."

She tilted her head and smirked at him. "Now why would I do that? Didn't I make myself clear? This can only end one way. The blonde can't hold on forever."

Miranda knew that only she could see Nancy Vernon. To Denny, his best friend's daughter was ten stories and two tentative grips away from joining her father. A hole opened in the back of Ginny's tank top, but Miranda maintained her grip. She squeezed Ginny's forearm with her other hand in a feeble attempt to ward off the growing numbness in her fingers.

Denny stretched his arm. "Ginny, please."

If I can get her closer. Miranda braced her knees against the rail and arched her back, pulling Ginny upward until she was within Denny's reach. Nancy made no motion to hinder her effort. She merely allowed Ginny's body to hang like dead weight, waiting for Miranda's grip to fail.

"That's good." Denny slid his way closer along the rail. Miranda marveled at his courage but feared for him nearly as much as for Ginny. "Just a little higher."

Somewhere below them, excited voices chattered and metal rattled. Miranda pressed her foot against the rail for support. Denny clutched Ginny's bicep and began to lift her —but Nancy wouldn't have it. She yanked her arm from Miranda's grasp and gouged the back of Denny's hand with her fingernails. He grunted in pain and recoiled, dropping her arm.

Fabric tore.

Amy gasped.

And Ginny fell.

CHAPTER 15

NO GOOD DEED

Miranda staggered back, the drenched remnants of Ginny's tank top clutched in her numb fingers. She dropped to her knees and doubled over, succumbing to the pain in her stomach. She fought the urge to vomit. *She's dead. Oh, God, she's dead...*

"Pull us in!"

A commotion erupted around her. More people yelled and something that sounded like aluminum clanked and scraped against the building. Denny climbed back over the rail and helped Amy to her feet. Miranda lowered her gaze to the asphalt, ran a finger over its coarse surface, and envisioned Ginny's broken, lifeless body ten stories below.

"Randy?" Amy knelt beside her. Blood clotted on her lower lip where Ginny, or rather Nancy, had punched her. "You OK?"

"Ginny," Miranda croaked.

"I think she's all right."

"She's good," Denny confirmed. "Over ten years on the force and I've never seen anything like that." He leaned over the rail. "Ginny, can you hear me?"

The pain had subsided enough for Miranda to stand—with some assistance from Amy. They joined Denny at the edge of the roof. "Where is she?"

"I'm not sure," Amy shrugged. "I heard something but by the time I turned to look, it already happened."

"What already happened?"

Denny pointed to the open panes of a large casement window about three feet below the edge of the roof. "Some guy was lying on one of those heavy-duty aluminum extension ladders sticking straight out that window. He caught Ginny and slid back inside. Friggin' wild. Let's get down there."

A ladder? It made no sense. *Who would have known—* "Where's Eddie?"

"No way," Amy said. "He was up here with me."

"Eddie," Miranda called.

"Yo."

"Do you have Ginny?"

"Yes, ma'am."

"Is she all right?" Denny asked.

"Yes, sir."

"Are *you* all right?" Amy shouted.

"Best ghost hunt ever."

Twisting her lips in a wry grin, Miranda held up Ginny's shredded tank top.

Denny bolted toward the stairwell.

"We're coming down," Miranda said.

"Take your time."

Denny spun in mid-stride and returned to the edge of the roof. "Hey, kid, hands off."

"That's kind of impossible given the situation."

"I have a gun."

"Point taken."

DENNY BARGED into the apartment ahead of the women. He unclipped his badge from his belt and held it up to a pair of bewildered painters who parted to reveal Eddie and Ginny seated on the floor. Ginny was wrapped in a canvas drop cloth, her ginger hair darkened and disheveled from the rain.

Denny lowered himself to one knee and met her dejected gaze. "Hey, sweetie. How do you feel?"

"To be honest, I think she's going to puke," Ginny said.

"She?"

Miranda stepped forward. "Nancy, let this one go."

The cop glared at her. "Her name is Ginny."

"I know what her name is, but she hasn't been herself lately." Miranda cocked her head at the girl. "Has she?"

Denny sighed. "What the hell are you talking about? Who are you friggin' people?"

"This one was obvious," Ginny said. "I practically gave her to you on a silver platter, or in this case an aluminum ladder, but there are two more and you won't get to them before I do."

With that, Ginny's eyelids fluttered closed. She fell sideways into Eddie, her body limp.

Denny brought his face close to hers. "She's still breathing but I want to get her to a hospital."

"She'll be fine," Miranda said.

Denny rose to his feet. "And how do you know?"

"I've been through this before."

"Oh, really, well I can't wait to hear all about it, lady, 'cuz you and I are going to have a conversation."

"I couldn't agree more, but maybe we should get Ginny back to her place first." Miranda held Denny's furious gaze for a few seconds until he snapped his fingers at Eddie. "You were the one on the ladder."

"Yes, sir."

"Nice catch."

Denny turned to the painters. "Thank you for your help, gentlemen."

"It's not every day we get to save a damsel in distress," the younger one said. "I know it's none of my business, but will she be OK?"

"She should be right as rain in a few hours," Miranda answered, much to Denny's annoyance.

Minutes later, after helping Ginny to her bed, Denny pulled a random T-shirt and shorts from the top drawer of her dresser. He stepped out into the living room and approached Amy.

"What's your name again?"

"Amy. Amy Healy."

"Amy Healy, I'm going to give you and Ginny ten minutes of privacy while you help her out of the drop cloth and into these dry clothes. Can you do that?"

"Uh, sure."

"Thank you. I'll get some ice for your lip."

Amy completed the task in less than the allotted time. She emerged from the bedroom carrying the balled-up drop cloth under her arm. Denny handed her an ice pack from Ginny's freezer.

"Should I take the drop cloth back to the painters?"

Denny nodded. "And come right back here."

Miranda was not pleased with the idea of a stranger ordering her team about, even if he was a cop. Under the circumstances, she had no choice. Besides, it was obvious that Detective Teelko cared for Ginny as if she were his own daughter.

Denny grabbed a chair from the dining nook and propped open the door to Ginny's bedroom. "You, ladder boy."

"Eddie Reynolds."

"I don't care. Sit."

Eddie flopped onto the chair. The detective leaned in, his face within inches of Eddie's. "Now, since you saved her life, I'm going to trust you to make damn sure she doesn't do anything crazy when she wakes up. Are we clear?"

"You know, since I saved her life, you could be a little nicer."

Miranda stifled a chuckle.

Denny allowed a thin smile. "OK, ladder boy, how's this? If I come back here and find your ass anywhere else but in this chair, I'm going to put a bullet in it. Your ass, not the chair. Once more, are we clear?"

"As the air between us."

———

IN THE LIVING ROOM, Miranda wanted nothing more than to peel off her drenched clothes and slip under warm sheets. Her entire body ached. Worst of all, her hair was a disaster. *I really am getting too old for this crap. No,* she chided herself. *Not as long as I can still save lives.*

"How are you feeling?"

Miranda turned away from the window and spread her arms. "Like a wet mop."

"Aren't we all."

"Before you ask, it's Miranda Lorensen."

"Well, Miranda Lorensen, you took a hard kick to the gut and risked your life."

"The pain's almost subsided." She pointed to Denny's hand. "What about you?"

He inspected the fresh scabs and broken skin where Ginny had gouged him. "Yeah, she really dug in there. Nothing that some antiseptic and band-aids won't fix. So, Miranda, are Amy and Eddie your kids?"

"No. They're friends. Team members."

"What kind of team?"

Miranda hesitated. *Oh, what the hell...* "We're paranormal investigators."

Denny's eyebrows shot up. He burst into laughter. "Hot damn, this gets better by the minute. You're ghost hunters? Like those people on TV?"

"Not exactly like them, but same concept."

"That is wild. You must have some amazing stories."

"A few, yeah."

Denny's smile vanished. "Well, I'd like the hear the one that explains what the hell you're doing here and why my best friend's daughter tried to toss herself off the roof and while you're at it, you can tell me why you called her Nancy, and what did she mean by 'two more people left?'"

"Anything else?"

"That about sums it up."

Thirty minutes passed, during which Amy returned and stood by Miranda as she recounted the events that had transpired since Tammy's phone call. She spared no detail other than the death of Frank Knedlhans. She knew to tread lightly where Ginny's father was concerned. Denny was speechless for nearly a full minute as he absorbed it all.

"When exactly were you at Elias Gray's house?"

"Two nights ago," Miranda said.

"Did you see anyone hanging around outside?"

Miranda and Amy shook their heads.

"But I know Frank was there," Miranda said. "He followed us from The Pressroom."

Denny leaned forward in his chair. "Be very careful here. If you never saw him, how did you know he was there?"

"She's psychic," Amy blurted.

"I sensed someone watching us at the restaurant and then again when we arrived at Mr. Gray's house. I didn't know who it was until the next afternoon, when we returned to present the results of our investigation. When I walked over to the cornfield, I had a vision of Frank's body lying there. He was murdered by Nancy Vernon."

"Frank Knedlhans died of a heart attack."

"No, he didn't." Ginny dropped onto a chair across the room.

Denny rushed to her. "How do you feel?"

"A little nauseated, but otherwise I'm alive." She looked up at Eddie standing a few feet away. "Thanks to him."

"So we should be nice to ladder boy?"

"His name is Eddie."

"I like ladder boy."

"Denny, I'm serious. Miranda's right."

"Sweetheart—"

"Don't sweetheart me, I'm not a child. My dad was killed by the same bitch that got inside my head. It was Nancy Vernon. I saw everyone she murdered, people I never met. How else would I know that? I saw my dad." Ginny's eyes glistened and her voice cracked as she continued. "She reached into his chest and crushed his heart."

Miranda knelt down and took Ginny's hands in hers. "I'm so sorry. I lost my father at a young age, too. You're strong, more so than I was. We know that Nancy has two more victims on her list. I have to ask, did you happen to glean anything about who they might be?"

Ginny shook her head. "No, I'm sorry, but I do want to help stop her if I can. If there's anything I can do—"

"No, there's nothing you need to do," Denny said. "Because this is all bullshit. The Vernons have been dead and gone for decades. Look, Ginny, you've been through hell these past few days. You're grieving, confused. Anyone in your state of mind would be easily influenced by crap like this."

"That's not—"

"I think you should stay with Liz and me at least for a few days."

"Denny, I appreciate your concern but I'm a big girl."

"It's a good idea, actually," Miranda said. "Just to be safe."

"Why don't you pack an overnight bag," Denny suggested. "You can always come back tomorrow for more after the storm clears out."

Ginny ambled to her bedroom. Once she was out of earshot, Denny whirled on Miranda. "I appreciate everything you've done for Ginny today, but I can take it from here. She needs counseling, not some whack job ghost hunters."

"I think Ginny can decide that for herself."

"Not in her current state, she can't. I've been a cop long enough to have seen a lot of people in crisis. She needs real help. I've known Frank and Ginny for years. I'll do what it takes to protect her."

"I'm glad to hear that."

"That includes telling you to stay the hell away from her. Do you understand me?"

"No good deed goes unpunished," Eddie muttered.

Miranda held up her hands. "We won't take up any more of your time."

Ginny returned to the living room and tossed a small duffle bag to the floor.

"We have to leave, Ginny," Miranda said. "Again, we're sorry for your loss. Please take care of yourself."

"Thank you, I will." Ginny glared at Denny. "And I apologize for him."

Miranda smiled. "He means well." She glanced down at Ginny's pink sneakers. "Your dad bought those for you."

"What?" Ginny glanced down at them. "Oh, yeah. How did you know? Oh my God, you *are* for real."

"He's just happy to see you wearing shoes for a change."

OUTSIDE, the rain had stopped, at least for now. Miranda slipped an arm around Eddie's shoulder. "You must be feeling like a stud with all these women falling into your arms lately."

Eddie blushed.

"That thing with the ladder was crazy and dangerous... and amazing." Miranda pulled him close and kissed him on the side of the head. "You're my hero."

Eddie reached into his pocket. "Ginny said the same thing after she woke up." He held up his phone. "In fact, I got her number."

CHAPTER 16

LAST STAND

With a few taps on his tablet screen, Elias Gray and his partners were officially retired. In the comfort of his sitting room, he turned the screen to Leland and Hagen. "Twenty million dollars wired to each of your accounts. Gentlemen, this concludes our business. You have my gratitude and congratulations on a plan masterfully executed."

All three men raised their glasses.

"God bless the Internet," Hagen said.

"How does it feel to be a multi-millionaire at twenty-eight?" Elias asked.

"Liberating. I just can't believe how smoothly it all went down."

"Don't jinx it, boy," Leland said. "We're not home yet."

Elias squeezed his friend's shoulder. "Always the cautious one. So where to now, old man?"

"Maybe I'll go to Disney World."

"My parents never thought I'd amount to anything," his nephew said. "With this kind of money, I can tell them to fuck off and then disappear for the rest of my life."

"Yes, disappear." Elias shot a sidelong glance at Leland. "Sounds like a grand idea."

"We should get on the road." Leland struggled out of his easy chair. "Our flight leaves in three hours from Philadelphia."

Hagen excused himself to use the restroom. When the door was closed, Elias held up his tablet. "Look, I never actually completed the transfers." He tapped the screen to cancel the pending transaction and began a new one, depositing Hagen's share into Leland's account. "Forty million dollars, all for you."

Leland smiled. "Excellent."

"You'll take care of our young partner?"

"What partner?"

The pair shook hands as Hagen returned.

"See you in Madrid next week, old friend," Elias said.

"God willing."

AFTER AN HOUR on the eastbound Pennsylvania Turnpike, Leland pulled off into a parking area bordered by dense, verdant woods. He had marked this exact location on their previous return trip. At four o'clock in the morning, traffic was sparse, and sunrise was an hour and a half away.

Leland reached over and shook Hagen's arm. "Hey, wake up."

Hagen sat ramrod straight, eyes wide open. He rubbed his face and peered through the windshield. "Are we there yet?"

"No, we're about forty-five minutes away," Leland said. "But my leg is cramping up. I need you to take the wheel."

"Yeah, sure." With a yawn, Hagen unclipped his seatbelt and slid out of the van.

While he did so, Leland reached beneath his seat until his

fingers found the handle of the Ruger P95 semi-automatic. He tucked the weapon under his polo shirt before leaving the van. He made a cursory inspection of the highway before rounding the front of the vehicle just as Hagen approached.

The headlights illuminated the younger man's face, casting it in an ashen pallor as the bullet pierced his forehead. Blood sprayed from the back of his head, yet his weary expression remained unchanged even as he bounced off the van's front bumper on his way to the ground.

In Leland's peripheral vision, a pair of distant headlights grew brighter. He estimated approximately ten seconds until the car reached his position. Hooking his arms under Hagen's, Leland dragged him to the passenger side of the van. He rifled through the pockets of his nephew's cargo shorts and removed his wallet, passport, and phone, leaving nothing with which to identify him. He opened the passenger door and tossed it all onto the seat along with the Ruger.

The car sped past and was quickly out of sight. Grunting and cussing under the exertion, Leland dragged Hagen's body deep into the thicket until he was sure it wouldn't be visible from the road. Sweat dripped from his nose and chin. *Good enough.* He dropped his burden and stretched his back and arms. *I'm too old for this shit. Thank God it's over.* High above, swaying branches cast a gamboling shaft of moonlight across Hagen's face. His glazed eyes shifted until they focused on his uncle—or perhaps it was Leland's imagination. *I need to get the hell out of this business.* "Thanks for all your help, kid. We couldn't have done it without you."

"ARE you sure you're up for this?"

Lori Switzer cocked her head at her fretful assistant. "Maggie, it's World Youth Day. You know I volunteer every year.

Father Federico is counting on me. Besides, maybe if I show a little leg, I can get a ride in the Popemobile."

"You just didn't seem yourself on Friday."

"I was tired and babbling. Trust me, I'm not going senile yet. Now, I have to get in line to be groped and scanned as if there's a surge of little white septuagenarian terrorists running amuck. Thank God I remembered not to wear an underwire bra. They might ask me to take it off."

Maggie's lips curled into a smile. "Have a safe trip, ma'am."

An hour later, Lori boarded Spanair Flight Twenty-Seven and settled into a window seat near the front of the plane. As other passengers filed in, she donned her reading glasses and slipped a folder out of her attaché. As she began to review the schedule for the coming events in Madrid, someone stumbled into the aisle seat. A plump, middle-aged man shoved a small duffle into the overhead compartment. He lost his balance for a moment as if the experience had caused him vertigo.

Or he's already drunk at seven in the morning. The man steadied himself before dropping into the middle seat beside Lori. His thinning hair was matted to his head and his breath reeked of alcohol. *And of course, he sits next to me.* She greeted him with a thin smile and returned to reading. After nearly a full minute of fidgeting, the man leaned toward her and spoke in a distinct German accent. "Maybe if no one takes the aisle seat, I can move over and give us some more room, you know."

"Yes, that would be nice," Lori said.

"My name is Leland."

"Lori."

"Have you been to Spain before?"

"I have, yes."

"Beautiful country. I live there now. Are you going on holiday?"

"In a way, yes," Lori replied. "Attending World Youth Day."

"Ah, very nice. I just closed a major deal that allowed me to retire."

"Congratulations. What kind of work do you do?"

"I trade in art and rare antiques. Something of an importer-exporter, you might say."

Lori's disdain turned into genuine curiosity. "That sounds fascinating. You know, my parents were from Norway. They escaped to England when the Nazis invaded in 1940, but not before the bastards stole everything they owned, including some valuable art that had been handed down through generations. I've checked with the German government, but they claim to have no record of these pieces. Would you be someone who could locate such things?"

The man's complexion turned rubescent. "Uh, no, ma'am, I don't deal in Nazi stolen art. It's bad for business. Whenever I come across it, I always report it to the authorities. Would you excuse me? I need to use the lavatory before we take off."

Lori wondered if she'd touched a nerve. So much the better, maybe she'd get some peace for the next eight hours.

Murmuring voices entered her consciousness. Lori opened her eyes and looked out upon a blue sea. At this altitude, low scattered clouds resembled white islands or perhaps, fluffy icebergs.

"Ma'am?"

One of the flight attendants took the aisle seat. The intoxicated antiques trader was nowhere in sight. Fighting the haze in her head, Lori regarded the young brunette. She couldn't recall seeing her before, even when the flight attendants gathered at the front of the plane to offer the standard preflight speech.

"Can I get you anything?"

"Maybe just a Coke, dear. Thank you."

"You might want something stronger for your last drink."

What? I couldn't have slept for eight hours. She checked her watch. They were only three hours into the flight. Maybe there was a problem. "Are we landing soon?"

"In a manner of speaking."

"I don't understand."

The young woman cocked her head. "You don't recognize me, do you? Well, it's no surprise. We only met twice I think."

Confused now, Lori shook her head.

"Since you only have about twenty minutes to live, I'll be blunt. I'm Nancy Vernon. You destroyed my family thirty-three years ago and now you're going to pay."

Jesus Christ, it is her. It's been her all along, not her husband.

"That's right, Mrs. Switzer. I've been killing everyone you conspired with to frame Jeff for embezzlement back then. You could say I've been climbing the corporate ladder. Now you definitely look like you could use a drink. How about a little scotch in that soda?"

On unsteady legs, Lori pushed herself to her feet. The rest of the plane was empty. "Somebody help me," she called. "Please!"

"Ma'am?"

She found herself staring at Leland. Passengers milled about in the aisle, conversing with one another. A movie played on the small LCD screen embedded into the back of the seat in front of her.

"Are you all right? Should I get a flight attendant?"

"No," Lori snapped. Then, in a softer voice, "I'm sorry, no. I'll be fine." She stiffened as her gaze came to rest on the glass of Coke bubbling on her tray. "When did that get there?"

"About five minutes ago," the man said. "You ordered it."

Lori shook her head. "I didn't."

"I was right here. You asked for a scotch and soda." The man raised his glass. It was half full of a clear liquid. "And I ordered a Himbeergeist. I couldn't believe they had it. But if you'll excuse me, I need to use the lavatory again. This stuff goes right through me sometimes."

Lori started to cry.

LELAND OPENED the door to the lavatory and found himself face to face with Hagen. Blood seeped from the bullet hole in his forehead. Leland screamed, but no one heard him over the explosion.

HIS HAND WAS WET.

Somewhere nearby, a woman's voice droned on about... something. Elias opened his eyes and winced against the stark pale glow of the television screen that provided the only light in the room. It was ten o'clock in the morning and an anchorwoman was delivering a special report. Windswept rain spattered the windows.

He lifted his hand from the ring of condensation left by the glass that had been knocked to the floor when he'd dozed off a few minutes ago. He wiped his hand on his jeans and rubbed his face. He had been unable to sleep since Leland and Hagen left, such was the excitement of finally obtaining his goal.

"Spanair Flight Twenty-Seven made a safe landing in Madrid this morning," the anchorwoman said. "But only after the loss of approximately a dozen passengers who were violently ripped from the plane when a lower cargo door malfunctioned, causing explosive decompression. An investigation is underway, and sources tell us that US naval divers have been dispatched in an attempt to recover the bodies of passengers lost at sea. This tragedy occurred on the eve of World Youth Day, an annual gathering of Catholics from around the world, scheduled to kick off tomorrow in Madrid.

"In local news, a severe thunderstorm has reached Eastern Pennsylvania, bringing with it..."

Elias leapt from his seat. He needed to call his contacts in Madrid to confirm Leland's safe arrival. He reached for his phone on the end table.

"Where's my money?"

On the television, a commercial for laundry detergent was just finishing, followed by another for breakfast cereal. So who said that?

"I asked you a question, Elias."

The voice was Hagen's, and he was seated exactly where he'd been before departing with Leland last night. A chill descended over the room.

"When did you get back?" Elias asked. His nearest weapon was a Grand Power K100 semi-automatic pistol. Unfortunately, it was concealed behind Hagen's chair.

"I'm not sure," the kid replied.

"Where's Leland?"

Hagen's eyes glazed over as if he were struggling to remember. "He was somewhere over the Atlantic last I checked."

"Shouldn't you be with him?"

"But you took my money."

"No. Your share is in the Swiss account I set up for you. Same with Leland."

Hagen rose from the easy chair, which should have rocked when he stood, yet it remained still. "Then why did my uncle do this to me?" A hole opened in his forehead. Blood streamed down over this face. "He dumped me on the side of the road like garbage. Why?"

Realizing the nature of what confronted him, Elias backed away toward the dining room. "I don't know."

"Liar. You two plotted against me. After all I did for you. It wasn't enough to take my money. I had my entire life ahead of me, and you took that, too."

By now, Hagen's face was all but completely streaked in dark crimson, making his wide-eyed expression of fury all the more terrifying. "You owe me, Elias." The apparition lunged toward him. "You owe me!"

Elias threw himself to the left, evading Hagen's outstretched hands. He stumbled as he skirted the dining room table but regained his balance. Upon reaching the far wall, he slapped the light switch. Hagen was nowhere in sight. From the sitting room, the voice of a shouting reporter described the scene at a storm-ravaged beach along the Delaware coast.

It was just a nightmare, like the others. Elias had been well aware that Leland would eliminate Hagen. It had been part of their plan since they'd recruited the naïve little bastard. In this case, it must have worked its way into his subconscious and become a dream when he'd dozed off. But just in case...

Elias made his way to the head of the dining room table and pushed aside the chair. He reached underneath for the Browning 9mm stashed on a hidden ledge.

A hand grabbed his wrist and forced his arm to the floor. "Janos! *Hilf mir!*"

Elias gasped as he stared into the frightened eyes of his oldest friend. The man's face and hair were sopping wet and the dank air around him was redolent of saltwater. It was pointless to call Madrid now.

"Janos, it's so cold." Leland shivered as he spoke. "I can't feel my legs."

It didn't take long to discover why. Elias dragged him out onto the open floor with little effort—because Leland's lower half was gone. Nothing remained but severed entrails and jagged bone protruding from the end of his torso. Elias thrashed and flailed his arm to break Leland's grip.

"No, Janos, you can't leave me like this."

"Get away from me!" He kicked Leland in the face over and over until the man released him. Elias staggered back, clenching his jaw to keep from vomiting at the grotesque apparition crawling toward him.

The back door was the nearest escape route. Elias side-stepped Leland and darted into the kitchen. He opened the bolt lock but the door refused to budge. "Dammit!" He peered over his shoulder, expecting to see Leland in the kitchen doorway, but like Hagen, he had also vanished. The dining room was empty. Walls and windows rattled and creaked as fierce winds battered the house. *Think! I've been through worse. There's more to fear from the living than the dead.* Nevertheless, Elias pulled his phone from his pocket and called the only person left who could help him.

"Hello?" the tired voice answered.

"Tammy, it's Elias." His words rushed together. "Are you at home?"

"Where else would I be? You sound out of breath. Are you all right?"

"I'm sorry to ask you this, but could you come over?"

There was a pause. "I'm already there. I've always been there, Janos. Always watching."

Elias frowned. "Tammy?"

"Guess again, *verbrecher*."

"Who is this?"

"Do you really have to ask? Shame about your friend Leland. He wasn't my target, more like collateral damage. Then again, no great loss."

"What the hell do you want from me?"

"You've brought the blood of millions into my home, Elias. I won't have it."

"This is not your house, you fucking bitch."

At that, the door to the basement opened.

"Why don't you come down here where we can discuss the matter? Unless you're afraid."

Don't do it. Get out now. But ego swallowed fear. It was time to fight. "On my way."

RAIN POURED INTO THE BASEMENT. The open cellar doors rattled and shook against the power of the storm but remained steadfast. Elias made no move to close them. He observed that the few pieces of unsold artwork had been rearranged. One large framed piece, nearly as tall as he and covered in a white canvas sheet, stood apart from the rest against the far wall. It was the first piece that Leland and Hagen had carried into the house before Nancy appeared to him at the van.

"Nancy Vernon," Elias called out against the din. "Show yourself."

"In good time." The words were a whisper, carried on the wind.

Elias lifted the sheet from the painting. A gust of wind swept through the basement, sending it fluttering from his grasp. The stench of rotting flesh permeated the air. He covered his nose and mouth but could not tear his gaze away from the canvas. A haphazard pile of naked, emaciated corpses lie in a gaping hole in the center of a field. Hundreds of them began to writhe, to crawl and slither over one another—men, women, children. As they drew nearer to the foreground, serial numbers tattooed on the ashen flesh of their forearms became clear.

Nancy's voice filled the basement. "These are the victims of Chelmno, Majdanek, Treblinka, and other Nazi extermination camps. Millions butchered, my parents among them. Much of the artwork you sold belonged to such people. It's only fair that you meet them, don't you think?"

The bodies crawled off the canvas onto the basement floor. Those who could stand upright slouched and limped. Many were mutilated, missing limbs, ears, eyes, breasts, testicles. Elias found himself unable to scream, to move, as these impossible horrors surrounded him.

"I'm... I'm not a Nazi," he croaked.

"You are like Mammon, profiting from the inhumanity of sadists and murderers." The voice was Nancy Vernon's, but the words were a chorus spoken by each member of the advancing mob.

A torrent of windswept rain drenched Elias as he backed up toward the open cellar doors. "That was half a century ago. It's long over."

"It is never over for those who suffered and died at the hands of evil."

"It wasn't my fault."

"That's what they said, too. 'We didn't do it, someone else did' or 'we were only following orders. It wasn't our fault.'"

"What do you want from me?"

"Give back what you took from us."

"I didn't take it from you to begin with." Elias's voice quivered. "I only... I only sold it."

Cadaverous faces stared back in silent indictment.

Elias pointed to the few remaining pieces of art across the basement. "That's all that's left. I swear to you. Take it. Take it all."

"It isn't enough. There is only one way to repay us."

From the darkness behind the stairs, something small and metallic skittered across the floor toward Elias. The Luger stopped at his feet, the gun he had lost days ago when the cellar doors dropped on his head.

"Pick it up."

Elias hesitated, his mind racing for options. It was only five steps to freedom. If he ran now...

"Pick it up."

Nancy Vernon appeared at the top of the steps, unfazed by the storm's fury. "I tried to warn you. You're all alone here, Elias. Alone among the dead. Would you like to leave?" Nancy stepped to one side and extended an arm toward the driveway. "As the expression goes, don't let the door hit you on the way out."

He knew there was no escape. He lowered himself to the steps, head in his hands, and wept as the rain drenched his back.

"No?" Nancy sat beside him. "Elias, if you were anyone else, you wouldn't even know I was here. I wouldn't have bothered you at all. I'm grateful, really. You helped me in ways you'll never know, but you used this house to make blood money. Like your friend Leland, you're just collateral damage."

There was no point in arguing. He no longer had the strength. Nancy was draining his energy. She crammed the pistol into his hand and curled his fingers around the grip. He gazed into her soft eyes as she pressed the muzzle to his temple. "No, *please*..." He recoiled, jerking his head back. Nancy placed a gentle hand on the other side of his face to stop him.

"It'll be okay, Janos. Soon, you'll no longer be alone among the dead. Trust me."

A moment later, Elias Gray no longer felt the rain.

CHAPTER 17

LAST ON THE LIST

The following morning, dawn brought with it pastel clouds, a gentle summer breeze, and a partially flooded basement complete with a corpse. Debris from the neighboring cornfield lay scattered across the driveway and side yard of the art dealer's house. Dried specks of dirt and strands of hay clung to the home's vinyl siding.

"Freakin' mess." Denny Teelko trudged through the swamp that had once been a lawn. As he walked beside the house toward the open cellar doors, he couldn't help but gaze at the cornfield where his best friend had been found dead just a few days ago.

Two uniformed officers flanked the entrance to the basement. They nodded as Denny approached. "Mornin', fellas."

Yellow caution tape crisscrossed the opening but did not obstruct the view. At the bottom of the stairs, Elias Gray lay prone in a puddle of ruddy water. *Christ, I just talked to this guy three nights ago. This can't be a coincidence.*

"Conroy in there?"

"Yes, sir," replied one of the uniforms. "But you'll need to go in either through the back or front door."

"Right, thanks."

Denny made his way around to the back door, which was also wide open. Conroy stood in the kitchen, waiting for Denny.

"Sorry, there was a tree down on Beechdale," Denny began. "Then another one on Church. So let me guess, the Amish guy found him."

"Close." Conroy led the way down to the basement as he continued. "Mr. Zook's grandkids were cleaning up some debris along the property line. One of them got curious and wandered over. He ran back to Zook, who called us... again."

"That guy's three for three."

"He's probably sick of us English by now."

Denny crouched to examine the body. Gray's clothes were intact, no tears or signs of a struggle. No bruises on the hands or neck. Just one bullet hole on either side of his head. Entrance and exit wounds.

"This house is bad news." As he stood, a glint of metal caught his attention. He peeked between the open risers of the wooden steps. A silver revolver lay on the floor behind the stairs. "I'd like to see whose prints come off that gun."

"The rest of the house appears untouched," Conroy said. "The television was on upstairs when we arrived. We found a bottle of whiskey on an end table and a glass lying on the floor. Seems he was drinking and watching TV, then came down here with a gun, opened the cellar doors in the middle of a thunderstorm, sat on the steps, and popped himself." Conroy spread his arms wide. "What the hell sense does that make? He could just as easily have shot himself in front of the TV."

Denny thought about Ginny. "Maybe he wasn't himself."

"What?"

"Never mind. Just something a woman said to me yesterday. We need to see if this fits the pattern of the other suicides."

Conroy snapped his fingers. "Right. Find out if he had a death in the family recently."

"Or a close friend, girlfriend, business partner, whatever."

"But just in case this wasn't a suicide, we'll get fingerprints. I have the guys upstairs taking samples from every room in the house."

"You know, I met some people who were here the night Frank died," Denny said. "Some ghost hunters. Seems Mr. Gray thought his house was haunted."

"Well, this was the old Vernon property," Conroy reminded him. "Both the husband and wife killed themselves about a week apart. In fact, if memory serves, the wife was found in the basement after she shot herself in the head." He pointed to Gray. "You think these ghost hunters had anything to do with that?"

"Not at all. It was a little blonde and two teenagers. They were adamant that the Vernons came back from the dead after this house was built and have been going around town taking revenge on people who screwed them back in the seventies. Some pretty wild shit."

"Well, my mom thinks my dad is still hanging around the house. Once in a while she smells the scent of the pipe he smoked for thirty years."

"Yeah, but your dad isn't killing people from beyond the grave."

Conroy shrugged. "Not that I'm aware of. Although he had one hell of an anger management problem right up until the day he died."

Denny nodded to several large rectangular objects leaning against the side wall of the basement. All were covered in canvas drop cloths. "What are those?"

"Paintings," Conroy replied. "Probably inventory for his art gallery. Should I bag the gun? The coroner's on his way to remove the body."

"Yeah, that's fine, and seal the house when we're all finished here. You know the drill."

Denny strolled over to the largest of the paintings and lifted the drop cloth, folding it back over its thick wooden frame. The painting was turned on its side. He stepped back to examine the piece. Bold brushstrokes captured a cobalt blue sky overlooking an expansive field of amber grain. A coppice of trees and overgrown shrubbery filled the background. The edge of a pond was visible on the far right, reflecting scattered clouds.

"Looks peaceful," Conroy said.

Denny ran a gloved finger over the ornate floral carving that twisted and wound its way around all four sides of the frame. "And old. Good thing the water didn't get this far. I wonder how much these things are worth."

He tilted the painting forward. A sheet of brown paper, flat and smooth, covered the back of the frame. "This, on the other hand, does not look very old at all. It looks like it was just glued on recently." At the bottom left corner, the paper was torn and folded back.

"Help me turn this over."

The men lifted the frame and rotated it, bringing the torn paper to eye level. Denny peeked inside. The yellowed edges of the canvas were stapled around a thin wooden frame. Stamped on the back of the canvas was an insignia, partially faded but no less recognizable. An eagle, its wings spread wide, perched atop a swastika.

Beneath it were the words, "*Dienststelle Westen. Eigentum des Drittes Reiches.*"

"Hey, check this out." Denny stepped aside as Conroy craned his neck to peer through the flap.

"Those are called stretcher bars, very common way to mount canvas in—"

"No, look toward the top corner in there."

After a moment, Conroy's eyes widened. "No shit. 'West office. Property of the Third Reich.' Well, the Nazis plundered artwork from all over Europe during World War Two, stealing it from museums and people alike. Once in a while, I catch articles online about pieces like this turning up and being sold or auctioned for millions."

Conroy's face lit up as he glanced from Elias Gray to the painting. "Maybe someone knew that Gray had this stuff and broke in here last night. Maybe he heard something and came down to investigate, but they got the jump on him. They could have executed him with his own gun and made off with a few million bucks worth of Nazi stolen art. We should see what this guy has in his gallery downtown."

"Why didn't they take all of it, then? There are only three pieces left here."

Conroy shrugged. "Don't know. Just thinking out loud. I'm not a psychic."

"SHOULD I take this as a sign that you're a bit more open-minded?" Miranda closed her car door and met Lieutenant Teelko in Elias Gray's driveway. "How's Ginny feeling?"

"Better today."

"Why did you ask me to come alone?"

"Officially, you're not here at all. This is off the record."

Miranda shifted her gaze from Denny to the house. "Why? Did something happen?"

"You tell me."

"Are you testing me?"

Denny folded his arms but said nothing more. Miranda strode over to the side of Gray's house. As she approached the cellar doors, dread consumed her. The perimeter of her vision blurred and swirled.

Of course, Miranda knew that Elias had suffered a nasty blow to the head when the doors closed on him earlier in the week, but there was more to it now. She pushed forward despite her mounting fear and knelt before the entrance. She laid a hand on one of the beige metal doors and closed her eyes. Though it was hot to the touch, a shiver blasted through her. When she opened her eyes, she found herself standing in the basement with Elias, a silver revolver in his right hand. He sat on the steps that led to the outside. Above, the cellar doors were wide open, quivering against violent winds. Rain poured in. Elias wept.

Miranda was aware of other bodies crowded around her, all watching him. They were naked, skeletal. Most were scarred or burned, some dismembered. She peered down at her own body. She could count every rib under her pallid flesh. Where her breasts had been, crooked incisions had been crudely sutured. A number was tattooed on her forearm.

Nancy Vernon sat beside Elias. As if playing with a doll, she lifted his arm and pressed the barrel of the gun to the side of his head. He struggled to no avail. Nancy cupped her hand over his and pulled the trigger. There was an initial spray of blood and brain matter from the opposite side of Elias's head before he tumbled off the stairs. The gun dropped through the open risers. Blood mixed with rain on the basement floor.

A pair of hands gripped her shoulders. She jerked away. "Leave me alone."

"Ms. Lorensen, calm down."

She stiffened as Denny helped her to her feet. "Please let me go."

Denny raised his hands and backed away. "Sorry, but you were crying and shaking. I didn't know—"

"Didn't know what?" Miranda snapped. "Didn't know how Elias died, so you called me here to figure it out for you? I ask again. Are you testing me, Lieutenant? Do you want to know if I'm a fraud?"

"What did you see?"

"I saw Nancy Vernon assisting in yet another suicide. She forced Elias to put a gun to his head, just like the ghost of her husband did to her all those years ago. Nancy Vernon did not willingly kill herself."

"So if she's taking revenge on people for something that happened in the seventies, why did she kill this guy?"

Miranda twirled a lock of her hair. "I don't know. Nancy wasn't the only one there last night. There were others, could have been a hundred of them. I don't know who they were, but it was like those pictures from World War Two with piles of dead bodies in Nazi concentration camps. It was as if they were there to witness Elias's death. I don't understand it."

"So how do we stop Nancy Vernon?" Denny asked.

"Oh, you believe me now? Because yesterday you told me to get lost."

"Let's just say I'm trying to keep an open mind."

"Let's just say that you have no suspects and you're getting desperate after almost losing Ginny."

"Are you always like this?"

The conversation was interrupted by the whimsical chime of Miranda's phone. She pulled it from her purse and glanced at the screen.

"Excuse me. I need to take this." She pressed the phone to her ear and turned her back to Denny. "Amy, were you able to get through to Lori Switzer?"

"No. I talked to her assistant again, Maggie. You're not going to like this. Lori died yesterday morning."

Miranda rocked her head back as she recalled Nancy

Vernon's threat. *I'm not yet finished with the people in this town, but thanks to you, I'm forced to accelerate things.* "Go on."

"She took a flight out of Philly bound for Spain. Somewhere over the Atlantic, there was an explosion on the plane. It ruptured the fuselage and several passengers were ejected, including Lori. They've been declared lost at sea. It's all over the news. Do you think Nancy Vernon could've caused that?"

Something materialized in Miranda's peripheral vision. She shot a sidelong glance at the house. The Vernon girls, Carla and Natalie, were sitting on the cellar doors staring back at her.

"I'm almost certain of it," Miranda replied.

"Maggie was in tears on the phone. She unloaded on me about how Lori's eight-year-old grandson is dying of a brain tumor and how the family is devastated and she's—"

"Matt," Miranda blurted.

"What?"

"Matthew Meade."

"The boy who had the visions? Are you sure?"

Miranda faced the girls. "There were other children at the cancer center. Other boys who were terminally ill. You didn't just seek out Matt because he reminded you of your brother. You knew he was related to one of your mother's targets. It all makes sense now. Adults couldn't see you, only Matt. Until I came along."

Carla—or was it Natalie?—nodded. "And now his mom is next. You need to go now."

"Where are they?"

"Are you still talking to me?" Amy asked.

"Carla and Natalie."

"The Vernon girls? Are they there with you?"

"They were."

"Randy, what's happening?"

"Elias Gray is dead."

"*What?*"

"I'll explain later. I need you to call Tammy and find out Matt's home address. Tell her about Lori, but not Elias. The police are still investigating his death. Make it clear that Matt's mother is in danger. She's going to attempt suicide today. By the time I get back to the hotel, I want both of you ready to move. I need all hands on deck for this."

Miranda ended the call and turned to Denny. "That includes you. If you want proof of everything I've told you, and you want to save a life, follow me."

"YOU HAVE ARRIVED AT YOUR DESTINATION."

Miranda pulled in behind Denny's unmarked Dodge Charger, its red and blue lights flashing from the rear window and bumper.

Unlike the rural area where Tammy and Elias lived, the Meades resided in a typical suburban development of cookie-cutter homes with gray or almond siding and two-car garages surrounded by perfectly manicured lawns.

"Boring neighborhood," Eddie remarked. "I bet nothing happens here."

Miranda climbed out of the driver's seat. "The day is still young."

The nearest cross street was a busy two-lane highway complete with speeding cars and tractor trailers.

"If you're going to put in an upscale development," Amy said. "Why would you build right up to that? The noise must be unbearable."

"Now what?" Denny asked as he approached the group.

"Well, I'm the last person these people want to see on their doorstep."

"April, stop!"

The shout was followed by the crash of broken glass.

"Did that come from their house?" Amy asked.

"Nancy's already here." Miranda took off on a dead run for the front door. She found it unlocked and charged inside.

Denny was close behind her. "You can't just barge into someone's house."

"Arrest me later." She darted toward the sound of scuffling. Denny followed her through the dining room and into the kitchen where Robert lay on the floor, his forehead bloody.

"April, what are you doing?" he cried.

Standing over him, his wife held an iron skillet. She leered at Miranda. "How did you figure it out?" As it had been with Ginny, the voice was Nancy Vernon's. Miranda held out a pleading hand. "Nancy, all the people that destroyed your family are dead now. There's no need to kill anyone else. This family is suffering enough."

"Don't you tell me about suffering."

"Shut up!" Heat rose in Miranda's face as her words tumbled out. "I've had enough of your shit. Do you think you're the only one who lost someone they love? I'm tired of trying to reason with you. Life isn't fair. Suck it up. These people don't owe you a goddamn thing. This ends right now."

"No, but it will in a minute." April hurled the skillet and threw open the back door. Miranda ducked as the cookware sailed past her head. She peeked through the curtains at the kitchen window to see April running straight for the highway.

"Dammit!" Miranda leapt over Robert and took off after his wife, ignoring Denny's angry shouts.

Outside, April stopped at the edge of the road and turned to face Miranda. She spread her arms wide. "Now, it's over." With a smile, she stepped backward into traffic.

CHAPTER 18

A CHILD FOR A CHILD

Its horn blaring, the red pickup swerved as Miranda charged onto the highway just ahead of the tractor trailer bearing down on April. Without hesitation, she tackled the woman around the waist. Both were off their feet as they barreled into the left lane and toppled onto the hood of a gold BMW. It screeched to a halt, hurling them to the asphalt in a tangle of limbs.

Someone screamed. There were shouts. Miranda opened her eyes. A face hovered over her. "Colin?"

"You give a whole new meaning to go play in traffic. You have three kids. What were you thinking?"

"I'm not letting Nancy claim another life."

"At the expense of your own? Do you think mom can handle losing another child?"

"Then help me, Colin. Do something. Please."

Her brother faded from view as Tammy knelt beside her. "Jesus, Mary, and Joseph. I thought I killed you both."

"I'm fine," Miranda groaned. "Just help me up."

"You're not moving until an ambulance gets here."

"That might be a while." Denny appeared beside Tammy.

"Some of the major roads are flooded out, not to mention fallen trees. I can't believe what you did. That was stupid."

"How's April?"

"About the same as you," Tammy said. "Could be worse. What the hell happened?"

Miranda winced as she propped herself up on her elbows. April was sitting with her back against the concrete divider. Robert was at her side, blood-stained gauze taped across his forehead. Denny waved traffic by in the right lane. Gritting her teeth against the stabbing pain in her knee and shoulder blade, Miranda struggled to her feet.

"You shouldn't move," Tammy warned.

"I grew up with an older brother who tossed me around like a rag doll. I can take a few bumps."

She limped over to April with assistance from Tammy. The woman's navy-blue Capri pants were torn over one bloody knee. Her left forearm was discolored with bruises and already beginning to swell.

April glared up at them. Despite her injuries, her face betrayed no pain at all. Nancy Vernon was still in there. "You think this is over, blondie? I warned you what would happen if you interfered with me." She nodded toward Tammy. "Did you tell her about Elias yet?"

Robert frowned. "Who's Elias?"

"Tell me what?" Tammy asked.

"Your new boyfriend is dead." April smirked. "Seems he succumbed to the guilt of his crimes and shot himself in the head last night."

Robert stared wide-eyed at his wife. "April, what are you talking about?"

"How did you know that?" Denny asked her.

"I'm sorry, Tammy," Miranda said. "I was going to tell you, but there was no time. I had to get here and stop her."

"And you haven't done that either." Nancy continued.

"There's someone else in that house. A boy near death, just like my own son was. Adam died alone in that hospital because of a false accusation. It's what pushed Jeff over the edge. I think it's only fair I repay that favor. Wouldn't you agree?"

Miranda shook her head. "No. You need to move on. Matt has nothing to do with this."

Robert glared up at Miranda and Tammy. "What the hell are you talking about?"

April's head slumped forward.

"Oh my God." Robert reached out to steady her.

Tammy pressed two fingers against the woman's neck. "She has a pulse. It's strong. I need to get my first-aid kit."

"Nancy left her," Miranda said. "She's going after Matt. I need to get back in that house. You two stay here with April. She needs more help than I do."

"You're not going anywhere except in an ambulance," Denny said. "We need to get April off the street, it's too dangerous here." He tapped the hood of Tammy's car. "Ma'am, I want you to pull around the corner."

While Denny waved oncoming traffic to a stop, Tammy and Robert lifted April and carried her off the road. Miranda limped along behind them.

"Be right back." Tammy returned to her car and drove off.

Denny signaled traffic to proceed as Eddie and Amy hurried to Miranda's side.

Screeching sirens in the distance grew louder as an ambulance rounded the corner at the far intersection. April groaned and began sobbing.

"What happened in the house, Robert?" Miranda asked.

"I don't need to tell you anything."

"Then tell *me*," Denny said.

"I don't know." Robert shrugged. "One minute she was fine, loading the dishwasher and the next she was upset. It was like flipping a switch. She said she couldn't live like this anymore and wanted to kill herself. First, she broke a drinking glass and tried to slit her wrist with it. I managed to stop her, but then she hit me with the skillet. That's when you two showed up."

"She wasn't herself." Miranda said. "Once her injuries are treated, she'll be back to normal."

"Why were you calling her Nancy?"

Robert's question was drowned by the blaring siren of the ambulance as it came to a stop. Miranda stepped back as Denny engaged the EMTs. She leaned toward Eddie and Amy. "Help me into the house."

With all attention on April, the trio slipped away unnoticed.

They made it as far as the living room before the air turned frigid. "Do you feel that?" Amy asked. "I take it that's not the air conditioning."

Miranda glanced up the steps to the second floor. "It's coming from up there. Nancy's here. I need to find Matt's room." She pulled away from Amy and Eddie and leaned against the newel post at the bottom of the stairs. "This could get dangerous. I can't ask you to go with me."

"You don't have to ask," Eddie said.

"Besides," Amy added. "You know the drill. No one goes anywhere alone."

They held out their arms.

"OK, but let me go in first and scope it out."

A few minutes later, Miranda came to an abrupt halt on the second floor. "I'll be damned."

Jeff Vernon made his way toward the end of the hall. *To Matt's room, I'll bet.* He appeared confused, disoriented.

"What do you see?" Eddie asked.

"Someone who shouldn't be here."

"Hey!" Robert bellowed from the bottom of the stairs. "Where the hell do you think you're going?"

"To save your son," Miranda said.

He took the steps two at a time with Denny on his heels. "Like hell you are." He pushed his way past Eddie and Amy and backed Miranda against the wall. "I want some goddamn answers. What the fuck happened out there and what do you want with my family?"

Denny stepped in front of Robert and spoke in a slow, measured tone. "Sir, I understand you're upset, but this woman just saved April's life. I need you to calm down."

After a moment, Robert held up his hands. "Fine. Since when are the cops using psychics?"

"Ms. Lorensen is consulting with me on this case only."

"Well, can your consultant give me an explanation? I think I deserve that much."

Miranda leaned against Eddie as her injured knee gave out. "The truth, Robert, is that your wife was possessed by the spirit of a woman named Nancy Vernon."

"Who the hell is that?"

She told him, summarizing as best she could. "I'm very sorry for the loss of your mother-in-law, but Lori conspired to frame Nancy's husband, Jeff, for embezzlement and—"

"And he went crazy and shot his kids, then killed himself," Robert finished. "I remember the story now. His wife committed suicide shortly after."

"Nancy and Jeff had a son named Adam who, like Matt, had an inoperable brain tumor. He died alone in the hospital. The day he and his family were to visit Adam for the last time, the police arrived to arrest Jeff for a crime he never committed. Nancy wants to make sure your son dies alone like Adam. For her, it's payback."

Robert shook his head. "I don't believe what I'm hearing. This is bullshit. None of you freaks are getting anywhere near my son. I'm going to check on him right now, and when I come out, I want you all gone."

He stormed past her but was hurled back by an invisible force, taking Eddie with him. They plunged down the steps, bouncing off the railing and wall before landing in a crumpled heap. Denny charged after them.

With a gasp, Eddie turned over and lay on his back. "You call this ghost hunting?"

"Amy, go make sure he's OK," Miranda said.

"What about you?"

"I can take it from here—alone."

"You can't go up against Nancy in your condition."

Miranda twisted her lips in a wry grin. "Maybe I'm motivated by guilt and an obsessive need for redemption."

"I'm never going to live that down, am I?"

Eddie sat with his back against the front door, while Denny struggled to move Robert. He lay on his side, trembling and sweating as if exerting himself yet he was utterly still.

"Sir, are you all right?"

"I can't move. It's like something's pinning me down."

That would be Nancy. Miranda hobbled into Matt's bedroom. Jeff stood at the foot of the boy's bed. Matt was asleep. With any luck, Miranda could end this without disturbing him.

"What are you doing here?" she whispered. "More to the point, *how* are you here?"

"I don't know. I was reminiscing about Adam in my house and the next thing I know, I'm here." He looked down at Matt and frowned. "Who is this boy?"

"My final revenge." Nancy stood in the doorway. As she sauntered over to stand beside the bed, the door slammed closed behind her. The air turned frigid. Miranda could see her breath.

"Nancy, what have you done?" Jeff asked.

"I killed them all, Jeff. Every one of those fucking liars who destroyed our family."

"I don't understand."

"Our son died alone. I think a little retribution is in order."

Jeff held up a hand. "No, wait. This is wrong. I never wanted any of this. You made your point with the others, but this boy is innocent—"

"So were our girls. So was I, but that didn't stop you."

Jeff fell silent. Nancy seemed to regard this as a minor victory. "That's why I trapped you in our old house all this time, Jeff. So I could get even with them on my own and keep you away from Adam. You'll never understand a mother's instinct to protect her children."

Jeff took a step toward Nancy. "You kept Adam from me?"

"It took every ounce of strength to hold you there, but I wanted you to see this one, Jeff. The last one."

"Where is Adam?" he seethed.

"That's all you ever cared about, isn't it? What about the rest of us?"

"Dad? Mom? What's going on?" In the far corner of the room, Natalie and Carla materialized.

"It's all right, girls," Nancy said. "We're just chatting about your brother."

"Are you finally going to let Dad see him?"

Jeff approached his daughters and lowered himself to one knee. Both girls flinched as he placed gentle hands on their shoulders. "Natalie, Carla, do you know where Adam is?"

Carla gazed past Jeff, eye wide. Nancy shook her head.

Jeff pushed a lock of her hair behind her ear and placed a

finger under her chin until she met his gaze. "Carla, please. I'm begging you."

"Don't answer him," Nancy commanded.

"Has Adam been with Mom all this time?"

Carla nodded. "But we weren't allowed to say anything."

"You can tell me where he is then?"

"If you tell him, I'll kill this boy." Nancy pointed to Matt.

"No!" the girls shouted.

"I know the two of you have been talking to him," Nancy said. "Warning him about every move I make." She glared at Miranda. "And getting her involved." Then to Jeff, "This is our chance to get even. Let this boy die alone. Let his family feel the pain that destroyed ours, that destroyed you."

"You were always the strong one, Nancy." Jeff stood and drew his shoulders back. He smiled at Miranda. "Please find my son."

With that, he lunged at Nancy.

And the room exploded.

CHAPTER 19

LAST DANCE

Miranda arched her back against the razor-sharp pain between her shoulder blades. She dug her nails into the carpet. A kaleidoscope of light and shadow swirled beyond her clenched eyelids. Around her, Matt's bedroom had become an ethereal war zone between husband and wife. She opened her eyes as a full-length mirror took flight, flipping end over end on a collision course with a bookcase across the room. Action figures and stuffed animals pelted her from every direction, passing right through a familiar figure kneeling over her.

She reached up for her brother. "Colin. You're really here?"

"You need to get on your feet," he said.

"I don't know if I can. Jeff and Nancy are draining my energy to fuel their battle."

"There's no giving up now. You can do this." He grinned. "It's as easy as jumpin' out of a tree."

"Will you be there to catch me?"

"Have I ever let my little sister down? If Jeff and Nancy are draining you, what do you think they're doing to that kid? His life is slipping away. He's gonna die alone, just like I did."

Like a ragdoll lifted by an invisible hand, Matt began levitating.

"No, he isn't." Miranda shielded her face as the window shattered above her. She scrambled across the floor on her hands and knees, ducking a whirlwind of children's books and DVDs. She wrapped an arm around Matt's waist and lowered him to the bed.

"Mom," he whispered. There was no fear in his weary eyes, no acknowledgement of the spectral conflict erupting around him—only peace. The peace felt by someone preparing to die.

"I'm here, sweetie."

"What's going on? There were people here. Was I dreaming?"

"Yes," Miranda said. "It's all a dream."

Natalie and Carla sat in the corner huddled in each other's arms. Colin was nowhere in sight. Miranda wondered if he had truly been there, or if her imagination conjured him up to give her the courage to finish this.

"Look out!" one of the girls cried.

Miranda threw herself over Matt, shielding him from the floor lamp that sailed over her head like a javelin and crashed against the wall. It snapped in half and fell across her back before sliding to the floor.

"Girls, where's your brother?"

Natalie and Carla shook their heads.

"Please. You know where he is. If we can bring him here, maybe he could help us stop your parents."

One of the girls stepped forward and reached out. Keeping one arm around Matt, Miranda took her hand.

"HE'S PROBABLY HIDING in that stupid fort that Dad built for him. He's always in there."

"What else is new? I'll go get him."

One of the twins trudged off, dried leaves crunching underfoot. The sky was overcast and the chill of late October raised goosebumps along Miranda's bare legs and arms.

It's always autumn here.

The stabbing pain between her shoulder blades was gone. The swollen, discolored bruise on her leg had vanished.

"Carla, hurry up!" Natalie demanded.

Her sister peeked into one of the fort's windows and muttered to Adam.

"I don't want to come out," he insisted.

"Mommy and Daddy are fighting. You have to help us stop them."

"Mom said I'm not supposed to talk to that woman, and neither are you."

"We can trust her. She's trying to save the other boy."

"What other boy?"

Carla stomped her foot. "His name is Matt and he's been sick, just like you were, and Mommy's trying to hurt him. Daddy wants to stop her and so do we."

"That's not true!" Adam cried. "Mom wouldn't hurt anyone. She told me Dad was the one who hurt her and you and that's why she won't let me see him."

Beside Miranda, Natalie sighed. "This is getting nowhere."

"Maybe I should try." Miranda sauntered over to the fort and placed a hand on Carla's shoulder. The girl moved aside as Miranda knelt down and peeked over the top of the fort. Adam sat with his back against the wall, refusing to meet her gaze.

"Hello, Adam."

"I'm not supposed to talk to you."

"I heard, but your sisters have been chatting with me for

274

days. They helped me save some people's lives. Would you like to help save people, Adam?"

He shrugged. "I don't know."

"Adam, please," Natalie said. "Matt's very sick. He hasn't got long to live and if we don't stop Mommy and Daddy from fighting, he'll die alone without *his* mommy and daddy there to say goodbye."

"That would be terrible," Miranda added. "Wouldn't it, Adam?"

The boy rose to his feet and stepped out of the fort. In a voice that conveyed more sorrow than any child should have to bear, he replied, "I can't think of anything worse."

STANDING at the foot of the bed, Adam stared in wonder at the aftermath of his parents' battle. The violence had ceased, leaving an uneasy silence in its wake. Miranda knew that Jeff and Nancy were watching, invisible but not absent. Undoubtedly, they had all but squandered their energy. Yet, the air in the room remained thick with the intensity of their rage—and the infinite sorrow that drove it.

Adam made his way to Matt's bedside. "Are you his mom?"

Under Miranda's bruised and swollen arm, Matt's chest rose and fell as he drifted in and out of consciousness. "No."

"Where is she?"

"In the hospital. She was badly hurt."

"Did my mom do it?"

Miranda shot a sidelong glance at Natalie and Carla. "Yes."

"Why?"

"You'll have to ask her."

"What about his dad?"

"Your mom won't let him in."

"Why not?"

"She's very angry."

"Why?"

"You'll have to ask her."

"I don't know where she is."

"I'm here, Adam." Nancy materialized a few steps behind her son.

Adam turned to face her. "Is Dad here, too? Natalie and Carla said Dad was here."

"Move away from the bed, Adam."

"Why?"

"I want to see Matt."

"Why can't I stay here?"

"Because I said so."

"You're fine where you are, Adam," Miranda said.

Nancy glared at her. "I thought I told you to mind your own business."

"You don't have the energy to stop me."

"You'd be surprised what I can do."

The heated exchange confused Adam. "Natalie and Carla said you wanted to hurt him."

Nancy shifted her burning gaze to her daughters. "Of course not, why would they say that?"

Rather than shrink away, the girls joined their brother, flanking him in defiance of their mother and obstructing her access to Matt.

Good for you.

Nancy seemed to sense Miranda's satisfaction. "I see you've managed to turn my children against me."

"What happened to you and your family was horrible, and you have every right to be furious, but we both know that taking it out on this family won't change any of that."

"I don't have a choice."

"Of course you do. You can move on."

Nancy shook her head. "I'm not finished yet."

"Yes, you are." Jeff's voice boomed from everywhere. Behind Nancy, the wall undulated as a portal opened but rather than a warm, inviting glow, this one was an ominous gray that emanated misery and hopelessness. Nancy charged toward Matt's bed—or tried to. An unseen force dragged her back toward the portal. She threw herself to her knees and grabbed Adam's outstretched hand, pulling him with her. Natalie and Carla threw their arms around their brother, holding him in place.

Once teeming with hatred, Nancy's gaze now held only sorrow. "I did it all for you. Please forgive me." With that, her hand slipped from her son's grasp and she was gone. It felt like an eternity before her screams faded. Jeff was there now, standing to one side of the portal.

"Dad!" Adam ran to him, tears streaking his face. Jeff dropped to his knees and for the first time in thirty-three years, father and son embraced.

"I never thought I'd see you again." Jeff waved his daughters forward. "Come here, all of you."

Adam peered up at the portal. "What happened to Mom?"

"It's hard to explain, but she and I need to leave for a while. I just wanted to see you one more time to tell you how much I love you and no matter where I am or where you are, I'll always be with you."

"Will I ever see you again?"

"I promise."

Adam threw his arms around Jeff. "I love you, Dad."

Jeff closed his eyes and pulled his son close. "Go with your sisters now. They'll take you home, OK?"

Adam stepped back. With a final wave to Miranda, the Vernon children vanished.

Jeff rose to his feet. "I'm sorry for everything you went through because of us."

Despite the twinge in her back, Miranda shrugged. "It was enlightening, if nothing else."

"Maybe we'll have another dance someday."

She smiled. "Sounds like a plan."

Jeff nodded toward Matt with a solemn expression. "He doesn't have much time. He should be with his family."

With that, he stepped through the portal. After it vanished, Miranda slumped against Matt's bed. Behind her, the bedroom door opened.

"Randy?" Eddie poked his head in. "Oh, shit."

Robert barged past him, gaping as he took in the state of the room. "Christ, what the hell did you do?" He hurried to his son's bedside. "Matt?"

After a moment, the boy opened his eyes. "Dad."

"How are you feeling?"

"They were here. All of them this time, not just the girls."

"Who was here?"

"The Vernons."

By now, Amy and Denny had joined Eddie in the doorway. As Matt closed his eyes and drifted off once more, Robert lowered his son's hand and gestured toward the hallway. After closing the door behind him, he aimed a finger at Miranda. "What the hell did you do in there? It looks like a goddamn tornado hit that room."

"Sounded like a war from out here," Denny said.

"It was," Miranda confirmed. "But it's over now. The Vernons have moved on."

"The Vernons," Robert spat. "Don't give me that shit again. I'm so friggin' close to filing charges against you."

"For what?"

Robert counted off on his fingers as he spoke. "Vandalism,

trespassing, harassment, endangering my son, oh, and not to mention assaulting my wife."

"She *saved* your wife," Eddie said.

"Shut up, kid," Robert snapped. "Adults are talking, or at least this one is, the one who lives in reality." Then, to Denny. "And what the hell good are you, letting these freaks disrupt my family and tear my house apart? My son is dying. Do you think I need this shit? Get the fuck out of here and leave my family in peace or I will sue all of you for every goddamn penny you have. Do I make myself clear?"

OUTSIDE, Miranda found herself in Eddie's arms once again as she limped along the walkway toward the curb. With every step, pain flared through her neck and shoulders. *What I wouldn't give for an out of body experience right now.*

"I'm taking you to the hospital with me," Denny said.

Miranda ignored him. "What happened to you guys while I was in the room?"

"After you went in there *alone*," Amy began. "Eddie and I tried to follow but something pinned us against the wall."

"Same here," Denny added. "But after all the noise in the kid's bedroom stopped, we were... let go, I guess you'd say. Robert flew up the steps as soon as I helped him off the floor. Ms. Lorensen, are you going to let me take you to the hospital or do I need to arrest you?"

Eddie shook his head. "You know, I feel bad for that guy, but what an ungrateful douche bag."

"Robert is scared and exhausted," Miranda said. "He's already mourning his son."

"I don't think he understands what happened today any more than I do," Denny said. "He wouldn't be out of bounds to file charges."

"Randy did not assault his wife," Amy insisted. "You were there."

"Of course not, but it would be hard to dispute the vandalism charge, not to mention endangering a minor. There were no credible witnesses to say otherwise."

Miranda threw up a scratched and battered arm. "Jeez flippin' Louise! You're the one insisting I go to the hospital. Do I look like I'm in any shape to inflict that much damage to a room? Oh, that's right, I was hit by a freakin'...'"

Miranda's gaze fell on the gold Mercedes parked in front of Denny's unmarked patrol car. "Where's Tammy?"

Heads and bodies turned in every direction. Tammy was nowhere in sight.

"I don't know," Amy said. "She wasn't in the house."

"Eddie, turn me around... gently."

"Did you see something?"

Miranda's father stood beside the Meades' house. The expression on his face was grim as he nodded toward the backyard.

"Behind the house?" Miranda said.

"What?"

"Tammy's behind the house and I think she's in trouble."

"On it." Amy bolted off with Denny on her heels.

As they passed Miranda's father, he lowered his head and vanished.

"Eddie, get me back there *fast*."

MIRANDA HEARD Amy's frantic voice even before she and Eddie rounded the privacy fence. Tammy lay drenched on the concrete beside the in-ground pool. Denny rolled her over onto her back and checked for a pulse. He began CPR while Amy called for an ambulance. Miranda pulled away from

Eddie and limped the short distance across the patio. She fell to her knees beside Tammy.

Amy lowered her phone, clothes and hair dripping. "I found her floating face down in the pool. No idea why she was in there."

"I know why." Miranda took Tammy's hand in hers and made no effort to hold back her tears. *This is my fault. I didn't listen. Just like with Colin, my abilities failed me. God, please don't take someone else from me. Don't trade her life for the ones we saved here.* "Don't let it end this way."

Tammy's body convulsed. She squeezed Miranda's fingers as her eyes bulged open. Denny backed off as she inhaled covetously the humid summer air before launching into a fit of coughing and gagging. Her body shuddered as she flopped onto her side and curled into a fetal position.

"Let her clear her lungs for a minute." Denny said. "She needs to get as much water out as possible."

"What hap—" Tammy's attempt to speak only resulted in another violent bout of hacking.

"Don't talk, ma'am," Denny said. "Just breathe. Ambulance is on its way."

Tammy settled into a steady but voracious panting.

Miranda leaned forward, brushed aside her friend's matted auburn locks, and kissed her lightly on the forehead. "Welcome back."

"What happened?" Tammy wheezed.

"A parting gift from Nancy Vernon."

CHAPTER 20

PANCAKES

I t was well past sunset by the time Miranda had been discharged from the hospital. Tammy would not be released until the following morning. They wanted to check for possible brain damage and pneumonia, although the early prognosis indicated no reason for alarm. Tammy had been cognizant enough to send Amy across the street to the cancer center for a duffle bag of clothes she had stashed in her office.

Detective Teelko had informed Miranda that he would call her the next day. He had no idea how to report the events at the Meades' house and had decided to sleep on it. Whether he believed in Miranda's abilities or the fact that a ghost had been responsible for multiple suicides was another matter, but at least he had softened up to her.

Lying atop the creaky bed in her hotel room, Miranda lifted her leg and scratched just above the brace that sheathed her knee thanks to a minor patella fracture. Then there was the brace on her sprained ankle. Her left arm was in a sling, compliments of a hairline fracture of her scapula. All told, she was lucky. A few weeks of physical therapy should have her up and around in time for the school year. *What a way to end the summer. Eddie's right. You call this ghost hunting?*

It could've been worse. At least every member of the team would be returning home in one piece. They had saved some lives, but others had been lost—Ginny's father, Elias Gray, Lori Switzer. Perhaps Miranda could have saved them too had she acted sooner, had she paid more attention.

Someone else was in the room now, sitting on the other bed, staring at her. She forced herself up. "Matt."

"I saw the light again today, just like it came to the others. Not the cold, gray light that took Natalie and Carla's parents. This was bright and warm. It was for me this time."

Miranda began to weep. She reached out to him with her uninjured arm. Matt slipped off the bed and took her hand.

"Don't cry. My dad told me why my mom couldn't be there. He said you saved her, and that she's gonna be OK when she got out of the hospital."

"Yeah. She will."

"Wanna see where I'm going?"

SHE FOUND HERSELF STANDING, unscathed and pain-free, at the edge of the clearing. The ground was covered in a carpet of orange, gold, and red. A temperate breeze rustled the trees, sending more leaves into a twirling descent, their colors made more vibrant as they passed through sunbeams that would never dim, never darken. Not here.

Matt stood beside Miranda, still holding her hand. He pointed to the fort, Adam's hideout. Somehow it seemed larger than before. Enough room for friends.

"Isn't that cool?" Matt said.

"Sure is."

Adam poked his head up from the top of the fort. "Matt,

come on. My sisters will be back soon, and I want to scare 'em with our Halloween masks."

"I gotta go," Matt said.

"Of course." Despite her tears, Miranda laughed as she released his hand. "You have important things to do."

Matt started off toward the fort. Halfway there, he turned and ran back to Miranda. She lowered herself to one knee as he threw his arms around her and kissed her on the cheek.

Don't start crying again, woman.

"Thank you," he whispered.

"You're welcome," Miranda said to thin air as warm tears trailed down the side of her face and dripped onto the bed.

Pushing the wheelchair aside, she hopped over to the desk, opened her laptop, and scrolled through the latest vacation pictures posted online by her daughter. Her kids had concluded their whirlwind tour of Europe in Madrid at World Youth Day. They would be home tomorrow night. *Not soon enough.*

IN THE ADJOINING ROOM, Eddie and Amy sat on one of the double beds, channel surfing and eating room service pizza.

"You think we should check on Randy?" Amy asked.

"She said she wanted to be alone for a while. She'll text us if she needs something. You know, I wonder how much of this case I'll be allowed to post on our website."

"The best you can hope for is the footage from Elias Gray's house. No one would believe the other stuff. Maybe if you changed his name to protect his privacy, Randy would OK it."

"What privacy? The dude's dead."

Amy scrunched her face in a look of annoyance. "Do you

have no respect at all? I mean, do you really think Ginny's going to find your attitude charming?"

Eddie's brow furrowed. "What?"

"You *are* going to call her, right?"

"Uh, well. I think so."

"You think so? You've had my number for months and you never called me."

"What?"

"You heard me."

"Well, yeah, everyone on the team has each other's numbers. It only makes sense if there's an emergency or a new hot spot to check out, we—"

Amy grabbed the front of Eddie's T-shirt and pulled him close. "Shut up already."

His eyes flew open as she pressed her lips to his. Somewhere beyond the sound of his racing pulse, a pizza box dropped to the floor, someone on TV was babbling about Nazi stolen art, and Miranda was buzzing his phone. Eddie didn't give a damn.

By the time Amy pulled back, Eddie was near suffocation. "Are you all right?"

Eddie slowed his breathing in a feeble attempt to regain his cocky façade. "You taste like pepperoni."

"Is that a complaint?"

"Not at all. I'll take seconds."

BEFORE CHECKING out of the hotel the following morning, Miranda received a call from Denny bright and early. To her relief, April Meade had suffered only a shattered patella and a mild concussion. She would recover after knee surgery tomorrow. Tammy would not be charged in the accident.

Matt's funeral would take place in three days. Miranda wanted to attend the viewing, but thought better of it.

"I'm just curious," she said. "What did you put in your report?"

"Only the events that occurred outside the house, because that's all I witnessed. You saved Mrs. Meade's life and Dr. Schell, who was coming to look in on her former patient, was unable to get a response at the front door of the Meades' home. When she went around back, she began to feel light-headed, possibly from the shock of the earlier accident. She stumbled and collapsed, falling into the pool where she lay unconscious and nearly drowned until found by Amy Healy and me. I already discussed this with Dr. Schell before calling you and she agreed that's exactly what happened."

Miranda chuckled. "That's some creative writing."

"Well, it's a hell of a lot more plausible to my superiors than ghostly possession."

"What do you believe?"

Denny left the question hanging in silence for a moment. "The jury's still out on that. I should tell you, there may be more questions down the line."

"Well, you know where to find me. Give my best to Ginny."

After hanging up, Miranda checked her messages. Tammy had called while she was on the phone with the lieutenant. She had been discharged at four in the morning with a clean bill of health. She insisted that Miranda and the team stop by her house for breakfast on their way home.

When they arrived, Tammy greeted them in her driveway. She hung her head as Eddie pulled the wheelchair from the trunk and brought it around to the passenger door. "Oh my God, I am so sorry. Is *everything* broken?"

"Nope," Miranda said. "Just sprained and fractured."

"What can I do to help?"

"You didn't happen to make pancakes, did you?"

Twenty minutes and two stacks of pancakes later, the four were seated at Tammy's kitchen table.

"How did you feel right after you found out about Elias?" Miranda asked.

Tammy stared at her glass of cranberry juice for a moment. "To be honest, it didn't sink in right away. I was still too distracted by the fact that I'd just run you and April down with my car. All I cared about was getting you both to safety. Then I pulled around the corner and as I started walking up toward the Meades' house, this feeling of hopelessness and dread overwhelmed me. Correction, it assaulted me. I don't think I ever felt that much despair in my life. It was as if the will to live was just ripped out of me."

"Nancy Vernon got in your head, although you probably didn't realize it until it was over. You felt bad about Elias. She made you feel worse."

Tammy exhaled, puffing her cheeks. "What now? Did you get a call from that cop?"

"Yeah, he read his report to me over the phone and told me about Matt. God bless him. He's in a better place."

"One of my most adorable patients." They ate in silence for a few minutes before Tammy turned to Eddie. "So, are we OK after that little bathroom incident?"

"Oh, uh, yeah." His face reddened. "I mean, yeah, we're cool."

Amy glanced from Eddie to Tammy. "Seriously, what did I miss?"

EPILOGUE

The sunlight was almost blinding as it shone through the windshield of Colin's car. He pulled out of the garage, braking for a wild rabbit that darted across the driveway. He leaned over the steering wheel and watched as it ducked beneath a lavender plant in the neighbor's front yard.

"I wish you'd stop and listen to me for a change," Miranda muttered as Colin turned onto the street.

"Of course." He eased the car to the right and parked along the curb. "So, what should we talk about?"

Miranda clutched her brother's arm. "You can see me now?"

"Well, considering that we're having this conversation." Colin flashed that lopsided grin that Miranda missed so much. It was the way he always smiled when he was happy. "I've been watching you these past few days. You did good. Saved a lot of lives."

Miranda lowered her gaze. "Still, others died."

"You can't save the world."

"I never wanted to save the world, just you."

Colin nodded. "It's generally easier to save someone from being victimized by others than it is to save them from themselves."

"Meaning?"

"You were always there for me when I needed you. You were the only one who understood me. God knows Mom didn't, and Rebecca had to take care of the children practically alone during this last year. She did her best to shield them from my... problems."

"Mom doesn't have the capacity to understand depression, or she just refused to," Miranda said.

"And despite the fact that you understood, there was still nothing you could do to save me. I didn't care about living anymore. I went to bed every night hoping I'd never wake up the next day. You can't imagine what that's like."

"No, I can't." After a moment of silence, Miranda continued. "Dad came to see me a few days ago. He said you were distressed because of me."

"I am. You're holding me here in this moment, in this car, on this day. You weren't even here when it happened. I need to move on, Randy, and it would help me greatly if you would, too."

"You don't understand. I have this ability to see things that most people can't—past events or brief flashes of what's to come." She squeezed his hand. "Conversations with people on the other side. I use this gift to help total strangers but when it came to helping you, it failed me."

Miranda sobbed as she continued. "Don't you think if I'd known what you were going to do, I would've run to your house and tied you to a chair or tackled you to the ground and held you there for as long as it took to—"

"To what? To convince me that suicide isn't worth it?"

"Yes!"

"It would have happened at another time in some other

fashion. You can't always be by my side. The meds weren't doing anything for me, and therapy was going nowhere. What next, institutionalize me? That's no life and neither is existing in this moment."

Colin pounded on the steering wheel with his palm. "You don't belong here. This was the end of my journey. You still have a long way to go. So, please, get out of my car and get on with your life. You have an amazing gift, Randy. Make a difference as only my little sister can."

"What about you?"

He smiled. "I'm going home."

Miranda tilted her head to glance past Colin as a familiar silver Buick rolled past and parked in front of them. Her father emerged from the driver's seat. She lowered her window as he approached. He reached in and wiped a tear from her face.

"How's my Miranda Panda?"

"You tell me."

"Well, despite the fact that you didn't listen to your old man and almost got yourself killed, you made me proud."

Miranda gave a half-hearted smile. "Funny, you never believed in my abilities when I was a kid."

"Death has a way of changing people." He opened the passenger door. "Now, out you go."

Miranda glanced at Colin one last time before stepping out of the car and into her father's arms. He kissed her on the forehead. "Give my love to the grandchildren." With that, he started back toward the Buick.

"Will I see you guys again?"

"When you need us." He ducked into the driver's seat and drove off.

Colin flashed a smile before pulling away from the curb and stopping at the intersection. Miranda steeled herself, anticipating that final left turn and the explosion a moment later when he would send his car head on into the concrete abutment. The pickup truck that had always stopped behind them in her visions came to a halt on the cross street.

What? No, that's not how it happened. Miranda stepped off the curb for a better view.

After a few seconds, the driver of the pickup waved at Colin and continued on his way. Her brother's car lurched forward through the intersection, following their dad's Buick. *I'm going home,* Colin had said.

Miranda waited in the middle of the barren street until their cars had disappeared around a bend, realizing in her heart that she had, in fact, made a difference.

ALSO BY PHIL GIUNTA

Available now from Raging Seas Press

AMERICAN BOOK FEST 2023 BEST BOOK AWARD
FINALIST

TESTING THE PRISONER

A Paranormal Mystery

Daniel Masenda thought he had made peace with his dark past when he left his home for a better life fourteen years ago. As the mayor of a small, tranquil town along Virginia's Eastern Shore, Daniel has everything he ever wanted—until a series of haunting visions, coupled with the death of his estranged mother, pits him against two ghostly entities at war with one another. Each has its own agenda as they force Daniel to relive moments from his violent youth and push him to the edge of insanity. As his idyllic life begins to unravel, will he be able to decipher the message behind the hauntings before they destroy, not only him, but the soul of someone he left behind?

"... *Testing the Prisoner* is so much more brilliant than just a terrific piece of fiction. It's about the crossroads that we all eventually end up at and the decisions we make when we get there... The character development is masterfully done, with character growth of not only the protagonist, but almost every single character in the story... And it's a damned good ghost story, too. Five stars is usually my top rating, but this one gets six. I couldn't possibly recommend it more highly. You can thank me later."

—As reviewed on Hellnotes by Carson Buckingham, author of *Too Late for Prayin'* and *Noble Rot*

ALSO BY PHIL GIUNTA

Available now from Firebringer Press

LIKE MOTHER, LIKE DAUGHTERS

A Paranormal Mystery

After her lover is found murdered during a paranormal investigation, Andrea Lorensen is determined to find the killer with some help from her lover's ghost. Meanwhile, her mother Miranda travels to Salem, Massachusetts where she reunites with the gentle spirit of a young woman executed for witchcraft in 1692. This time, however, the encounter reveals an astonishing truth about Miranda's past life —a truth that could kill her.

Read on for the opening scenes of *Like Mother, Like Daughters*...

"Phil's capture of the unique bond between a mother and a daughter is spot-on. The paranormal scenes are a splendid mix of horror and ghostly wonder... Once again, Phil has written a page-turning, eyes-wide-open, paranormal novel."

— Dawn Sooy, author of *From the Darkness*

LIKE MOTHER, LIKE DAUGHTERS

Andrea Lorensen considered giving a whole new meaning to the term "touchscreen"—with her fist.

Instead, she restrained herself to a sigh as the dashboard GPS announced for the third time that it was "recalculating." *Sure, get me this far then screw me over... bastard.* She knew it was just embarrassment and frustration getting the best of her, especially since she was now 20 minutes late. The fact that her mom was with her didn't help.

"Lost in the woods on a frigid February night. Not how I prefer to start a paranormal investigation." From the passenger seat, Miranda Lorensen glanced at her daughter. "Just saying."

"I can barely see the street signs, okay? It's pitch black out here." Andrea pulled her mother's SUV onto a dirt road and turned around. "We must have passed it."

"Again."

Andrea rolled her eyes. "Don't be a smart-ass."

"Takes one to raise one. I thought you knew how to get there."

Andrea turned left onto what qualified as the main road in this podunk town, probably because it was the only one that was paved. "I've only been to Wendy's place once for a Halloween party and I had a hard time finding it then. Can't your psychic mojo give us some direction?"

Miranda nodded toward the GPS. "That's what he's for."

As if on cue, the British baritone voice spoke up cheerfully. "In point one mile, turn left onto Pine Swamp Road."

Miranda snickered. "Now that's a name that inspires confidence. Just take it slow and let's keep our eyes open." In unison, both women perked up and pointed ahead. "There!"

The tree line parted just enough to reveal a narrow gravel road.

"Turn left," the GPS instructed.

"Now you tell me." Andrea swung the vehicle hard.

Miranda gripped the door handle with one hand while pressing her other palm against the dashboard. "Jeez, girl, who taught you how to drive?"

"You did."

"It shows."

Ahead of them, the high beams bounced and shook as they illuminated a well-traveled path of dirt and stone bordered by patches of snow and dead grass. Beyond that, more impenetrable darkness.

"And Wendy lives all alone out here?"

"Her parents own this little one story ranch. It's a tiny place, two-bedrooms, one bath. They use it as a summer getaway, but Wendy lives in it during the school year. It's haunted, or so she says."

"Right. She hears voices and her cats get spooked."

"More than that. She also sees lights in the woods behind the house, and not flashlights either. They're up high near the treetops. They just float around and then vanish. She's dealing with it, but I think she's freaked—"

"Slow down."

"Why?"

"Something's coming. I can feel it."

"Where?"

Following the curve in the road, Andrea turned the vehicle slightly to the right—and screamed as a pair of headlights suddenly flashed on directly ahead of them before swerving to the left. Andrea was momentarily blinded as she veered the SUV wildly to avoid a collision. Just as quickly, she straightened out the wheel, narrowly missing a cluster of pine trees. Finally, she stomped on the brake pedal, propelling both women toward the windshield. Andrea's seatbelt sank into her chest before her body snapped back into the seat. She turned to her mother. "You okay?"

"Fine." Miranda nodded, pushing disheveled blonde locks away from her face. She reached over and did the same for her daughter. "You?"

Andrea slapped the steering wheel. "Bastard!" She threw open the driver's side door and leapt out.

"I'll take that as a yes," Miranda muttered. She followed Andrea's gaze to the fading red glow of taillights. "They're already gone. Nothing you can do now."

Using the flashlight app on her phone, Andrea inspected all four sides of the vehicle before climbing back in. "No damage that I can see. Friggin' redneck was driving with his lights off!" She sighed and sat back in her seat. "Sorry about this."

"Not your fault. That was some quick thinking behind the wheel."

"I had a good teacher, remember?"

"Did you happen to see what kind of car it was?"

"I think it was a pickup. I caught a flash of silver." Andrea narrowed her eyes. "I wonder if that was Ross."

"Ross?"

"Wendy's boyfriend or maybe ex-boyfriend by now—you never know with her. I only talked to him once at the

Halloween party, but he picked Wendy up from campus a few times. I remember he drove a silver Chevy truck." Andrea exhaled sharply and frowned. "Mom, are you sure you're fine?"

"Yeah, why?"

"You're twirling your hair. You only do that when you're nervous. I know, because I do it, too."

Miranda dropped her hand. "Like mother, like daughter."

"I think we're both a bit rattled. Let's just get there and have a good night of ghost hunting."

As Andrea turned the SUV back onto the gravel, Miranda put a gentle hand on her forearm. "I can't pin it down, but something's wrong. I'm getting that old familiar pressure behind my eyes."

"The tunnel vision, too?"

Miranda shook her head. "Not yet, but the feeling is oppressive. The driver of that truck was running from something. Whatever it is, it's expecting us and it isn't very happy."

Andrea's shoulders slumped. "Thanks, mom. You're giving me my second scare of the night and we're not even there yet."

Wendy was waiting for them. She stood just outside the front door in a loose-fitting sweatshirt and jeans that hugged the curves of her full figure. The cuffs were tucked into thick plush boots that were all the rage with young women today. Miranda had never understood the appeal in them. The girl's fiery red hair spilled around her shoulders and chest from beneath a gray fleece cap complete with earflaps and tassels.

Even as Miranda and her daughter approached, Wendy didn't smile. Standing beneath the exterior light, she regarded them with a detached expression, her hazel eyes glazed and distant.

"Hey." Andrea threw her arms around Wendy and pulled her close, yet the other woman's posture remained rigid as she returned a tepid embrace.

Andrea pulled back. "Are you okay?"

"I have a skull-splitting headache after dealing with my ex. You just missed him."

"Only by a few inches. He damn near ran us off the road. Didn't even have his lights on until we almost collided head-on."

"Doesn't surprise me. We ended up in an argument. It was an ugly scene."

"If he was angry, that would explain his reckless driving," Miranda chimed in.

"Oh." Andrea stepped back and gestured to Miranda. "Wendy, this is my mom."

"Nice to meet you." The girl smiled wanly and extended a hand. It was gelid to the touch and for a moment, the pain behind Miranda's eyes flared sharply. It subsided as soon as their hands parted.

"Sorry if this is a bad time."

Wendy's gaze snapped into focus as she looked from Miranda to Andrea. Wincing slightly, she raised a hand to her stomach. "No, you need to be here. Tonight of all nights, I need your help."

Miranda and her daughter exchanged puzzled glances.

"Uh, sure," Andrea said. "Has there been more activity lately?"

"You could say that." Wendy opened the door. "Come on in, I'll give you a tour, although there isn't much to see. This place is just one giant box."

The living room was a narrow rectangle that spanned the entire width of the house. An entertainment center and sofa took up the left side. Behind the sofa, a vase filled with tiger lilies sat atop a half wall that opened to a small kitchen. To the right, in front of a cluttered desk, one of Wendy's cats was curled up on an office chair watching the visitors as they entered. The other cat was likely hiding elsewhere in the house.

Andrea pointed to an acoustic guitar suspended upright in its stand beside a small brick fireplace. "Oh, cool. When did you get that?"

"My mom brought that with her the last time she visited. I played a lot in high school. Don't get as much time with it anymore, but I wanted to get back into it. Actually, since it's been here, it strums every so often by itself as if someone's lightly running a finger across the strings. It only happened a few times, but I can't explain it."

"I suggest we leave a digital voice recorder on the floor in front of it," Miranda said.

Wendy led them down a narrow hallway toward the back of the house. Silhouettes of the women reflected in the glass of the storm door that opened out to the backyard and woods beyond.

Just past the bathroom, Wendy stopped and waved to her right. "I occasionally hear voices in this bedroom, which is why I sleep in the other one. I can never make out what they're saying and when I go to the doorway to listen, they shut up."

"Sounds like another candidate for a voice recorder," Andrea said. "What about the activity outside? You mentioned seeing lights in the woods."

The color vanished from Wendy's face as she turned to gaze toward the back door. When she spoke, her tone was pensive. "Yeah... there was activity out there earlier tonight, in fact."

Miranda could sense Wendy's mounting fear. Whatever awaited them, it was in the woods—and Wendy knew it.

Andrea stepped up beside her friend. "If you don't want to go outside, it's fine. My mom and I can—"

"No." Wendy lowered her head and massaged her temples. "It's just this damn headache, but I want to show you where I see the lights."

"Take your time," Miranda said in a soothing tone. "Is there something about the lights we should know?"

Wendy didn't answer right away. With a sigh, she leaned against the wall.

Miranda looked at her daughter. Andrea shrugged and shook her head. From what she had told Miranda on the way here, Wendy was not normally so withdrawn. She was known to be vivacious and cheerful. Recently, however, something had changed. Andrea didn't know what.

After a moment, Wendy raised her head. "This is going to sound crazy, but I think they show up specifically for me. That's just an impression I get because my parents and brother never see them when they stay here."

"You think they're trying to communicate with you?" Andrea asked.

"I'm not sure. Maybe you can help me figure that out tonight."

"What do they look like?"

"Small bluish orbs that hover above the trees. They never make a sound. Eventually, they fade away. It's comforting but eerie at the same time. You know this area is haunted for miles around. People have seen spirits of Indigenous People and Civil War soldiers. Twelve years ago, two hikers were murdered on the Appalachian Trail not far from here. Their souls are supposedly still roaming the woods. It's an active area."

"I can feel it," Miranda said. The pressure behind her eyes returned, blurring the edges of her vision. "There's definitely something here."

Andrea pulled a small LED flashlight from her coat

pocket. "Let's go then."

Miranda held up a hand. "Hold on. Before we explore the woods, I want to get a few things from the car." She nodded toward the spare bedroom. "Andrea, can you please leave your voice recorder in here? I'd like to put the mini DV in here, too. Wendy, would you mind if I set up my laptop on your desk?"

"No problem."

"I have a night vision camera we can take with us outside."

"Do you need help?" Andrea asked.

"No, I'm good. Just stay put. Don't venture out there until we're set up in here. We'll all go together, okay?"

Andrea waited until her mother was out of earshot. "Wendy, are you sure you're all right? You've been down for weeks and I'm really concerned."

Wendy turned her head slowly, her expression inscrutable. "We need to go out there *now*."

"You're starting to freak me out. Can we just—"

Wendy gripped her hand with surprising strength. Andrea drew in a sharp breath. "Your hand is freezing. Don't you think you should put a coat and gloves on first?"

Wendy moved toward the door, dragging Andrea behind her. "Wendy, what the hell? We should wait for my mom. She's psychic or a medium or whatever. If she thinks there's something wrong—"

"She's right," Wendy opened the door, "but it can't wait any longer."

Andrea glanced over her shoulder to the front door. "Fine. How far into the woods are we going?"

"Not far at all. He didn't have much time. I told him you were coming."

Andrea frowned. "What are you talking about?"

Wendy said no more as she stepped outside and strode across the small yard. Andrea followed her and noticed several pieces of firewood scattered across the frozen ground. She brought her flashlight to bear on the scene and noticed a half-cord of wood stacked neatly in a rectangular rack against the fence. It was obvious that one side had been disturbed.

"What happened here?"

"I was gathering wood for the fire when he showed up. I dropped some pieces during our argument. Come on."

Wendy opened the gate and hurried into the thicket.

"What's the rush?"

"You'll see."

Andrea weaved and ducked her way around bare branches while ice-frosted snow crunched under foot.

Wendy needed no illumination to make her way. For a minute, Andrea lost sight of her until the path curved to the right. There, Wendy stood with her back to Andrea, peering up into the sky.

At the lights.

Andrea gasped. "No shit." Two bluish-white orbs hovered above their heads. They seemed to pass through the branches as they glided among the trees. "Oh my God, they're just like you described."

Wendy didn't respond immediately. She seemed to be mesmerized. "They're here for me."

"What?" Andrea pulled her phone from her coat pocket and aimed it at the orbs. She took several steps forward, tracking them as they began to move out of view. When she spoke again, it was in hushed tones. She was afraid of scaring them off. "Damn it, mom, get out here with that camera. My mom got this cool night vision camera for Christmas. This is our first ghost hunt of the year and we were hoping to test it—"

Andrea turned around. Wendy was gone.

She aimed her flashlight along the path behind her. "Wendy?"

———

Miranda shook her head as she gazed down the empty hallway. She called out to Andrea and Wendy, but there was no response—which only meant one thing. "These kids have no damn patience."

Carefully pushing aside a haphazard stack of notepads and index cards, Miranda placed her laptop and mini-DV camera on Wendy's desk. She made her way toward the back door, hoping that the girls were merely waiting outside.

A distant, terrified shriek told her otherwise.

Miranda threw open the storm door and bolted across the yard. "Andrea!"

She stepped on something solid that rolled under her foot, sending her stumbling forward. Snow-patched earth rose up to meet her. Miranda yelped as her chest landed squarely on another piece of firewood. She pushed herself up just enough to slide it out from beneath her and push it away.

"Mom, where are you!"

"I'm here," Miranda croaked. Wincing against the pain, she rolled onto her side and wrapped her arms around her chest, forcing her breaths into a calm rhythm.

When she opened her eyes again, two people stood above her a few feet away. The closest was a tall, stocky man wearing a leather jacket and baseball cap. He turned away just as Miranda gazed up at him, making it impossible to see his face. The girl, however, was unmistakable.

Wendy.

She cradled a few pieces of firewood in her arms as she stared wide-eyed at the man who was shouting at her. He was young, judging by his voice.

"You're fucking with the wrong family, bitch! You better keep your goddamn mouth shut."

"I'm not talking to you about this." Wendy held up a hand as she sidestepped him and made her way toward the house. "Just get the fuck out of here, before I call the—"

"Lying whore!" In a blur of motion, the man grabbed her arm and jerked her backward toward him. He brought his other hand up to her chest and shoved her effortlessly into the rack of firewood, knocking several pieces to the ground.

Miranda reached out to the chain link fence and pulled herself to her knees, all concern for herself forgotten. No one turned to look at her. This was a vision of events that must have occurred shortly before Miranda and her daughter arrived.

Wendy cried out as she crumpled to the ground. The young man moved in and grabbed her by the hair. She picked up a hefty piece of firewood and swung, but he anticipated her. He caught it easily and yanked it from her grasp, then raised it above his head. "You're not calling anyone, bitch."

"Oh, God, no..." Miranda could only watch in disgust as he clubbed Wendy in the stomach. She groaned and doubled over, but that wasn't enough for him. He continued his assault, beating her in the back of the head even after she collapsed into the snow. He stopped only when her body began twitching.

Seconds later, that stopped too.

The man tossed the firewood aside. It landed precisely where Miranda had tripped. Despite the pain in her chest, she forced herself to her feet. "You son of a bitch."

He lifted Wendy over his shoulder and carried her beyond the yard and into the woods. Miranda watched until they vanished into the darkness.

Wendy's words from earlier came back to her. *You need to be here. Tonight of all nights, I need your help.*

"Andrea!" After following what she hoped was the right path, Miranda spotted the boots first. She slid to a halt in the snow and traced her flashlight along the body. Wendy's face was obscured by her thick mane of saffron hair, made crimson by congealing blood.

Andrea knelt over her friend. She looked up at Miranda. Her mouth hung open in confusion and horror. Tears fell from her face. "Where the hell were you? I was calling for you!" Struggling to catch her breath, she held out her hands above Wendy's prone form. "She's..."

"Dead, I know."

As Andrea broke down into quiet sobs, Miranda moved beside her and took her into her arms. "Honey, I'm so sorry. I would've been here sooner, but when I stepped outside, I... I had a vision of what happened."

Her daughter pulled back. "Tell me."

Miranda wiped the tears from Andrea's face. "It can wait. We need to—"

"No, I want to know who did this!"

Miranda hesitated. "The guy driving that truck killed Wendy in her backyard and dumped her out here just before we showed up. Problem was, it was too dark to see his face."

Andrea fell silent as she began to tremble, eyes wide. Miranda could only watch helplessly as cruel realization seized her daughter. "That means we were talking to her *ghost* the entire time?"

"That would explain a lot, like why I felt such heightened stress and fear when we first arrived, and why Wendy was so cold to the touch."

"Oh, God."

Miranda remained silent as Andrea stood and turned away. She leaned against a tree until she regained her composure. "At first, I thought she just tripped and fell, but I would have heard that. Then I saw the blood on her head... and she wasn't moving and..." Andrea doubled over, gritting her teeth. "Damn it."

Finally, she stood and ran a sleeve across her eyes. "We saw the orbs. Wendy said they were there for her."

"It's possible. They could have been the souls of just about anybody who lost their lives in these woods. Maybe they were here to shepherd Wendy to the next life, I don't know." Miranda glanced at the sky, but saw only the stars. "I really wish you'd waited for me before venturing out here."

"You're going to start on me now? It's not like I expected *this* to happen."

"Exactly. You're not experienced with the paranormal and even if you were, investigators should never go anywhere alone because you never know what to expect. You've heard me say that more than once when I bring new members onto my team. At minimum, we work in pairs."

"I can handle myself, and Wendy was with me... sort of."

Miranda held up a hand. "We'll talk about this later. Right now, we need to go inside, put the equipment back in the car, and call the cops."

Andrea shook her head. "I'm not leaving her."

"You don't have to. I'll go to the house and call from the landline. There's no cell signal out here."

"What are we going to tell them?"

"Well, they're not likely to believe that her ghost led you to her body. It's probably better to say that the house was wide open when we got here. We noticed the firewood in disarray and the back gate open so we went looking for her."

"And tell them about Ross."

"We'll tell them about the truck."

Mother and daughter shared another embrace before Miranda started back toward the house.

Andrea dropped to her knees and closed her eyes. "I'm so sorry we were late. Please forgive me. It was my fault we got lost. I'm sorry." After a silent prayer, she opened her eyes and reeled back as a bluish-white sphere, no larger than a child's fist, hovered over Wendy's body.

"Wendy?" Andrea slowly reached out, but before she could touch it, the orb floated skyward and eventually joined two others that materialized above the trees. After a few seconds, all three faded into the night.

Four hours later, Wendy's body had been removed and the property cordoned off with caution tape. In the backyard, the cops had found blood on a loose piece of firewood. It had been bagged as evidence. In the living room, Miranda sat with one arm firmly at her side and the other around her daughter. In keeping her hands away from her head, she hoped to stifle her hair-twirling habit in front of the sheriff as he reviewed their statements.

Of course, that didn't stop her from fingering a lock of Andrea's hair instead.

Finally, the sheriff nodded grimly and closed his notepad. "Well, thank you both for your help. We'll contact her family tonight. I'll be in touch if I have more questions."

"Absolutely." Miranda and her daughter rose from the sofa. "Whatever we can do, please let us know."

"Actually, sir," Andrea spoke up in a timorous voice. "Before we leave, would you mind if we feed her cats?"

"Unfortunately, ma'am, this is a crime scene now. I'm not supposed to let you touch anything," the sheriff tapped his notepad against his other hand, "but you ladies don't seem like killers to me. Just make it quick. I need to go talk to my deputy. I'll be back in a few minutes to escort you out and lock up."

In the kitchen, the women kept their voices low as they filled food and water bowls and cleaned litter pans.

"You didn't tell him about your vision in the backyard," Andrea said.

"That would only have complicated things. Besides, I didn't see the guy's face. We told the sheriff about the truck. They found the firewood. Let them do their jobs. I'm more concerned about you right now."

If you only knew... "I'll be all right. I just need time, and I think I owe you an apology."

Her mother frowned. "For what, sweetie?"

"All these years listening to your ghost stories, I never really knew whether to believe you or not."

"Oh, I know, and now that you've had your own experience, you're finally convinced that your old lady isn't an embarrassing whack-job."

"Something like that."

"If the spirits know you can see them, more will come. Most will be like Wendy, innocent lost souls just looking for help."

"Most?"

The sheriff stepped through the front door.

"We'll talk more about it later."

"Do you think I'll see her again?" Andrea whispered.

As if in response, a single, gentle strum startled both women. They turned to look at the guitar in the far corner of the living room. Even the sheriff was startled.

"I think you just got your answer."

About the Author

Phil Giunta's novels include the paranormal mysteries *Testing the Prisoner, By Your Side,* and *Like Mother, Like Daughters.* His short stories appear in such anthologies as *Love on the Edge, Beach Pulp, Space Opera Digest 2022, A Plague of Shadows, Scary Stuff,* the *Middle of Eternity* series, and more. He is a Pushcart Prize-nominated author and member of the Horror Writers Association, the National Federation of Press Women, and the Greater Lehigh Valley Writers Group.

Phil is currently working on his fourth paranormal mystery novel while plotting his triumphant escape from the pressures of corporate America where he has been imprisoned for thirty years. Visit Phil's website at www.philgiunta.com.

facebook.com/writerphilgiunta

instagram.com/phil_giunta71

youtube.com/@philgiunta

bookbub.com/profile/phil-giunta

linkedin.com/in/phil-giunta-997856a2

goodreads.com/phil_giunta

amazon.com/author/philgiunta

www.ingramcontent.com/pod-product-compliance
Lightning Source LLC
Chambersburg PA
CBHW031154050726
47495CB00019B/1723